THE EMPTY PLACES

LANDON CROOK

THE EMPTY PLACES

First edition. January 11, 2024.

Written by Landon Crook.

Copyright © 2024 Landon Crook.

All rights reserved.

This is a work of fiction. Similarities to real people, places, or events are entirely coincidental.

Edited by Raigan Nickle.

Book cover, title pages and graphics by GetCovers.

For my girls.

PART ONE

1

Baggage

FEAR IS A FUNNY THING. Because it's uncomfortable, we pathologize it by labelling it as negative—something to be avoided. But like physical pain, fear is adaptive and helpful. Fear is simply information—a signal to react, to move, to adapt. It is a call to action. With fear and anxiety, well, we generally see the call to action as a call to run away. Sometimes, however, it is a call to be courageous—to move forward regardless of the fear felt.

- *The Garrison Theories* podcast, Episode 1: "Our Weird Frontier"

"**C**all mom."

The sound of her own voice in the small space of her hatchback startled her. The last six hours since her singular, brief stop passed in complete silence, save for the droning music coming softly through the speakers and the roar of the highway as it ran under her tires. And those six hours were only a chunk of the overall thirteen it took her to journey from Vancouver—yet Sara sat wide-eyed and white-knuckled from the start.

Only her anxiety had nothing to do with the road conditions or the maniacs that ripped past her in their oversized trucks. It had everything to do with the trees that pressed in on both sides, gathering in tight, furtive groups that seemed to bend into each other like they conspired against her. It wasn't true, of course. But fear had a way of displacing the truth. She needed to push back, to challenge the lies her brain told her. *That's just your phobia talking, Sara. They're just stacks of wood with some greenery and snow on top. They can't hurt you.*

What's more, she had to keep telling herself that this would all be worth it in the end.

Buzzing, her phone stared at her from the dash. Her travel app reduced her to a small dot on a winding blue line. *Almost there*, she thought—the same words recurred the last few hours. *How many more trees stand between me and this godforsaken town?* She pinched the screen, and it climbed away in a satellite view. There civilization lay, waiting at the edge of the device. At least what passed for civilization this far north. The ringer continued its chime over the speakers, humming low through the subwoofer. It stopped, and the atmosphere changed.

"Sara?" came her mom's voice after the buzzing ceased.

"Hey, mom. It's me."

"Oh, it is you." The signal crackled, with motes of sound dropping out, fracturing her mom's words. "Well, how have things been since your last check in? That was... how many hours ago? Six?"

"More or less. Things are OK."

"As good as can be expected, I would imagine." In the background, water rushed, and dishes clinked. "Really, though, Sara—how are you doing with all the..."

"The greenery?"

Her mom gave a sombre chuckle. "That's one way of putting it."

"Yeah," said Sara, her voice trailing off. She leaned forward slightly, craning her neck to take in a larger view through the windshield. A great swath of trees rolled over the mountainside to her left, their white tops dusted with gold from the sun disappearing behind the mountains. The beauty of it captured her for a second before a wave of fear dashed it. "It's going OK." She squeezed the steering wheel, her knuckles rising like whitecaps.

"I still think you should have flown."

"I know you do," Sara said flatly. "And I said it was too expensive, remember?"

"We could have helped you out," she protested. "And you should have broken it up, Sara. It's been, what—ten hours of straight driving?"

"Maybe. Thirteen, likely."

"Oh, Sara. That's reckless."

Sara rolled her eyes like her mom was there in the passenger seat. "And yes, I know you could have helped me out with the plane tickets," she repeated. "But I wanted to do it my way, remember? Who knows? Maybe I'll conquer some fears."

A fuzzy sigh came through the speakers. "Hopefully that includes your fear of actual work." The water stopped, but the dishes kept on clinking. "Well, how long is your little vacation going to last, do you think?"

Sara sighed right back. "Ah, I was wondering when my supportive mom was going to show up." She cut her eyes to the trees and a pang of anxiety ran through her. Her eyes drifted back to the asphalt that stretched out ahead and grew into a deeper shade of grey by the minute. "It's not a vacation. I'm working, remember?" Even as the word working left her mouth, she didn't believe it herself. Maybe this was a big mistake—just like her mom had said in the days leading up to her departure.

"Right," said her mom through the speakers. "Sometimes, Sara, it's like I don't even know you."

The question haunted her daily, too: who was Sara Garrison? Her graduation ceremony over three years ago had left her with an English major, a journalism minor, and precious little else while she floundered in her parent's house and served coffee a few times a week.

She spent the rest of her time meticulously crafting a creative world steeped in the paranormal—*The Garrison Theory Podcast*. It was her baby, her escape—and if backed into a corner, she would sheepishly admit that she hoped it would be her future.

"I can relate," Sara finally admitted in response.

She left Vancouver thirteen hours prior, having decided that she would treat her dream with the reverence it deserved. She had an interview—a real interview—and with it she would make an amateur journalist of herself and send her struggling podcast to new heights. Something weird was happening in the sleepy town of Coalbrook, British Columbia. And she wanted a piece.

"So, this interview for your podcast—is this a safe person? Will you be meeting them somewhere public, maybe?"

Sara sighed. "It's all taken care of, mom."

"Didn't you say the articles said police did all they could? Why put yourself into the mix?"

Sara frowned at the blurry road ahead. "I'm not solving a case. Just going to give someone an opportunity to tell their story." She waited for her mom's response, running her fingers over her mouth and face, adjusting her glasses, and thumbing her septum ring. But the silence only stretched. The knot in Sara's throat cinched.

"Well," her mom continued, "let me know when you've settled into your ho—"

Like a dead radio station, a piercing static tore through the speakers. The pools of light cast by her headlights flickered in the dimness of the now-shadowed road, blinking slightly like the backlit instruments on her dashboard. Sara tensed as the power steering died along with everything else, but before fear took root, everything went back to normal save for her dropped call. Breathing a sigh of relief, she brought her eyes back to the road.

A massive antlered elk stood clear in the centre—not crossing but standing right in the middle of her lane. It stared her down, teeth bared, and eyes reflected yellow in her headlights as if daring her to make the first move. She only had the length of a few blinks to see it, but the creature looked sickly, almost skeletal. She jammed her boot into the brake pedal and swerved hard to the right. The road fell away as her car continued off the shoulder.

Seconds before everything jolted down with a crunch, it occurred to her that she should have sprung the cash for a flight.

Buried in the lavender duvet his wife had picked out, Steve lay with his eyes wide open, staring at the swimming murk of their bedroom.

A few feet away and threatening to roll into the depression he made in the mattress, Vanessa lay curled under the sprawled duvet, her breathing coming in quick gusts. It was her typical position; one he came upon often after late nights at the detachment or on patrol. Usually, she looked so peaceful that he refused to disturb her, settling for the couch in the living room. Recently, he couldn't help himself. He needed to be close.

Steve studied his wife's gently rising frame, almost imperceptible in the dimness of their bedroom. *How did she sleep so easily?* He sighed and rubbed his eyes, stars dancing in his vision. Sleep had a way of eluding him. It was his nemesis—how could it be so hard? It seemed so simple. It wasn't like a skill, some discrete choice he made in the darkness. Sleep was an absence of something; you simply lay, eyes closed, and hoped that your brain did the job.

He wondered if his brain was broken.

The frustration over his inability to pass out had an agitating effect, which made him wake up even more, which made it more difficult to sleep, which had an agitating effect... and so on.

So, he had taken the advice of online sleep hygienists and rose from the bed to busy himself with something else. But his frustrations with the entire process pushed him to a place of avoidance, cutting into his sleep by the hour until he collapsed. And recent events didn't help, either.

And if he came clean with himself, that was the biggest reason for his sleeplessness: he couldn't shake the feeling of being an imposter. He felt he was a fraudulent peace officer, a fake member of the Royal Canadian Mounted Police, despite being the local commander and highest-ranking officer.

Steve pushed himself off the bed in frustration and moped out of the bedroom, down the stairs and around the corner into the kitchen. The room glistened ice blue in the moonlight. He stopped in the doorway, unsure what he hoped to accomplish, then shook his head and flicked on the light before going to the refrigerator, grabbing the nearly empty jug of milk on the top shelf. Squinting, he poured himself a glass and slumped into a chair at the kitchen table, leaning his head against the wall. The weary man simply sat, breathing deeply, and looking out the back window at the blackness of the deepening night. The space between him and his next shift thinned. The internal clock kept ticking.

His mind raced along with the blood in his veins that burned his skin as he booted up his laptop. As it hummed to life, a voice came from the shadows outside of the kitchen entrance.

"Steve?"

He looked up to see Vanessa, standing bare legged in one of his shirts, squinting into the light, looking like she did twenty years ago when they married. The look screamed exhaustion, but clearly she didn't want to be apart. Sometimes he found it annoying when he wanted some time alone.

Tonight, he welcomed it.

"Hey, honey. I couldn't sleep." He took a long drink of milk and then set the glass down on the counter. "Sorry if I woke you."

Vanessa stepped into the kitchen and moved to the fridge to retrieve her own milk. She stood in silence for a few moments, sipping. "You feeling okay?" she inquired at last with a thin voice. "Is being on call tonight messing with you again?"

He watched her from over the dark rims under his eyes. He slapped his laptop shut, cutting off the startup sequence. "No, it's not that. Just frustrated."

"Thoughts racing?" she said, wrinkling her forehead like his words were going to be predictable.

"Yep," he said, rubbing his eyes.

She sat down at the table, clinking her glass into his. "Cheers," she said, her eyes still half-shut like they refused to adjust.

He gave a mirthless smirk, then planted his head into his hands as he propped his elbows on the table.

"So, what sort of thoughts are you having?"

Steve sat back in his chair, throwing up his hands in defeat. "Nothing, really. There's nothing specific, just the... I don't know." Only he did. The ghosts of old choices howled at his heels. "Like my brain wants to think, but it doesn't know what to think—only that it should be thinking."

"And what does that tell you?"

He shrugged, spinning his glass in his fingers on the table. "Something's wrong, I guess. Something I need to figure out."

Vanessa gave him a sympathetic look as she pushed up from the table, coming around to sit on his lap. He gave her a weak smile as she rested her head on top of his.

"Can I take a guess?"

His eyes didn't move from the table. He nodded, shifting her head along with his.

"Is it about last Fall? The missing boy?"

Another nod.

Her voice grew quiet. "Steve..." Her tone came with empathy, threaded with impatience. "Steve, honey—I'm telling you: you've got to talk to someone about this."

"I wouldn't even know what to say," he half-whispered. Her breath rolled hot over his scalp.

"Then you tell them there's nothing to say." She paused, taking a moment to run her fingers around the back of his neck. "About the fact that sometimes in life there are no good choices to be made, and that's that."

Steve gave a scant nod again. "I made the right call, didn't I?"

Vanessa leaned back on his lap, staring him full in the face. "To call off the search?"

"To bring us up here." *But yes, that too.*

She hugged him again. "I love it. The girls love it." Her chin dug into his shoulder. "It hasn't been without its challenges, sure—but it's what we wanted, right?"

"Away from the hustle and bustle."

"No hustle, no bustle. That's right. Plus, we can finally afford a house, be more independent, spend more time with the girls..."

Steve frowned. "Seems like there's more bustle up here than we wanted."

Vanessa sighed, this time with less empathy. "Honey, what happened was terrible. But those kinds of things... they are once-in-a-lifetime town tragedies." She pulled back, looking at him once again. "Something like that isn't going to happen again."

He scoffed. "I'll hold you to it."

"Well, you can't fix it in the dead of night." She scratched his head, and he closed his eyes. "Come back to bed, and I'll let you snuggle me."

"OK," he said, staring up into her face. She showed the signs that come from being on the cusp of middle age, but he still saw the same Vanessa. He kissed her, and she slid off him, giggling at her own clumsiness. "I'll be there in a second," he reassured.

"Don't wait too long."

He slumped forward as she disappeared, allowing his thoughts to wander into uncomfortable places. The burden within him shifted, as if aware of his attention and trying to hide somewhere among his organs. Even though he had come to Coalbrook nearly eight years ago with his wife and two young children to avoid the crassness of metropolitan life, the deep dissatisfaction that hounded him there sniffed him out, following him to these northern woods. Perhaps the city wasn't to blame after all.

Maybe it was him.

He quietly made his way to the master bedroom. Vanessa was already asleep. He climbed into bed and lay down against her. She had her back to him, curled up in a pose that he gratefully aligned himself with.

But sleep still escaped him. He draped his arm over her, wondering if he would always be like this. Wondering about the boy he failed. If he wasn't already dead by the time Steve called off the search a year ago, he was certainly dead now.

Kimberly sat on the end of her bed and clutched her arms tightly in front of her stomach. It was late, and she would probably be easing into sleep if it wasn't for the screeching woman standing in the doorway to her room.

Kim stared at the floor, sometimes cutting her eyes to her mother as she continued screaming from the hall. The photographs tacked up, down, and across the doorframe framed her mom's tirade, acting like talismans to keep evil from entering her room. Didn't seem to work with her mom, although it wasn't lost on Kim that she hadn't yet crossed the threshold.

The words came in red hot and oh-so-predictable, punctuated by the demand that Kim look her in the eyes as she talked. Kimberly quietly declined and kept her eyes on the rusty shag, as she always did. It was something about her performance at school, followed by something about her taste in men, followed by something about her attitude. The tirade reached an ironic crescendo with some Biblical wisdom relating to authority, which may have been powerful if either of them attended church and if her mother wasn't an emotionally abusive alcoholic.

Still at the threshold of the room, her mom's hands flared in front of her, finally arriving at their destination at the top of her head as she ran her hands frantically through her hair.

"I have no idea how to help you, Kimmy," she cracked desperately. "God knows I've tried."

"This doesn't help, you know." Kim's voice shrunk, her hands tightened into fists, knuckles barely visible under the too-large sleeves of her friend's charcoal sweatshirt—he was a boy, incidentally, and mother didn't approve. Her watery eyes lingered on the portraits of her friends she had drawn and scattered with pins on the cork board above her desk. Each of them looked on as an empathetic audience, helpless to intervene.

"Oh, what a surprise," came her mom's raspy voice. She threw out a hand and started counting off her fingers rhythmically. "Counsellors, doctors, medication, endless sacrifices and accommodations—I could keep going, Kimmy." She thrust the splayed fingers into the room. "I could finish on this hand and the next, and probably have to move onto my toes!"

"Give it up, Sharon," said Kimberly to her carpet as she rubbed her elbows through her cavernous sweater.

"I've told you a thousand times, don't call me that. I'm your mom, Kimmy."

"Then act like it."

Silence stretched between them. Her mom still hadn't stepped into the room. "Just keep taking your meds, then," she huffed. She left without looking back, slamming the door hard enough to send one of Kimberly's portraits gliding down onto the carpet.

The row was complete, but the tension lingered. Glass clattered somewhere in the kitchen. Likely more wine.

Like a compressed spring, Kimberly coiled tight on her bed. With arms cinched even tighter across her chest, she stared at her collections through tears. Her clothing hung on the overhead rack in her closet, her moccasins kicked off on the floor right beside her nightstand, her books and old DVDs, sketches and papers scattered across her desk.

The words inside her head tried to make themselves known, but she pushed them out of her mind, shoving them back down into her subconscious where they belonged. The words would tell her to kill herself or to break things or to run away; they would attack and drag down the other words and tell them they were worthless and should die.

Kimberly shook her head and took a deep breath in the way her counsellor taught her to. *Create an antithesis to the thoughts. Challenge them. Don't let them in unless you check them at the door.* In slowly through the nose, hold, and out from the back of the throat over a few seconds. Her breath gusted out of her as she gave up on the exercise—if deep breathing made her mom work through her bitterness, then it might be worth it. Gathering herself, the desire to

11

go after her mom tempted her, but it seemed futile. It occurred to her at that moment that her mom's protestations—although different in tone and content—weren't all that different from those of the school counsellor.

"Take your medicine and it'll all just go away," she mimicked her mom as she organised the clutter on her desk. "And what about you?" she screamed across the empty room. "What medication can I take to make you go away?"

Her door didn't budge.

"Yeah, that's what I thought," she said to no one, tears glinting at the bottom of her eyes; her sleeves rubbed against her face, stopping them before they fell. "Stop it," she said to herself under her breath. "Just stop it. It's not worth it."

She sat back down in her chair, staring at the surface of her desk, the clutter now slightly more organised. Her eyes lifted, taking in her drawings that hung on the wall, crawling up the cork like vines. These were the many faces of her friends and acquaintances. They cared about her, the ones whom she ran to when things got hard. They understood; many lived it themselves. Her friends gave her warmth and hope; here, she only found ice and disappointment. Why had she tried so hard to keep things patched with someone who never seemed to think she was good enough?

Her mom probably saw herself in her: a naïve young girl, unprepared for the larger world, eyes filled with nothing but paper dreams. It's like she tried to prepare Kim for disappointment by making sure she never climbed higher than she ever did.

You'll be eaten alive out there, she had said once. *You've got to take care of yourself because no one else will. And those drawings won't get it done—get that homework finished!* Kimberly imagined a younger, fuller version of her mom in those moments. She must have been naïve too, because the man who was partially responsible for her existence was, as her mom so strangely put it, an emotional cannibal.

Unsatisfied with the chaos, she pushed the desk against the wall and threw herself backwards onto her bed. A loose book fell from the bedside table and hit the soft carpet with a muffled thud, but she paid it no mind. She stared up at her bedroom ceiling, unseeing.

A coldness came over her, wrapping her in a blanket and cutting her off from the rest of humanity. It was like the threadbare connection to her mother was severed, like their argument had been the last push that would send her over the edge.

She pulled her phone in front of her face. Her thumbs flicked over the glowing screen.

On second thought, count me in

2

Dead to the World

WHY DO THE WILD AND empty places of the world hold such mystique and menace? I believe it's because it provides much-needed mystery to our banal and predictable lives. To believe in one's heart that this world still holds secrets, like buried treasures clamouring for discovery, is a driving force all to itself—an energy perhaps akin to what the centuries-old explorers felt when they saw new land on the horizon.
-The Garrison Theories podcast, Episode 5: "Here Be Dragons"

Sara's eyes fluttered open, stinging under the assault of the yellow buzz of fluorescents. She winced her eyes closed again, rubbing at her sockets, dragging numerous tubes with each movement of her arm.

"Hey, look who's awake," came a youthful man's voice from her left.

She jerked her head towards him, eyes still narrowed. The movement rattled her brain in her skull, and she groaned.

"Hey, take it easy, Ms. Garrison. You were in quite the wreck."

Carefully, she pushed herself into a more upright sitting position. Sara pulled on her glasses and then felt around her body, making sure everything still worked. "Is everything—?"

The man chuckled. His muscular frame, still somehow visible beneath the bulk of his uniform, filled the unmistakable trappings of an officer of the Royal Canadian Mounted Police. He sat with one leg rested over the other, revealing the tell-tale yellow streak of his iconic pants. He was only slightly older than her, although his baby face that bulged beneath his toque made it difficult to discern just how much older. It must have been hard having such a cherubic face in the RCMP—probably explained why he grew such a cheesy moustache. If only it helped.

"Well, you should probably wait for the doc for the official report. But from what they've told me, I think you'll be out of here in no time." He stood and ambled over to her hospital bed from his seat in the corner. "I'm Corporal Reid." He tapped the stack of two chevrons on his shoulder. "Or Cameron, if you'd prefer." He extended a hand, and she shook it with what little strength she had.

"And I'm assuming here is—?"

"Coalbrook. You're in the medical centre at the moment, right in the heart of town." He raised an eyebrow. "Surprised?"

Sara let out a weak chuckle. "To be in Coalbrook, no. The hospital? Yes." She eased back into the pillows of her metal frame bed. "And my car?"

Corporal Reid grimaced. "Yeah, I'd guess that's a write off for sure. You hit that tree super hard, Ms. Garrison." He gestured with his hands, making motions to match his words. "What sent you off the road?"

Sara looked down at her hands. "I saw a deer, and I panicked."

"Swerved to save it? What a bleeding heart you are—all for a deer, eh?"

"Whatever it was. It had horns—antlers, I mean. Big ones. And it looked pretty nasty... almost infected. Is that normal here?"

His animated style seemed to fall away at the mention of the details. His jovial expression vanished, too. "A bull elk," he said with a nod. He licked his lips, and his gaze floated away like something more important had come up. "Yeah," he continued, "yeah, that'd do it. I wouldn't want to hit one, either. Probably better off with a tree..."

"Huh," she grunted. "Um—sorry, corporal—don't mean to be rude, but why are you here with me in the hospital?"

"Fair enough question." He ambled back to his chair and smoothed his young moustache. "I found you off the road. And once you were here, I wanted to make sure you didn't wake up filled with questions."

"Thank you," she said. "I appreciate the care. You must have other things to do... especially during ski season—there's a ski hill here, right?"

"No problem. Staff Sergeant would have wanted me to hang around and ask a few questions, anyways." He paused, removing his toque and scratching his head while he looked at her. "And no, the ski hill has gone defunct in recent years."

Sara strained to be polite. "Is it because of what happened last fall?"

Corporal Reid hesitated. He put his toque back on and shook his head. "Blue Hills has been abandoned for longer than that."

"Oh, OK. And the questions? From your... boss, presumably?"

"That's right, Ms. Garrison. Staff Sergeant Stephen Boyko, he's the commander of our detachment here. And the main question would be to ask you: what brings you to sleepy Coalbrook?" He crossed his arms. "Most just pass on through. Where you coming from, anyways?"

"Vancouver. And I'm here for work."

He looked surprised. "That's a ways. Got a job at the mill?"

"Nope. I run a podcast."

He pursed his lips. "Is that right? What about?"

She looked away, grinning, and she asked, "I don't think I have to answer these questions, do I?"

Corporal Reid smiled, but his eyes seemed to harden. "I guess not. But why do work here, though? Not much going on here for podcasting."

16

Sara shrugged. "Change of scenery." He was pushy, that was certain. There was something about him that seemed uncertain, like he was uncomfortable with the whole exchange but felt like he had to press her for answers. *Well, it is his job, after all. Boss says jump...* But even in the pressing, it felt like it was more than just a run-of-the-mill, light interrogation. The pleasantries were beginning to have an air of inhospitality.

"I see," said the officer as he stood. "Well, stay out of trouble, eh?" He strode to the door, turning slightly as he slowed. "Ms. Garrison, once you are all rested up, give the detachment a call. If I'm available, I'd be more than happy to take you to the tow yard to collect the rest of your things and rent a car, OK?"

She hesitated. "Thank you."

He had scarcely stepped out of the room before she dug into her bag, the only piece of her effects she had with her. Her phone was the first thing out of her bag. She had countless missed calls and confused texts, all piled up under her mom's number. Her fingers bounced off the digital keyboard.

Got in accident on hwy, almost hit elk. In hospital but OK, police say car is write off. Will get rental and finish work b4 coming home. 2 weeks tops I hope. Luv u

Her mom would be mad that she texted a bombshell like that, but she didn't have the energy to talk. Her eyes drooped along with the rest of her aching body that melted into the thin mattress. She closed her eyes, but before she found any rest, her phone vibrated on her stomach as it hid beneath her folded hands.

Are you serious??

Her thumbs flicked over the screen.

Yes, but im OK. Just resting

It buzzed again.

Sara, just come home please. This is insane. Dad can book a ticket and have you home tmrw

She stabbed at the phone, sighing with frustration.

I want/need to go thru with this. Please understand, will keep u posted

The phone vibrated in a thrumming sequence, heralding an attempt by her mother to cut off the texting and talk over the phone. Sara ignored it, and a minute later, more vibrations came, this time in a frantic sequence of broken English.

You running from your responsibilities is going to get you killed. You are smarter than this. PLEASE come home. Dad and I are worried to death

Sara's jaw locked tight.

Appreciate concern, luv u both lots

She powered down her phone and closed her eyes. It kept buzzing, but eventually it all blurred together with the humming of fluorescents and the beeping of machinery.

From beneath her toque, Kim peered at the tight wall of towering evergreens. They could scarcely be seen in the near-absolute dark of the night, the tops just barely lit by the moonlight that cut through the slow-moving clouds. A breeze ran among the branches, sending the trees into a flurry of movement. She took a deep breath through her scarf, feeling the closeness of her own air as she breathed in and out. *Wouldn't want to be out in that.* Even standing at the threshold of the wilderness, with the sounds of her friends unpacking the vehicles a few steps behind her, she shivered. She shivered from the cold, certainly—but it was more than that. It was the same as the shiver that crawled up her back when she came up the stairs from the basement when the lights were out.

"It looks so different in the snow, doesn't it?"

Kim shook her head. "I can't believe we're up here. Have we ever done this in the winter before?"

Cara's laugh was snugly placed in her bomber cap. "*We* aren't doing anything," she said as she swivelled and gestured to the white SUV—David's. "*They* are." The two boys did their best to wrestle two portable power stations from the trunk, grunting as they heaved them by their handles.

"Whose idea was it?" asked Kim as she hugged herself tight. Her jacket said it handled temperatures up to below thirty Celsius, but even in the dry twenty below air they stood in, it seemed scant protection.

"Tanner's."

"Are those his power stations?"

Cara shook her head, her eyebrows rising over her frameless glasses. "David's dad's."

"He's dead meat."

Both girls laughed as David approached them, lifting his boots high to step down into the calf-high snow. He beamed at them beneath a ruby red nose. "Ready to head in?"

"The usual spot?" asked Kim.

"You know it. Doesn't look like anyone's been up here to board it up since the last time we were here."

Cara extended a hand. "Lead the way, mountain man."

David sauntered back and gave Tanner the signal before reaching into the cab of his truck. He killed the engine, plunging the surroundings into darkness and silence. Whatever moonlight remained barely touched this part of the forest. The vehicle waited patiently within the clearing alongside the snow-covered husk of the derelict ski lodge that used to be the workhorse of tourism during the colder months of the year. Blue Hills Ski Resort. *May it rest in peace.*

Their flashlights cut back and forth across the skeletal remains of the resort with its empty, boarded-up windows like watchful eyes over the tops of the plywood that couldn't quite get the job done. The cobbled base stood strong, marred only by graffiti, stacking up over Kim's head before they shifted to smooth lumber. The questionably coloured aquamarine tin roof made itself known through patches of snow that had fallen away—but she knew it well enough already. It was a common destination not just for them, but for many of the young people in Coalbrook. Common enough to be patrolled every once in a while by the brown-nosers at the Coalbrook RCMP detachment. But it wasn't a drive made by many in the winter; lots of effort, little payoff.

But for her and her friends, the effort always paid off.

Tanner bent over double beneath the covered drop-off entrance, nearly slamming David's dad's undoubtedly expensive portable power station onto the concrete. "And you girls say I never take you anywhere nice."

The front door stood dead centre, flanked by two large, many-panelled windows. Most of the glass stood cracked and boarded up. Countless memories flooded into discussion between the four as they neared the prize of their midnight commute.

"Oh," said David. "Someone's put some fresh boards on here."

"And they did a good job," said Tanner. "Those are some deep screws. Give me a sec. I'll check around the building real quick."

"Be careful," called Cara.

Kimberly wrapped her arms around herself, doing her best to not let her thoughts wander to the argument she had with her mom less than an hour ago. Even after her mom's worst moments, home always tugged at her. The same way that guilt did. Especially when it stressed her mom out when she would disappear. Thankfully, they had an unspoken agreement: if Kim came back within a day or two, it was acceptable. *Or, if not acceptable, just not worth talking about.* Sometimes, a person just needs some space. Sometimes they both needed a break from each other. Tonight was one of those nights.

Kim shivered, catching her thoughts wandering again. "Is that everything?" she asked David to shift her mind to other things. She wondered when her mom would notice her absence.

His eyes bulged. "Oh! Thank you, I almost forgot." He grunted his way back to the truck and returned with a small space heater and a few tiny tanks of fuel knocking together in a plastic bag. "Warm things up quicker!"

"Oh, good," said Cara through a mischievous smile. She crept close to David and rubbed her shoulders against his. "I was worried we were going to warm it up ourselves."

"Well, that too," he replied, grinning. He glanced at Kim—she pulled her face away.

"Any chance you'll give Tanner any attention tonight, Kimmy?" asked Cara.

She narrowed her eyes, smiling slightly. "I guess that depends on what you mean by 'attention'," she said. "I won't ignore him, if that's what you mean."

"That's a start," said Cara.

The crisp sound of crunching powder and shifting gravel caught their attention. Kim spun to see a red-faced Tanner appearing around the corner of the lodge.

"There's a rotten board at the back," he breathed. "I peeled the corner back, and it tore off, and there's no window behind—we've got our way in!"

Once around back, they took turns going through, awkwardly crawling like rats through an opening that started around knee height. Kim thrust herself through third, after David and Cara and the backpacks, and immediately collided with the thin stink of various kinds of rot. The musk of decayed wood and fabric—among others—pressed in and made it hard to breathe. Every step deeper answered the question as to what. Kim took care to step over a variety of dead rodents and birds in varying states of decomposition.

"I can't handle an entire night of this smell," complained Cara as she pulled her pack back on.

Tanner laughed. "Don't worry. Won't take long for us all to get nose blind to it."

"I don't think this is the smell you want to be nose blind to," said David. "But hey, we've come this far."

"The cops probably sealed the basement off." Tanner strode to the front of the group, sweeping his flashlight beam back and forth over the chaos of the main hall. The shadows responded to every sweep, shifting and stretching like they tried to hide from the four teenagers. "This way, right?"

As always, the hall looked war torn. Blotchy carpet—a hideous mix of reds and browns—blanketed the floor. Tables and chairs were overturned and stacked in places, their legs snapped and surfaces broken; the associated cushions punctured and gouged. The floor lay covered with the fragments of glass of fixtures, scattered like broken bones and crushed skulls.

Encircling it all were the peeling, sagging walls splattered with graffiti, like a guest book for those bold enough to trespass in such a place. Her own initials hid somewhere, thrown on with spray paint like so many others. Blue Hills served the youth of Coalbrook as a rite of passage, the go-to for the mutinously minded. And in a small town, that defined the bulk of the young population, for what else remained for them to do? Her mind drifted to her drawings, her books—among other hobbies and pastimes. Lots to do, actually, at least for her. But it didn't hurt to throw in one's lot with the rest every now and again.

That became especially true when one's friendships depended on it.

The darkness in the bowels of the ruin was absolute, and sometimes difficult to comprehend. When they came during the warmer months, the sun would find ways of penetrating through cracks and slivers in walls and windows, giving just enough light to navigate the murk. Without their flashlights this time of year, they would be groping and tripping, enveloped in the blackest of blacks. Kim peered after her beam, trying to remember which hall led where. She crept to the edge of the dining hall near the main entrance. Behind her, her friends still navigated the minefield of junk.

Her breath caught. A shuffling sound across the entrance drove a wave of heat across her face, and she followed it with her flashlight. She caught a shadow—maybe a bird? It was like a fluttering scramble.

"What's that?" called David.

Kimberly didn't take her eyes off the doorway a few strides in front. "Not sure," she shouted back, hoping the volume of her voice might keep whatever creature was there at bay. "And I don't really want to find out. Where's the lounge, again?"

Four different beams crossed and spread back and forth over the wreckage of the once-thriving dining hall. Eventually, they found their way to the least disgusting area: the lounge at the bottom of the staircase that at one point must have been the most luxurious basement in greater Coalbrook.

The French doors at the bottom swung wide beneath the once-fluorescent sign at the bottom of the shallow stairs, revealing the sprawling pit of relaxation. In the resort's abandonment, the owner's left much of the heavier fare behind, including the neglected and sad-looking trio of pool tables that still stood as if waiting for someone to give them purpose. And every now and again, the youth of Coalbrook would do just that. It always seemed to Kim that they were doing the place a favour.

"We should do this more often," declared Cara. "This place is too good to only use in the summer." The others agreed.

Tonight's plan was the same as always: the wet bar at the end would be stocked with cheap beer and cheaper spirits of their own supply; they would clear the compact stage of dust and dead things to make way for small, portable generators and sound systems; the cracked leather couches, although freezing to the touch this time of year, would serve as impromptu beds when the night deepened.

Cara shivered. "Let's get that heater going, eh?"

Kimberly smiled, almost unaware of her mother as the details of the argument faded to the background, displaced by a growing sense of excitement. This place served them in their celebration of youth, and tonight would be no exception.

3

Night Terrors

A MAJOR OBSTACLE TO legitimising paranormal investigation is the sheer volume of hoaxes that exist online. And intentional hoaxes are one thing, but beyond that exists content uploaded that is, unfortunately, mistaken. Pareidolia—the tendency we all have to attach meaning and form to ambiguity—is a filter that is difficult to remove. Or perhaps it's impossible, since we are meaning-making creatures, after all. We search for truth with such ferocity that in its absence we fabricate it to hold ourselves together.

-The Garrison Theories podcast, Episode 3: "Truth and Lies in Gastown"

Andrea was running again.

In the depths of sleep, Sara floated, disembodied in darkness, watching her sister sprint naked and helpless through the trees. Each step left bloodied footprints in their wake, but she didn't slow her pace. Looking through Sara, she threw her head this way and that, trying to see into the shadows. Trying to see something.

Sara, Andrea called, her voice hollow and distant, different than she remembered; it sounded older and strained. Sara tried to respond, but she had no mouth to work into words. She reached out to her, but her hands vanished. She wanted to rush to her sister's side, but she could only watch and wait, floating after her as if a ghost or a rolling camera rig. Just like that late Autumn evening over a decade ago, she stood helpless.

The branches raked against Andrea's body as she sprinted into the shadows, heedless of whatever waited ahead, doing everything possible to get away from unseen threats. She tripped and crashed into piles of tendrils.

Sara, her thin voice rose again, the squeak nearly swallowed by sounds of unseen crackling undergrowth. She scrambled to her feet, lumbering forward in terror, grasping for support as she collapsed against the bole of a branchless, naked tree that rose like a pillar until darkness swallowed it.

Her sister faced her, now looking right in where her eyes should have been. Andrea extended a pleading hand as a soundless scream emitted from her gaping mouth.

Don't let it keep me, Sara. The grate of her weathered voice smoothed as she spoke, shifting into the teenage voice that she remembered so clearly.

Andrea stabbed her arm forward, little finger outstretched. *Pinky swear!* The trees closed in and swallowed her.

Sara shot up in the hospital bed with a shrill gasp. For some time, she sat propped up by her arms, chest heaving as she remembered where she was and why she was there. Her sheets clung sodden to her legs with sweat.

She wiped away her tears, then fought her way back to sleep.

Kimberly's head swam as it lolled on her shoulders. She buzzed with liquor and excitement, weaving her frame back and forth with the beat of the music. It unfolded wonderfully: the heater pumped their corner of the lounge full of warmth as their own moving bodies contributed what heat possible. The cocktails crafted by Tanner worked their magic. They placed the lanterns strategically, along with the few strands of fairy lights hung according to Cara's keen eye. It was almost magical. Almost.

In the half-light and fog of liquor, Kim was caught off guard by how magnetic she found Tanner. His brown curls were falling just right over his forehead. Her inhibitions thinned along with the fresh memories of the conflict and grief of home.

The dancing hung for a moment as a melodic rhythm bridged the transition between the songs in the electronic mix. Tones shifted and climbed as the tempo increased, and the four bodies moved in kind. Tanner's body burned as he moved closer, Kim like a satellite caught in orbit, swirling around him as the lanterns cast bizarre shadows on the decaying walls.

Each beat prompted a shift from one leg to the other. With a hot sigh, Kim relaxed her neck and stared up at the web of fairy lights that criss-crossed from the low beams. She closed her eyes as Tanner's hands roamed across her belly as he pressed into her back. A gush of electricity pricked the nape of her neck and expanded like a ripple in a still pond over her skin, causing her pores to contract and hair to rise. She couldn't help but raise her arms. He kissed her neck, and she opened herself to it, dropping her head towards her shoulder.

The music crackled as it gushed from the corner, and along with the others she leaped and twirled. The rotten floorboards gave slightly with each landing. She flicked her hair back, leaving behind sweaty strands of streaking black on her forehead. Her mouth slackened as hot breath fired from her lungs into the warming air. Under her top, a bead of sweat drew a line between her breasts.

Then, the music softened, the last drop having played out and diminished, leaving a smooth melody in its place. It was perfect. For one meaningful, ponderous moment, significance gripped her. These three, at least, saw her. Knew her. They didn't demand anything from her except her presence.

A pair of hands wrapped themselves around the small of her back; she returned the gesture by wrapping hers around Tanner's neck. A smile said yes, so he kissed her. Kim did not know where this led, but she didn't care. Tomorrow would have its own problems—tonight, she had nothing to hold her back. Kim kissed him back, pulling back quickly with a giggle. He made a playful face, then tried to pull her back.

She didn't resist but hesitated momentarily when a sour smell cut through the room. She wrinkled her nose and tucked her chin into her neck, and judging by Tanner's expression, he smelled it too. Before she could identify the stench, something caught her attention.

In the corner of her eye, she saw someone standing on the other side of the French doors.

The blood that passion had awakened and warmed suddenly dumped into her gut, leaving her weak and cold and desperate to swallow the pang of nausea that threatened to overwhelm her. Eyes wide, she shoved herself back from Tanner, and stabbed her finger across the room.

"There's someone at the door!" she screeched as she stumbled back.

Tanner jerked himself around and stared. "What the f—" he shouted, cutting himself off as he burst towards the doors with David on his heels. Both grabbed pool cues on the way over, clicking on flashlights that served to only fill the glass with glaring, white streaks. "Who's there!" he screamed, his voice cracking.

David yanked the door open. Kim leaned forward, almost too scared to look but emboldened by her own curiosity. No one stood there, and certainly no one crested the top of the stairwell. Cara sidled close and gripped Kim's arm.

Tanner spun and stared, bewildered. "What did you think you saw?"

"Well," Kim hesitated, "I mean, I swear I saw someone. It was like a black figure." She turned to each of them, settling at least on Cara. "I'm not making this up. I saw a person there, just standing and watching us." Her pulse throbbed in her temples. A chill born of both nausea and fear swept over her once again.

David shrugged, offering her a sympathetic look. "I'm sure that's what you thought you saw. It's all good."

"I don't blame you," said Tanner, coming back to her side. "This place is spooky, I get it. And with these lights, and lots of movement—"

"And lots to drink," interjected Cara, giggling.

"—and lots to drink," repeated Tanner, "one of us was bound to freak out at one point."

"I'm not freaking out, Tanner," growled Kim. "I could have sworn..."

"Probably just a reflection." David's tone seemed uncertain, like he tried to convince himself just as much as the others.

Tanner looked suddenly remorseful, although Kim suspected that it was mostly because he worried he talked himself out of a date. "Sorry—I didn't quite mean it like that."

David laughed. "No worries, Kim. It's all good, like I said."

"Yeah," echoed Tanner pathetically. His smile entreated her. "It's all good, Kim."

Frowning, Kim crossed her arms. The others stared at her as if waiting for her to cut through the tension and allow the party to continue. Eventually, she scoffed and offered a thin giggle.

The small hours passed in drinking and discussion. The music that had penetrated Kimberly down to the bone had faded, leaving only the thin whispers that slithered among the wood and concrete. Night deepened. Young bodies crowded the warmer corner, pressing together to preserve heat. They cocooned in all manner of sleeping bag and blanket, tucked into nooks and hollows among the skeletons of old comforts.

The thought of finding a place to lay down and sleep seemed like an impossible task following such a sick fright. No one would entertain leaving now, so she didn't even bother to ask. *Just one night, Kimmy.* She looked at Tanner. The whole scare had dashed the romantic feelings, but as night fell in a place like Blue Hills, the thought of sleeping separate grew in its ugliness. Kim flopped down next to him and nuzzled in; reluctantly, at first, but then gratefully. Her gratitude blossomed when the generator tapped out and the hum of the heater faded—now she had Tanner to keep her warm.

Before she fell asleep, she reflected on the smell that had wafted through the lounge. It remained, hanging thinly in the air around her face, almost daring her to give it a name. Unequivocally, she named it as the stench of rot.

4

Small Town Problems

IF YOU WANT TO SEE a cryptid, here's my advice: get away from the city. Most encounters tend to occur at great distances from urban centres where the influence of humanity wanes. And do some research on what is local to you, as these occurrences tend to be regional. Hell, all my life I probably could have thrown a rock and hit a sasquatch.

- *The Garrison Theories* podcast, Episode 1: "Our Weird Frontier"

Steve's face split with a yawn too strong to stifle—and stifle it he often tried, especially when on duty. Anyone who witnessed a baggy-eyed officer of the Royal Canadian Mounted Police struggling to remain awake in his cruiser would probably have the confidence sucked right out of them. And that was the last thing Steve needed. The local faith in him and his officers had waned in the last year or so. He needed a win.

It was, however, only a few hours into his eight-hour shift, and that win was already eluding him.

He sipped his syrupy, extra large Tim Hortons double-double and glared blearily through his windshield. A greying, scowling woman lugging plastic bags glared right back over the hood of his SUV. The police radio buzzed in the background, a muffled fuzz over the idling engine; he ignored it, his attention drawn to the familiar face. He blew over the top of his cup, carefully replacing the lid before rolling the window down.

"Good morning, Nicola," he called, leaning his head slightly out the opening. A knife of wind cut across his scalp before he nestled his yellow-banded cap on it.

She came around his parked car, drowning in the pooling exhaust, standing a few strides away but talking as if she was right next to him. "My tax dollars at work," she said, bags outstretched. "Sittin' and sippin' on his Timmies. No wonder things have gotten so bad 'round here."

He gave her a polite nod, although anyone with an ounce of emotional intelligence would have taken his straight-mouthed smile as an admonishment. Nicola Cartwright was no such person, because she continued along the same line of interrogation without so much as a pause.

"Shouldn't you be patrolling?" she queried impatiently. "God forbid you actually help someone for once."

He opened his mouth but held his tongue—miraculously. "Have a good day," he squeezed out between his teeth as an alternative. She left in a huff.

Steve stared after the old woman as she shuffled away, huddled into herself with her bags. And really, why the fuss? Things here were as quiet as always—there was nothing bad about it. He took a deep breath, triggering another yawn, wondering if he had the energy to do this today.

It hadn't always been like this. Eight years ago, policing this area had been relatively easy, a nice change from the non-stop mentality in the big city. The Coalbrook detachment defined itself with shorter shifts, higher pay due to the remote posting and cheaper housing, to start. And the people? Mostly friendly, mostly quiet. It had all been smooth sailing—until the Johnstone boy disappeared. It was the town's highest profile case ever, and Steve ran the show.

Ran it right into the ground.

When search and rescue efforts failed, the town pointed their fingers at him. Steve was too slow to pull the trigger on putting together a search. Christian Johnstone perfected the tough guy act, so he figured it was reasonable to think he would show up. He always vanished for a few days and reappeared like a magician—always. Steve encouraged everyone to be patient, that it was just another disruptive escapade... and they listened. They listened reluctantly, but they listened. His fellow officers aligned with him, too. It just so happened that time that Christian decided not to come home.

Well, maybe not decided.

Nobody pointed a literal finger, of course—but the effect remained the same. While the unstable populace like Mrs. Cartwright had no issue taking him to task, the rest of the town had become decidedly more withdrawn. Polite nods and greetings were few-and-far between and had become so rare it was preferable to be confronted; otherwise, he simply didn't exist. Now he only found safety in his wife and kids, and perhaps the rest of the members at the detachment. But even some of the other officers doubted. He saw it in their eyes as they struggled to maintain eye contact.

Come on, Boyko. Snap out of it. He took another sip of his coffee and continued his patrol. Like most days, it would certainly play out as an uneventful one. *Just like Vanessa said: maybe they were ashamed because they agreed with me at first. Maybe they can't look me in the eye because they feel the same judgement.* The best thing about small towns is that everyone's close; the worst thing about small towns is that everyone's close.

Maybe. Or maybe I just made a bad call.

His utility vehicle grumbled as he slowly took it through town, nodding at every one who would give him the time of day, if they could even see him from under their hoods as they shuffled down the empty, salted sidewalks that lined Coal Street. Snow glared white

33

on the shovelled walkway, a thin layer that touched just above the soles. He rolled on, switching from street to street as he made his way through the heart of Coalbrook, eyes darting here and there to ensure nothing slipped past his attention, responding now and again to the radio buzz that came from dispatch and the other patrol; Corporal Friesen and Constable Campbell, patrolling on the edge of town. Both were young guys, but hard workers.

Most of the morning passed similarly, bringing Steve almost to the point of dozing. It reminded him of how things should be, the way he had hoped they would be when he first came here with Vanessa and the kids. It felt just a hair's breadth beyond his reach, pushed a bit further out by last year's harrowing. Still, he lingered in recovery mode, as did the town.

Maybe it wasn't so bad. Maybe he just had to keep a cool head and cool eyes. It's why he had the officers keep him in the loop whenever they saw someone unique come into town. Since the death of Blue Hills and the subsequent collapse of their tourism industry, interesting people seldom came to town—and if they did, they stopped at the gas station and were well on their way to where they really wanted to go.

At least, that rang true until yesterday. Now there was someone in Coalbrook with the possible intent to dig through the town's—and his—dirty laundry. And he had her description: mid-twenties, Caucasian, cropped black hair, about five foot five. Has a big bruise from the accident. Red toque, round glasses, black clothes all buried under a long, tan overcoat. Her name was Sara Garrison, and his main goal for the day was to find her. He presented—at least he hoped he did—as an attentive peace officer, but in truth he scanned for the telltale newcomer from Vancouver. Until he ran her out of town, his sleeping difficulties were going to compound—and as Cam mentioned, it turned out that her possible write off was now a two-week repair job. Two weeks of podcasting, including some interviews. Two weeks for someone to potentially fan the already crackling flames of discontent.

Interviews for what?

Steve sighed as he brought the Explorer around to grind down another street. Those two weeks stretched ahead like a tunnel—and there wasn't any light at the end. Suddenly, he needed another coffee.

Sara stared at the ruin of her little hatchback. It hunched in a heap in the elements, somewhat obscured by a grey tarp carelessly tossed over top, allowing a few vestiges of the 1998 Civic to peek out from below. It was like attending an old-fashioned, open-casket viewing—like maybe she should have brought flowers. Corporal Reid said it would be a write-off, but to her delight, it wasn't. The repairs would be around ten to twelve days, giving her a deadline for her project.

Rest well, Silver. I'll be back.

But as soon as she climbed into her rental, she forgot about her losses. It was a deep blue crossover, brand new from what she could tell. It had bells and whistles she didn't know modern cars had, her being the thrifty one who was more of a secondary market kind of girl. She pawed at the wheel as she took a contented breath. The leather, chrome, and black plastic bliss of the rental gave her the first sensation of safety since she'd arrived. The reunion with her luggage and other effects was sweet, even miraculous considering that they survived the wreck. Sara was back on track. She adjusted her mirrors.

I look like a pirate. The rear-view mirror revealed the dark bruise that covered her right eye and side of her face. The effort to cover it with foundation seemed Herculean, something probably not worth the attempt—so she wore it then as a badge of honour, the result of a hazing ritual concocted by the town itself as payment for her passage.

Could be a great intro. She made a note in her phone and backed the rental out of the autobody yard.

The main highway that cut through the town swelled with the contemporary staples that sucked the life and bespoke culture out of a community: fast food and big box stores. She ignored them, navigating through the blissfully short traffic lights towards the older centre of town where decades-old brick and stucco walls announced themselves with subtle decorum.

Corporal Reid had referred to Coalbrook as sleepy, and the first ten minutes of her ramblings around this part set that descriptor in stone. It was near winter, to be fair. Compared to Vancouver, this place was a ghost town.

Coal Street had the most character and represented the heart of old town. It was a luxuriously wide, two-lane road with ample angled parking on both sides. It spread out to the point that crossing on foot seemed like it would be an expedition; why they built so much space across was entirely beyond her. How the storefronts along the main strip survived was a miracle—or perhaps this was some form of Potemkin village, like she might walk up to the barber shop facade and push it right over onto its back. Unlike the outskirts of town where the architecture was utilitarian and identical from one lot to the next, here the bespoke spirit of Coalbrook's heritage displayed itself in the form of red brick and painted lumber.

Sara parked her rental and finally exhaled. *Not a tree in sight.* Nothing but concrete and mortar soaked in exhaust and snow—her bread and butter. And as said exhaust and snow wreathed around her groaning car as it settled into its downtime, she caught in her peripheral a light blue awning with black letters. *Anita's Bakery.* A mural of a huge cappuccino that had no right to be as good as it was in a town like this covered the towering bay window.

A small bell announced her entrance. The drawl of a country singer came from a small speaker on the checkout counter as the entire establishment glanced up, and in some cases did full body turns in her direction. At least one eyebrow rose after the eye it hung over did a snap assessment of her obvious out-of-town apparel relative to the mass of flannel and trucker caps that filled the plain interior. But it was quaint, filled with baked goods behind curved glass next to vintage furniture and local craft goods.

Feeling like an animal in a zoo, she quickly crossed the space and ordered an extra wet cappuccino—she ventured a request for soy milk—to go. One hand in pocket, one hand on her phone, she waited by thumbing through a bunch of content she cared nothing for. When her order came, the woman behind the counter—*was it Anita?*—made a show of her cappuccino artwork before placing the lid.

The bell chimed again, and she made for her car. Then she shot a quick glance across the street, and she went cold just as her lips touched the hot cappuccino.

That had to be him: Staff Sergeant Boyko, Coalbrook's detachment commander and apparent gatekeeper. He really embodied the look, too: salt-and-pepper hair, cut close in a pseudo-military style, like he was the kind of guy who spent a great deal of time after work waxing his mid-life crisis vehicle of choice.

Not my kind of person.

She strode to her crossover, her free hand buried deep in the pocket of her overcoat as she gave him the side-eye. He remained on the sidewalk next to his idling SUV, eyeing her over the top of his red cardboard cup as he drank. There was a distinct tightening of his eyelids as he watched her, undoubtedly noticing her bruise.

Sara ducked into her car. Like the final girl in a horror movie, she fumbled with her keys in the ignition. Was it nerves, or the chill? The key finally found its mark, and she pulled onto the road.

That was the thing about small towns: word travels fast, and everyone knows a bit about everyone. Back home, she was another face in the crowd—and that's how she liked it. You could pick and choose your friends and acquaintances and even drop them if you wanted. Back home, if she ghosted someone, there was a decent probability that she would never see them again. In a place like this? Not a chance.

She had barely dipped her toes in, and it was like someone put up a billboard with her face on it. *I just want my interview, maybe a poke around town for awhile as I wait for the repairs...*

She eased back onto the highway that pumped blood through the central artery of the city, branching off south to touch the industrial park where her car currently sat in disrepair and north into the greener part of town where most of the homes—and trees—seemed to lie. She would avoid that part if possible.

She glanced up at the mirror again to survey her bruise, as if she expected it to have gotten better by some miracle. To the left of her bruise, a pair of red and blue lights flashed. She jerked her head around.

Boyko.

He chirped his siren, and she responded by pulling over onto the side of the highway next to a snow-piled median. Other vehicles hissed mercilessly past on glimmering pavement, their drivers rubbernecking. Sara pushed on her steering wheel, pressing back into her seat while she drummed her fingers nervously on the leather.

A yellow-lined cap appeared, and its wearer tapped on the glass—his wordless command to lower the window. His open jacket revealed his tactical vest emblazoned with large white letters that spelled POLICE. She powered her window down as he leaned against the car, the stack of his four staff sergeant chevrons on his jacket shoulder staring her straight in the face.

He smiled. "Toque off, please."

She complied, but she made sure her face betrayed her desire to do otherwise—not that she could hide it otherwise. Up close,

Staff Sergeant Boyko looked surprisingly human, doughy-faced and cleft-chinned. And he looked just as tired as she did. The bags under his eyes—most certainly not the product of a collision with a tree—combined with the crow's feet that can only come with the advent of middle age told the story of a weary man.

"That's quite the bruise. You must be the podcast girl from Vancouver."

"That's me," she mumbled through a tight jaw. *Once again, Sara, wearing your emotions on your sleeve. Keep it up and you'll be heading to the detachment.* "Sara Garrison."

He smirked. "Welcome to Coalbrook, Sara Garrison. Are you planning on being here long?"

She shook her head. "Just passing through, really."

"On the way to where? Not much else this far north unless you're headed to Whitehorse."

"Well," she started, rolling her head side to side, "this was *kind* of where I was headed."

He looked up and down the highway. "So, we were a destination, eh?"

"Yessir."

"Imagine that. And for your podcast?"

She nodded.

"What's the subject?"

The words died in her throat. She felt compelled to answer, like if she answered enough questions that maybe he would leave her alone. But it didn't stop, and the tension mounted. Sara shifted in her seat, her clammy palms almost sliding off the wheel. This guy was pushing too hard, too fast. She locked up.

"What are you doing it on?" he asked again.

"If you're interested," she said, the words coming slowly, "I would encourage you to look up my podcast. The episode I'm working on should be out in a f—"

"I'm good, Ms. Garrison," he cut in. He tapped the top of her rental. "Sorry for the questions—us officers here tend to get a bit sensitive when journalists show up. Or when those who are kind of like journalists show up."

She raised an eyebrow, and the sting in her bruise flared up. "I have a degree in journalism, you know."

He raised his hands in exaggerated defence. "I'm sure, I'm sure."

"Wait—did you just stop me to ask me those questions? I don't think you can do that." She glared at him, emboldened by the sudden realisation of her rights. "If I didn't know any better, I would almost think that you were trying to intimidate me."

Staff Sergeant Boyko sucked his teeth. "Nope," he began, "I actually stopped you to make sure you were still feeling OK. From what Corporal Reid told me, you had hit your head pretty hard. Maybe even bordering on a concussion."

"Oh," she said. "Well, either way I don't appreciate being pulled over like this."

"Apologies, Ms. Garrison. I tried to get your attention while you were about to pull away back on Coal Street, but you were too quick." He shrugged his head down, searching her eyes. "Are you sure you're OK to drive?"

"Absolutely, I am."

He smiled. "Good." A soft groan escaped him as he straightened and tapped the roof of her rental again. "Good, good. Alright Ms. Garrison, sorry to keep you. Oh—by the way, where are you staying while you're here?"

Sara almost responded, the words just about to pass her lips—but she caught herself. "I haven't decided yet," she declared.

He looked incredulous. "You made plans to come here from the coast and you didn't book a place to stay?"

She shrugged. "Small town like this?" she said. "Didn't look too lively. I figured no one would be booking anything."

40

He scoffed, but not in a way that revealed offense. "Alright, then. See you around, Ms. Garrison." He tapped the roof again, stepped back and invited her to move on with a wave of his hand.

She took off towards the motel where her weeks-old booking waited. In her side mirror he remained on the side of the highway, watching her go for much longer than she would have liked.

5

Blue Light

THERE ARE SOME STORIES that are so beyond the pale of what we know to be normal, that they somehow circle back to being believable. After all, who could make this kind of thing up? Sorry, I had to laugh—clearly, anyone with half a brain could. But isn't it fun to believe that these kinds of things are possible? At any rate, at the end of the day, it's up to you.

-*The Garrison Theories* podcast, Episode 2: "What's Going on in Sasquatch Provincial Park?"

Sara slapped the spacebar with her forefingers. *Oh my god, I don't remember it sounding so cliche.* With a blowing sigh through pursed lips, she pushed herself away from the motel desk, the chair scraping on the cheap floral pattern of the motel carpet. A few sore steps and she entered the bathroom, snatching a cone cup from the dispenser and downing a mouthful of water. It went down wrong, and she hacked a cough. The cup bounced off the tiled wall and into the growing pile in the tiny tin pail next to the yellow toilet with the seat askew.

She stared at herself in the dim light. It wasn't just the toilet—it was all a diseased yellow in here. Behind her glasses, her face glowered bruised from the accident, leaving a purple crescent that wrapped around one of her eyes. She looked sick; she felt sick. Hard not to after no sleep on a thirteen-hour drive that ended with a bang.

Hard not to in a city—no, this was a town—like this. Coalbrook. Even sealed into this two-star room, the stench of wet dog chased her in and rolled like a miasma over her face, too thick to be natural.

And the surprise interview with the local commander didn't help either. She resisted the temptation to conclude that Coalbrook didn't want her presence.

According to reception, the stench was a part of the Coalbrook experience, and tended to be every winter. The pale dude with the patchy beard rolled his eyes when she made a show of wrinkling her nose at the obvious assault to the nostrils. He must have heard it all before. *You'll get used to it*, he said. *After long, you won't even notice.*

Liar.

She took off her glasses. The eyes that stared back at her sank into her face, the result of her thirteen-hour pilgrimage. Sara rubbed at the dark wedges of her lower eyelids, wincing as she touched her bruise. "You can do this, Sara. It's what you're here for."

She grabbed her face, pulling it down into a ghoulish mask, groaning. The ailing bulbs made her own pale skin look off. Sara longed for sleep, but her violent arrival in languid Coalbrook had jolted her awake as if she had moved through a wall of static. The hospital bed left a lot to be desired.

She sojourned in a new world, now—just her and Coalbrook and whatever else awaited. Another sigh, then a splash of foamy water from the blustering sink over her face. The towel raked her skin like sandpaper.

Back to it.

With her glasses returned to her face, she fell into the tiny desk chair with a creak. Alt-tabbing away from the podcast stream, Sara encountered a white rectangle, blinding in the murk of her motel room. The cursor blinked at the top left of the page. Two months. It had been two months since her last podcast episode, and she was all out of ideas. Like the litany of other horror podcasters, Sara plumbed the depths of the standard fare, doing her best to give her own twist to it. Cryptids. UFOs—or UAPs as they were now called. *Doesn't evoke the same mystique.* Ghosts and the paranormal—the basics, all filtered through a Canadian lens. It was her niche, and it had worked pretty well so far. Enough to keep her afloat while she worked part-time at a coffee shop. But now, the well ran dry. There was only so much Canadian high strangeness in the past to explore.

It was time to start chasing after the new stuff; time to put that journalism minor to use. No more armchair podcasting, not if she wanted to make it big.

You're kidding, Sara—right? Her mom's voice gripped Sara's head as she stared unblinking at the screen. Most parents, she imagined, probably didn't react well to their unestablished young adult children when they quit their jobs abruptly to "make it big". *Don't turn a hobby into a job, it'll make you hate it.*

She frowned, fingers hovering over the keyboard like a pianist's would hover over the ivories. For her, there were no illusions of making it big. Just to make it, to do something she loved instead of grinding herself down like the coffee beans that ruled over her weekends and Wednesdays. *Podcasting isn't a real job,* her mom's voice came again. *God, Sara, you can be so impulsive.* Sara shook her head like it might shake her mom's words loose out of her ears.

She cracked her knuckles. "Just a few words," she announced to no one in particular, "and the rest will flow."

So—Coalbrook. An old coal-mining town gone sour, with nothing left but lumber and a skeletal tourism industry to save it. And if the lumber industry was anything like the tourism one, well... it was good she came here when she did. This town wasn't long for Canada.

Of course, she wasn't here to experience the great outdoors, no—the wilds and she didn't get along, hadn't for over a decade now. Her white-knuckled driving north through the meandering, forest-clad wilds of British Columbia was proof positive that maybe her strides in therapy weren't as big as she thought.

So, what possessed me?

On the edge of fall and winter, just over a year ago, a young man named Christian Johnstone disappeared in or outside of Coalbrook. The RCMP and local search-and-rescue, complemented by myriad citizens, had searched for ten days. They never recovered his body, and they presumed him dead from exposure a few days later.

And she of all people had secured an interview with the remaining family, their contact information gleaned with a bit of internet sleuthing. They were suspects at first, but eventually passed over as the trail went cold. But after watching the interviews with them, it seemed clear that they were painted with a broad brush with a colour that didn't suit them. It seemed to her that there was a story there—one of a mismanaged detachment, poor leadership, and an unfair treatment of the next of kin. So, with her breath held tight in her lungs, she fired off an email with an invitation to clear the air with a fresh story. Their story. And if she embellished it slightly along the way to add a bit of mystique to the tragedy... well, that just came with the profession. *What is storytelling if not embellishment?*

She couldn't believe her eyes when she read that email from the boy's uncle—it was like an acceptance letter to a prestigious university, a document that held her entire future. The time and date were set, and she dropped her job—the real one, as mom liked to say—like she had never had it. Something told her that she needed to be there. To be here. To truly report on something, to get the feel of it... well, you've got to be there. Sara smiled softly as her fingers fluttered over the keys, the excitement of the adventure pouring out of her—

She startled as the window to her right groaned, creaking as wind buffeted the side of the motel. She jerked her head towards it, half-expecting to see the door open with the receptionist standing

45

there dumbly. Outside, through the parted curtains and across the poorly lit highway, a towering wall of evergreens churned in the breeze, revealing black patches in the spaces between the boles and boughs. Sara shivered, trying vainly to snap her attention back to the screen. But the trees held her gaze, taunted her with their dance, daring her to imagine what lay beyond them. Dared her to try to guess where the body of Christian Johnstone lay.

Edging closer, Sara fixed her eyes on the trees. *If I'm going to make it here, I've got to figure this phobia out once and for all. Time for a bit more exposure therapy, maybe?* Clutching the thick, brown curtains that flanked the large window, she stared at the churning wall of trees across the highway. As she held her gaze, a sense of disquiet grew within. Disquiet shifted into unease, which blossomed into anxiety—and then pitched into full-blown terror at the prospect of what was out there in the darkness. What was out there in the trees.

"Nope," she declared as she leapt to the window, snatching the curtains shut. She flung herself onto the bed.

Eventually, the laptop screen switched to black.

Vanessa's face beamed at him, cheeks squished as his two teenaged children sandwiched her between their own faces. The smiles were ensconced by trees with clear blue water stretching out before snow-capped peaks that in their altitude resisted the sun's attempts to melt the snow away.

The man who rested his chin on top of Vanessa's brown hair smiled, too. Steve looked like him. This doppelgänger wore the same summer clothes, had the same shock of silver dusting the sides and top. But he was a foreigner, someone he didn't know who was feeling and experiencing things that he couldn't understand.

That frozen moment in time was summer vacation over a year and a half ago, precious months before it happened. Before his career spun out of control and turned his peaceful life into a daily fire walk. He would have dinner with his family. He would laugh. Now he came home burned out and stretched thin like overcooked microwave bacon. The sleepiness that had once defined this humble town had crept into his house, killing the life that was once there. Vanessa hadn't bothered to print any pictures from their vacation from a few months ago in July.

Steve let out a grating sigh, eyes wide in the dark of the small room that served as both home office and music room for Vanessa. The working day had passed uneventfully after he had—as he lied—checked on the new girl to make sure she was fit to drive. Throughout the day, trying as he might to busy himself about his duties as an officer, he found that she lived rent-free in his head for the entirety of his shift, casting a grey cloud over his mind. How could he put last year's debacle behind him if people like her kept on trying to dig it up?

You don't have proof, buddy. She could be here for anything...

Now that he was home, and the house hushed with sleep—except for his, of course—he figured he would take some steps to extricate this young woman from his head. He had to know what she schemed. If she wouldn't volunteer the information, he would do a bit of seeking on his own time.

As he closed the door to his office, he stared at the thin laptop on his desk, waiting for him like a table setting. Steve swirled the amber contents of his glass, dreading the information that the small machine held for him, hoping desperately that it wasn't about to confirm his worst fears.

He peeled open his laptop and waited for it to boot up, taking a sip of what would have been a night cap if he had any intention of sleeping. The two additional monitors that swept across his desk flickered on simultaneously, and he leaned back in his chair to watch the brief startup sequence as he winced at the rye that ran burning down his throat.

No time was wasted in navigating to the search bar to punch in: sara garrison podcast. Steve pressed the enter key, and his search engine of choice introduced him to her pseudo-professional portrait on a gothic-looking site. The tabs invited him to read her short fiction, to click links to her YouTube channel, to see some of her photography, to see—ah, there it was: the podcast itself. He clicked it, and scrolled through the titles of episodes, like *The Jilted Bride, What's Going on in Sasquatch Provincial Park?*, and *Here Be Dragons.* Hell, there was even an episode on gnomes. His eyes bulged.

Gnomes?

This girl was all ghosts and goblins, so what business did she have here? She made it clear that she wasn't just passing through. Coalbrook was where she wanted to be—but why? This town was entirely inconsequential, except for the people that lived here.

In his mind, there could only be one reason, and one reason alone that a girl with a penchant for paranormal podcasting would be here. Probably for the only thing from Coalbrook that has ever reached national news: the disappearance of Christian Johnstone.

It screamed desperation. And if she was desperate, then maybe she saw Coalbrook as an opportunity, like a gold mine of misery just waiting for someone to jump a claim. A meal ticket to restarting this failing venture of hers. She *had* to be here to explore what happened to Christian. What other reason could there be, given her work? *Work.* He almost laughed.

A tightness grew in his stomach. He still reeled from the catastrophe of it all, even a year later. Every working day reminded him of his indecision, his bias, his unprofessionalism that may—*may*—have been at the root of failing to find the boy. And now this girl had the nerve to show up and dig up those old bones, like some sort of pain grifter?

He took another sip. Of course, Steve knew she wasn't without justification. The circumstances were strange and remain to this day to all involved without closure—including him. One theory was that Christian's aunt and uncle were involved, a theory that he entertained until the evidence didn't materialise. It fell to the simplest of answers: he was simply lost, or he took his own life.

That's the story Steve told himself. And it approximated the entire truth, knowing as he did that something about the whole thing was off in a hair-rising way. Even after pushing hard against Clayton and Rita—the aunt and uncle—there remained some strange thread woven through the entire event, something uncanny that he couldn't put his finger on. The days with search and rescue left an impression on him. *What was it that Sergeant Parenteau had said last year? Something like she felt the trees were watching them.* Either way, such oddities and fancies fell outside of their normal police work; it wasn't his place to explore hunches on zero evidence, and frankly he didn't have the energy to explore. *Don't forget the courage part, buddy. You were too chicken to take it to the next level.* He took a long drink from his glass and set it down empty on his desk.

Ultimately, it was the lack of evidence that made it so strange. Not so much as a footprint in the snow. The memories, the feelings, the ominous nature of it all... it had made him sick, and he had no intention of revisiting it. And if Sara was willing to face it, then maybe she was a better journalist than he gave her credit for.

If only she knew what I knew.

He had a feeling she'd know soon enough.

6

Interviews

MANY RESEARCHERS HAVE tried—and are still trying—to prove empirically the existence of the creatures we call cryptids. Sasquatch—or maybe Bigfoot for my American listeners—is a prime example. To prove that Sasquatch is a biological creature, researchers will focus on the physical evidence like foot castings but ignore the high strangeness surrounding so many sightings. For me, the most compelling evidence comes from the testimonies from those not boxed in by the primate paradigm—the stories of snowy footprints that suddenly end like the owner was sucked into space, or the glowing green eyes that beam like flashlights, or the smell of sulphur or strange lights in the sky. I believe that Sasquatch, with all his global incarnations, is more than just some reclusive ape. And I believe we can say the same for many of these other mysteries...

-The Garrison Theories podcast, Episode 1: "Our Weird Frontier"

He wore the same look on the highway billboards as he did in the newspaper—a slack smile on a long, asymmetrical face. A school picture, by the looks of it. An expression heedless of the future. He was the reason she was here.

MISSING. CHRISTIAN JOHNSTONE. HEIGHT: 5'8". APPROXIMATELY 180 LBS. LAST SEEN IN COALBROOK, BRITISH COLUMBIA, ON OCTOBER 12TH...

The image towered on stilts just off the shoulder of the road. It struck her as more of a memorial than a call for help, despite the words emblazoned across the bottom next to the number for the Coalbrook RCMP detachment.

PLEASE HELP US.

And help Coalbrook did—at least they tried, according to what she knew. The news covered the story briefly, describing a call to action that brought search and rescue and citizen volunteers out in droves. What defined a town's recent history, however, was just a blip on the national radar. First, a report on the disappearance; second, a report on the declaration that he likely died due to exposure. It hung over the tragedy as a controversial call, to be sure, one that offered no closure to family and friends. But the case closed with no more coverage. The billboards that remained all around Coalbrook testified to the opposite: the city had not forgotten. She marvelled at their continued presence along the highway before the built-in GPS commanded her in a soft voice to turn right onto Covey Road.

Immediately, she tensed. Like reporters leaning over velvet ropes on the red carpet, the boughs of the evergreens clambered over the road and hung over her, the weight of their presence pushing her deep into the upholstery. Sara cut her eyes to the GPS. *Ten more minutes.* She pressed her boot into the gas pedal. The potholes tossed her side-to-side, but she didn't let up. The crossover crunched over snow and loose rock as the snow-dusted trees slid past.

She checked the rear-view. *Maybe I should consider sticking with armchair journalism.* With lips pressed into a thin line, her mind lurched back and forth along with her rental, timed to flashing images of her mother's disapproving looks. *Remember the vagus nerve, Sara.* Slowly, she took in a shaky breath through her nostrils, making sure to focus on her diaphragm as she squeezed the steering wheel. The knot in her stomach quivered—the nearest to relief as she would get.

The trees pressed in on both sides, hiding the infrequent driveways until the last moment when it was suddenly too late to turn. Sara did her best to keep her eyes forward, mindful of the myriad potholes that stretched as far as she saw down the road like a minefield. The threatening posture of the trees made them impossible to ignore as they towered like old rivals that knew her weaknesses all too well. A quick glance to her right sent a jolt of fear through her.

In her mind's eye she visualised Andrea running through the trees, dipping in and out of sight as she passed behind each bole before eventually disappearing with a scream. Even the light of day did nothing to quell the menace of the trees.

Focus on the interview. You're a journalist. Kind of.

She took a deep breath, reactivating her vagus nerve and bringing her mind back to the present. Coalbrook wasn't much to look at, but these unpaved outskirts somehow managed to be even less. The soothing voice came again from her phone. *In 200 metres, turn left. You will have arrived at your destination.*

11 Covey Road.

Past the ditches, beyond the trees, the edge of the Johnstone property came into view, and then suddenly the trees fell away to reveal a sprawling patch of cleared land. It was a flat, mottled sprawl of dead grass and dead machinery. Decades-old vehicles sidled up against the outbuildings like they tried to keep warm. A large garden sat neglected on raised beds near the right side.

Good country people.

The house itself was precisely as she pictured it. The interviews on the CBC made Clayton and Rita look like they lived in a place exactly like this: the plaid of their jackets paired perfectly with the broken-down cars and gutted workshop. The red paint on the wavy wood siding was coming off in strips. Swallowing, Sara imagined the interior. She held her breath and rolled to a stop in the dirt driveway.

She crossed the yard, her eyes crawling over the uneven and snow-patched grass and up the front of the house where she caught some movement behind some curtains. *Another deep breath. Check bag for interview stuff. Don't panic, Sara—you're a journalist, remember?*

Her knocking rattled the glass covering the torn screen door. The moment on the steps stretched out, and Sara felt compelled to fidget with her phone in her jacket pocket to escape. A sigh of relief quietly left her when the front of the house shook at the arrival of whoever hid behind the door; it opened first, followed by the screen.

"Hi," she began, almost in disbelief at her lack of preparedness. Her voice sounded weak in her skull. "My name is Sara Garrison, and I am looking for—"

"Me." The man's face glistened, broad and dark. "Clayton Johnstone. And I could tell it was you. You look like a Sara from Vancouver."

She pasted on a smile. "Clayton—yes! Nice to meet you finally."

He flicked his head to the side. "Come on in."

Clayton ambled down the narrow hallway, the flared arms of his oversized t-shirt brushing against the walls and hissing against his puffer vest. Sara crept behind him, every step reminding herself of what this interview might do for her career—if she didn't repeat those mantras to herself, her lizard brain might have taken over and sent her running. It even sounded odd in her head, calling it a "career". She longed for the day it didn't.

"So, how was the drive? Not exactly a short one, eh?" He gestured to the tiny rectangle of a kitchen table then busied himself about the sink. A wall of shelving separated the space from the dining room. The shelves were packed with pressure-sealed jars of preserves, like he thought nuclear winter was just around the corner.

"It was… long," she said as she sat, dropping her messenger bag against the wall and tossing her toque on top. "And then I swerved to avoid an elk and hit a tree."

"Really?" he asked, gesturing down the hall to the front door. "Strong car you got."

"That's my rental," she said as she smoothed her cropped hair with both hands. "I totaled my car."

"Damn," he groaned as he returned to the counter. "Coffee?"

"Please!"

"Cream and sugar?"

"Do you ha—"

He raised a thin eyebrow, a hint of a smile pushing his round cheeks back and burying his tiny, dark eyes in the thick folds of his face.

She waved a hand. "I'll take it black, actually."

He poured her a cup and joined her at the table. His head was like an enormous, smooth boulder covered in hanging black moss. As if on cue, he took an elastic and tied it back in a ponytail. "I know I said this on the phone a few weeks ago," he said as he took his coffee and held it steaming below his chin, "but hell, that's a long way to go for an interview these days."

Sara suppressed a wince at the sip she just had, cutting a quick glance to the counter behind him. Nescafe—that explained it. "I guess I'm a bit old school." She took another polite sip. "Trying to be, anyway. A lot gets missed when you don't add the face-to-face."

"Right," he said with a nod. He left his mug on the table and leaned back in his chair. Sara braced for it to buckle. "You don't really strike me as the old school type, you know?" His eyes moved from hers, flickering to her glasses, her cropped hair, her overcoat that spilled like curtains on the tile. "But I'm glad you're here. 'Bout time someone gave a rat's ass about our perspective."

She smiled, genuine this time. "That's why I'm here," she said, a hint of triumph in her voice. *Already settling in.* "Thank you for the coffee." She emptied her pockets onto the table: notepad, pen, pencil, smartphone. "And thank you most of all for allowing me to interview you about this. It can't be easy to talk about, but it seems necessary based on the reporting done by the CBC. I can't believe the implications in some of the articles published."

A shuffling noise came from the room at the end of the hall behind him. "More than just implications," he challenged. "The cops here were almost downright saying it out loud with some of their questions last year."

"Right," Sara continued, "Shall we get into it, then? I don't want to jump too far ahead, and I want to be respectful of your time—"

"Please."

Sara slid her phone forward on the table, the screen indicating to them both it was recording their speech. "So, Clayton—tell me about what really happened to your nephew on October 12th of last year."

Clayton kept his eyes down, fixed on the steam rising from the mug of coffee before him. He took in a protracted breath, letting it out with a shaky sigh. "It was a regular school day. Rita drove him in."

"Oh, OK—so what happened? What went wrong?"

Clayton shrugged. "When I went to pick him up, he wasn't at school. Didn't come home. Which for a while wasn't unusual, since he sometimes would crash at a friend's house."

"When did it start to feel off?" Sara asked as she checked to make sure the phone was still listening.

"He wasn't responding to our texts."

"And who is 'our'?"

"Me and Rita. His aunt, my wife." He gestured over his shoulder to no room in particular. "Didn't want to talk."

The story grew, and Sara sat transfixed, eyes unmoving from Clayton. At times he laughed as if all was right with the world, like her presence in his home was the result of a neighbourly visit to discuss hockey or something equally mundane. As the story of the search for Christian seesawed, his face would often crumple along with an increasingly empty voice. And occasionally Rita would stride wordlessly into the kitchen, take some food, and leave. But each visit would stretch in length as she glanced at Clayton, at Sara, listening as she loitered.

"So," Sara said after a lengthy pause, "it seems pretty clear that you think the RCMP made the wrong call."

"Hell yes they did," he griped. "My nephew was probably still alive. One of his teachers saw him walk off from the school, thinking nothing of it. His footprints... they more or less faded."

"I remember the article said they thought someone picked him up in a vehicle."

"That's what they said. Rita and I spent weeks afterwards looking for him ourselves." He crossed his arms, shaking his head at her like she made the call herself. "The RCMP hears what we say, they smile and nod, but at the end of it all they just do what they want. They just saw us as an obstacle at best, and an alibi at worst."

Sara furrowed her brow. "Why would they try to pin it on you when you were pushing for a more thorough investigation? That doesn't make sense."

Another sip of coffee, another shake of his large head. "No," he responded as he licked his lips. "It's 'cause we think that it wasn't on purpose."

"Because he disappeared?"

"That," said Clayton, "but mainly because that ain't our nephew. He knows the bush around here, but no matter how much you know you can get lost out there. Happened to me before. So, they figured it must have been a suicide related to some psychosis, some mental break or somethin' or other. But me and Rita are his family, we know better. Christian had his struggles, like we all do. But he would never do somethin' like this."

"The articles published never mentioned suicide."

"Because suicide ain't the official word. But that's what they believed; I can tell. Steve and the others. Or at least that's what they pushed for, either suicide on his part or malicious intent on ours. Anything that would suggest responsibility on our end that would take away the burden from the RCMP and the search and rescue teams."

"Steve?"

"Steve Boyko. Commander of the RCMP detachment in town and the surrounding area. Sergeant or somethin' or other, not sure." Clayton looked out the window. "We talked to him the most."

She nodded. "Right. I've met him."

"What'd you think?"

Sara glanced at her phone. They had been recording for nearly fifty minutes. "I'm not one for authority, let's say. So, he made the final call?"

Clayton nodded.

"And you believe that by trying to explain it away with suicide or... murder, I suppose—that it took some of the heat off them?"

"That's right. Can't find someone that isn't meant to be found, right? Self-imposed or not. If my nephew was simply lost and wandering, then it was simply a lack of resources... time. Skill maybe. All things that reflect poorly on the RCMP and others."

"I see."

"They abandoned my nephew out there, Ms. Garrison." He drummed his fingers on the table. "Who knows how long he would have lasted." He glanced to the right, staring out the kitchen window to the woods beyond. "Certainly can't last a year. It's a closed book now." He turned back to her. "Well, maybe not anymore."

She smirked. "Maybe not." Sara lifted her phone and stared at the timer. *Lots of content to draw from.* It continued to count as she placed it down gently. "One last question, Clayton," she said as she spread her hands. "Obviously, I reached out to you. If you accepted my request for an interview this long after the incident, why hadn't you gone to another news outlet sooner? Wouldn't anyone want to represent you?"

Clayton sighed and his shoulders sank like he was a balloon letting out air. "Frankly, Rita and I were scared." He rubbed at his knuckles. "At first, we laid low because of the way the narrative was being spun. We were afraid of being implicated..."

"Even without evidence?"

He shrugged. "Who knows what they might come up with? Seemed like the media bought the idea that we were hiding something at the time. But then time went by, and we just slowly stopped going into town—"

Rita appeared from down the hall. "We were angry." She stared right at Sara through watery eyes. "We were so damn angry."

Sara struggled to find the words. "Oh—hi, Rita."

"We bunkered down. Stopped caring about this godforsaken place."

Clayton simply nodded.

She hung about for a bit longer, but the conversation became circular—Clayton was adamant that Christian wasn't the kind of kid to do something like that, despite the RCMP investigation suggesting otherwise. And the published news seemed to suggest Christian had an ongoing relationship with a counsellor at his school, calling into question his stability. She thanked the Johnstones and left, with a loose indicator of a desire to reconnect before she left town.

She sat in the loaner car and stared at the evergreens at the edge of the property as they shook in the midday wind. It was good content. And it was good to give the Johnstone's a voice. But the electric feeling from the interview, of being a part of something significant—well, now she tasted blood. She wanted more.

She pulled out her phone and thumbed her way to the location of the Coalbrook RCMP detachment. As she drove back into town, she scarcely noticed the trees.

When he read the Northern Lights community periodical—more of a bulletin than anything—Steve would often find himself lingering at the back, scanning for the small section of the obituaries. Often, it read empty. But each time he searched this sense of foreboding rose, some sick pull to the hidden depths of the starved periodical, some small-town expression of *l'appel du vide*. In an isolated place like Coalbrook, with its stagnant and ageing population, he was bound to see the name of someone he had come to know over the past eight years. He came across lots of faces in his line of work, and occasionally he received the ugly surprise of seeing them framed at the back of the single, off-yellow sheet of thin cardstock.

The radio on his lapel buzzed, and a male voice hummed through. Steve checked the chart on his desk. It was Corporal Reid and Sergeant Parenteau on patrol around the downtown core. Of course, patrol here largely meant pulling over and having a light conversation with a small group of teenagers, then popping into Tim Horton's for a coffee. Maybe a doughnut. The crackling faded.

There was one morning, about a year ago, where Steve's reading of the bulletin was hampered by the shaking of his hands. He had thumbed it over slowly, ignoring the sad attempts at local news and the discouraging federal occurrences. The bulletin lay face-down, his hand flat and covering the bottom right corner where he knew it would be. He lifted his cupped palm, peeking under it as if expecting to see a trapped insect. He remembered so clearly the feeling of his heart dropping into his stomach. There it was, the portrait of a young man who he had come to know deeply despite having barely interacted with him before he disappeared. The black-and-yellow print didn't hide the darkness of his skin, or the roughness of his features, or the shade of his obsidian hair which jutted out of his head like thorns. His narrow, youthful face wore a restrained, but hopeful smile. The town memorialised Christian Johnstone because Steve had declared him dead.

Steve had sat there for a time, back when the weight of the choice crushed him, and tried to discern what went on within. A twinge of grief. A pang of guilt.

A roiling mountain of shame.

Now, a year later, familiar sensations washed over Stephen, pooling somewhere below his heart. *You just need more time, buddy. Maybe a vacation.*

He placed the bulletin flat on his desk and sighed aloud to shake off the feeling. It didn't budge. With a creak he spun in his chair to meet the low sun that peeked at him over the sprawling woods that surrounded the small town of Coalbrook. The edge of the forest that he disappeared in, the unbroken labyrinth of green, grey, and brown that would go on to sprawl for countless kilometres in every direction.

Maybe a resignation.

A knock came from his door. Steve spun around in his chair and stared at the buzzed head of Constable Barchard. He was a young officer, nearly fresh out of depot. Most everyone just called him Matt.

"Staff Sergeant? You free?"

Steve planted his elbows on his desk. "Somewhat."

"Well, there's a woman out here who is interested in talking to you."

He frowned and crossed his arms. "Who is she?"

"An independent journalist, she says." Matt smiled. "I guess The Northern Lights wasn't good enough for her."

Steve rolled his eyes. "Don't tell me—is it a Ms. Sara Garrison?"

Matt nodded, furrowing his brow. "Yeah—how'd you know?"

"Call it intuition. Please tell me you grilled her for what she wanted to talk about."

"I did," he responded warily. "And when she told me, I told her you wouldn't be interested. But she won't leave, and I really don't feel like cuffing her." He scrunched up his shoulders. "She seems nice."

"You're a humanitarian, Mr. Barchard," he said as he pushed himself up. He strode around his desk, fingering his vest in his standard ritual to check his instruments. Sidearm. Taser. Cuffs. Spray. By the time he reached the cramped space that served as the lobby of the Coalbrook RCMP detachment, he felt secure—secure enough to frown directly at the red-capped young woman standing right in the middle of the thin carpet of the double-wide portable that gave them their workspace.

Now outside of her vehicle and standing up close, Sara Garrison seemed a bit waifish. She seemed paler too, made sickly by the awful lighting in their small detachment that drew the yellow out of her bruise. Her beady eyes peered at him through a pair of oversized round-lensed glasses, which for all he knew were nothing but a fashion statement along with her septum piercing, among others. Steve gave her his hand, and she took it.

"We meet again, Ms. Garrison," he said as he squeezed and pumped. "How can I help you?"

Weakly, she returned the grip and smiled with what looked like forced confidence. She had one hand over the strap of her messenger bag. "I was hoping that I could have the privilege of asking you a few questions about last year's event." The question came fast, as if she already knew the answer and wanted to get it over with.

"Well, Ms. Garrison, if you are referring to what I think you are referring to, we've already offered everything we are willing to share to the public. You can read about it online—the CBC even ran a few articles on it." She nodded, her lips moving as if she waited for her turn to interject. He shrugged. "So, at this point I'm not willing to comment further."

"I've read those articles, Mr. Boyko. They alluded to the fact that the families left very unsatisfied with the investigation, so it seemed like there was more of a story. And there's lots of buzz online if you know where to look..."

"Buzz?"

"Rumours, I guess. That maybe things didn't go very well, and that those involved obscured some bits of information... there are lots of fairly negative comments on the article."

"First, it's Staff Sergeant Boyko, Ms. Garrison." He resisted the urge to cross his arms, keeping his hands on his hips. Near his sidearm. "Second, you can't believe everything you—"

"Read on the internet. Yes, I've heard that one before."

He gave in and crossed his arms following a brief, annoyed glance at Constable Barchard. "And who are you representing? What do you want with this information? Is it just for your struggling podcast?"

She seemed to dodge the dig. "Yes, for myself. But for my audience, too. I don't know if you've had a chance to look for yourself, Staff Sergeant Boyko, but I run a very popular Canadian—" she paused, glancing between the sergeant and the very polite Constable Barchard, "—true crime podcast."

"I see. What's it called?" he asked, feigning ignorance.

"The Garrison Theories podcast."

"Right," he said. *True crime, my left foot.* "Maybe I'll give it a listen later—but either way the answer is no, Ms. Garrison. This kind of information is relayed through official press releases on our site." He gestured to her. "Not like this."

Sara furrowed her brow. "Fair enough. I just wanted to give you a chance to give your perspective, that's all."

"The RCMP has already given the facts of the case. There's nothing left to add to our perspective."

"Yeah—no, I just wanted to give you an opportunity to respond to some of the allegations coming from the Johnstone family."

Steve crossed his arms tightly over his vest. "Have you talked to them?"

"Just did. I wanted to give them a chance to voice their concerns freely." A tight smirk crossed her face, one that betrayed a shaky confidence. She was an adult but presented as a petulant teenager. "Are you sure you don't want to add anything?"

"No," he said through his teeth. "Is there anything else, Ms. Garrison? Or can we get back to some real police work?"

"Sorry to keep you," she said as she began to spin. But she hesitated.

The phone at the front desk had started to chirp. Constable Barchard stood over the reception desk, hidden somewhat behind a wall of plexiglass, and answered it. Steve kept his eyes on Sara as Matthew mumbled into the phone, doing his best to be discreet.

"Please, Ms. Garrison. It would be helpful if you would give us the space to—"

"Steve?"

He glanced back at Matt. "What?"

"It's Sharon Shaw. Wants you. Says Kimberly snuck out last night and hasn't come home."

"I'll take it," he mumbled as he came alongside reception. He cut a look to Sara, who loitered in the lobby. *This girl is going to be a thorn in my side, I can feel it already.* "Matt," he whispered, "get her out of here, will you?" Before he even brought the phone to his ear, he groaned quietly to himself as the other officer approved her request to use the washroom before she left.

The frantic voice that buzzed through the receiver was unmistakable. Sharon was a well-meaning single mother who could never quite pull herself out of crisis mode because she was too busy pulling herself down into liquor. These phone calls were a dime-a-dozen because her teen daughter's escapades were themselves a dime-a-dozen. And who can blame a young kid for wanting to get away? She was one of the local youths who found herself straddling the edge of lawlessness for much of her days, so Steve was well-acquainted with her. She was a sweet kid, though. Maybe bittersweet was a better word. Lots of potential, if only she would pull herself together long enough to realise it. The harried words came quickly, and Steve scrambled to keep up.

"Sharon," he started. "Sharon—Sharon!" He paused. So did she. "Sharon, as always, we'll get someone right on it. Any idea where she might have gone?" She relayed a few names, some whose parents she had already contacted. She said that the detachment might be hearing from them soon—they were in the same position. Teenagers, AWOL and zero contact. *That meant one thing...*

"Sharon, we'll find her. Hang tight, we'll be in touch. Do you need anything? I might be able to spare an officer to—no? OK. Yes, ASAP."

As he hung up the phone, Matt returned from down the hall. "She's still in there," he said with another trademark shrug.

Steve sighed. "Forget about her. Looks like Kim Shaw's whole group is missing, none of them checking back with home base."

"No other parents have called yet."

"Yet. We'll beat 'em to the punch hopefully. I'd be willing to wager..."

"Right," said Matt, his eyes lighting up. "Blue Hills?"

Just as the words left his mouth, the would-be-journalist Sara Garrison strode up behind him. She only smiled, giving them a little bow as she clutched her messenger bag. "Thanks again. And sorry for bothering you."

With a scamper, she left. Steve frowned at her back as she left the detachment, and then to Constable Barchard, who naturally only shrugged.

7

Every Nook and Cranny

WHEN WE THINK OF HAUNTINGS, we tend to move immediately to thoughts of old, creaky, and often gothic-looking houses. These tropes aren't arbitrary. They root themselves in the experience that many have had: older buildings contain more history, and lengthier histories contain more emotional energy. It's like the floorboards and the walls themselves hold memory, some sort of ownership over events witnessed—both good and bad.

-The Garrison Theories podcast, Episode 6: "The Jilted Bride"

I ntuition was a funny thing. It seemed so incidental, so untethered from anything solid enough to be worth grasping on to. But it never steered her wrong. *Got to trust your gut.* Mom's words, though hardly original. *Bet she regrets it now that I've taken them seriously.* Sara heard it in mom's voice as she threw the door to the Coalbrook detachment wide open and speed-walked to her car without a glance back. Staff Sergeant Boyko's gaze burned the back of her skull. Yet she couldn't ignore the stronger burning of her intuition.

The interview with Clayton left a lot to be desired, and the subsequent interview—if it could even be called that—that just finished was a complete non-starter. It seemed like her podcast might not get the boost she sought. Sure, Clayton had given her his side of the story, but it turned out to be a more granular version of the few dismissive lines of text in the published articles. It was a different opinion. It was possible for her to cut it to pieces and Frankenstein it back into something that might work for her podcast, but it would require embellishment and exaggeration to the point of discomfort. *And for me to feel uncomfortable about bending the truth... that means something.*

But more missing kids in Coalbrook? Almost exactly one year later? That was a nugget of content too rich to pass up. It could be a coincidence. Could be a twenty-four-hour runaway that will resolve with a tearful hug and apology. But the electric frisson that pooled at the base of the back of her neck told her otherwise; something was up, and she wanted a piece.

It was the hardest she had ever pushed a car, made easier by the fact that it wasn't hers. Sara had tried to press the gas lightly when she backed out of the detachment parking lot, but she rushed with an unfamiliar intemperance; the snowy gravel spat against the curb while she rolled back onto the road, her heart pumping adrenaline through her system, her eyes bulging like it was her first time on a new drug. She had done nothing illegal, yet she felt every bit the outlaw.

She cranked the wheel around and sped down the road towards the centre of town in the hopes of finding some nook to sidle her vehicle into. Away from those iconic, yellow-striped pants that for all she knew could be hot on her heels. Towering pines blurred in her peripherals. Nervous laughter escaped her as she took a right onto Coal Street and tucked neatly into an angled parking space.

After a brief struggle with her pocket for her phone, Sara brought up a local map, stabbing her forefinger shakily into the text box:

blue hills Coalbrook

An indigo line coursed from her location to a destination forty-four minutes out of town, right into the foothills of the nearest mountain where, according to her phone, the Blue Hills Ski Resort nestled and waited for her. She snapped her phone onto the dash and ripped out of the parking lot.

The hiss of the wet pavement beneath him was loud enough to drown out the grinding of his teeth. Alone in his work SUV Steve carved his way along a cold and serpentine passage, each rotation of the wheels plunging him further into the foothills of the Northern Rocky Mountains. The alpine road narrowed as it split, forlorn passages and logging roads dwindling and winding beyond into grey obscurity.

He left Matt and the other on-duty constables behind, choosing to call instead on Corporal Cameron Reid and Sergeant Lauren Parenteau to pause their patrol and give him a hand. They were both young, but not too young as was the problem with the others. A few of the other members at the detachment were still pretty green, only a few years out of depot and barely scratching the middle of their second decade—Matt included. Cameron and Lauren had more years and more wisdom. Cameron had a way with the youth; Lauren wasn't too bad herself, although her mid-thirties sensibilities may have made her too motherly for some. And Steve had about ten years on her. *Does that put me into grandfather territory?*

After forty-five minutes, the lovingly carved yet now cracked and discoloured sign of the Blue Hills Ski Resort appeared. It cowered on the side of the road, partially obscured by trees but exposed enough to give a reluctant welcome. Steve sighed. *What a waste.*

Around the bend, the main structure came into view. Backed by snow, the striking silhouette of the turquoise metal roof caught his eye first. It was entirely bare, giving the place an appearance of routine maintenance thanks to the natural ability for the smooth, angled top to dump the snow. That was where the illusion of care ceased: the rest of it was boarded, rotten, and shattered. It was a cobbled and timbered husk that crumbled alone on the border of a chewed-up parking lot and sloping mountainside.

Before the front doors, Sergeant Lauren Parenteau stood outside of her cruiser; blonde hair wrapped up in a black ushanka. She approached Steve as he rolled up to the front of the resort, tires crunching over snow and gravel. He lowered the window and met her clear blue eyes.

"We need a search warrant, you think?" she called into his idling vehicle.

He killed the engine and joined her outside, gathering the faux-fur collar of his jacket around his neck. Eight years, and his skin still refused to adjust to the hard-hitting cold of Canada outside of the Lower Mainland. "Not unless we have due cause. Looks pretty quiet."

"Steve!"

He spun and called out to Corporal Reid. "Canvass?"

"That I did, Sergeant," replied Cam as he came around the side of the building. He was red-faced beneath his toque. "We got two empty vehicles out the back and a possible point of entry."

Steve glanced at Lauren. "There's our due cause."

"There's another car, too," Cam declared. "But it ain't empty."

Steve frowned. "Let me guess—our nosy guest from Vancouver?"

The moustachioed officer blinked. "The journalist girl, yeah. I'm afraid so."

"Podcaster."

"What?"

"She's not a journalist," Steve growled. "She's an independent podcaster."

"Ah," said Cam. "How'd you know she'd be here?"

"Call it intuition." Steve worked his way down the lengthy south face of the building. The windows that he shouldered, now blanketed with OSB, would have nearly a decade ago given the three officers a glimpse into the vaulted space of the main dining hall; it didn't quite have the glory now. The interesting thing about the lodge was that every time they searched it—whenever they got a call or caught wind of a party—the interior had drastically changed. The rotten furniture was moved around, there were new things broken, new murals and graffiti, and so on.

He rounded the corner and stared at the blue crossover he saw less than an hour ago tear out of the detachment's parking lot. "Unbelievable," he breathed as he approached, shaking his head. "What is this girl doing?" He leaned against the side of the car, lowered his head, and stared into a pair of wide, hazel eyes centred in oversized eyeglass frames. With a frown, he tapped on the glass. She powered it down.

"Hello, officer." Her voice faltered. She was stiff, holding fast in her seat like it was the last place she wanted to be.

"Ms. Garrison, do I even have to ask?"

She looked back to her phone and hurriedly finished tapping the screen before tucking it between her thighs. "Just taking in the sights," she said with a gesture to the lodge. Corporal Reid smirked back at them while Sergeant Parenteau did her best to peer into the murky insides of the old resort.

He brought his attention back to the car, grateful for the warmth coming through the open window. "Are you aware that this is private property?"

"Isn't it abandoned?" Sara asked with an air of uncertainty.

"Abandoned? No. Derelict? Yes." He glanced away, eyeing the boarded-up windows and graffiti. "Parks Canada owns the property, so—"

"Oh."

"Yeah." He declared, content in his victory. "Ms. Garrison, we are going to enter that building and see if we can't find what we're looking for." Steve straightened and examined the opening to the inside of the lodge. Someone pulled back a rotten piece of OSB and snapped it at the corner, exposing a ragged edge of broken glass. Cam and Lauren waited expectantly. "And when we are done," he continued, louder, so she heard him, "please make sure you are gone."

Sara leaned over the passenger seat, craning her neck to look at him. "And if I am still here?"

"I'll take you into custody for obstructing a peace officer."

"Oh," she said again. "Is that a thing?"

"It is. Section 129 of the Criminal Code."

She pulled herself back into her seat. "Alright then."

He fixed his hat and joined the other officers. He bent over and clicked on his flashlight, peering into the darkness beyond. "Pretty quiet in there."

Lauren chuckled. "I'll bet they're in the basement again."

"Man, it stinks down there," Cam said. "I hope not."

"Remember," said Steve as he yanked the board free, throwing it to the snow-dusted gravel, "they're just kids. Let's not make a bad situation worse, eh?"

"Got it, chief," said Cam as he lifted a leg over the cobbled wall, moving into the building first through the towering window. He wasn't two steps in before he scattered something metallic with his feet. "Sorry," he hissed.

Steve entered last. He swung his head from the stark white of a clear northern day into the utter black of the lodge where his nose met the stink of must and metal. Slashes of light cut across the space, scattered with floating dust, giving form to the myriad objects piled around the vaulted space. Cam and Lauren whisked their own light back and forth, fixating momentarily on a spot where they thought they saw something before shaking their head and continuing into the dark. All three officers eyed their feet in equal measure to their surroundings, mindful of the rotten floral pattern beneath that was covered in debris. Steve didn't want a clear announcement of their arrival. *Well, no more than Cam did already.*

They scoured the familiar ruin of the first floor. The debris and broken objects were the same, just shifted slightly or repositioned to a different room. One table was upended on its side near the proper entrance, covered in yellow paintball splashes. *What didn't these kids get up to here?*

"All clear," said Cam as he crept to Steve alongside Lauren, who looked somewhat unsettled.

Steve ignored her expression, but only because he sensed something, too—but dread and professionalism held his tongue.

Cam nodded to the end of the room. "Basement next?"

Steve nodded back. "Like moths to a porch light," he said as he took the lead, weaving around a circular dining table.

At the end of the hall a broad stair cut into the earth like a wedge, leading down to a pair of French doors. Above, a stained sign read: LOUNGE.

Slowly, Steve descended the steps, resisting the urge to ready his pistol. *Easy, Steve—only teenagers, right?* Still, his fingers struggled to find a comfortable grip on his flashlight. He eased his shoulder into the door, sending a shuddering creak into the blackness beyond. He cocked his head, listening. Some white noise sounded a few metres away, like the rasping of radio static. He focused his eyes ahead—yet cold fear gripped him, almost billowing outwards from the space. It hung around him like icicles descending from rotten eaves. It was magnitudes colder in the space beyond.

He stepped in, sweeping his flashlight across the room. More rotten carpet. Splintered wood, punctured walls. Crude images spray painted on every surface.

"Smells like a meat locker in here," whispered Cam.

Something glistened in the pool of light cast by his torch.

"Is that—?" Lauren leaned in, focusing.

Steve crept further into the room. His eyes bulged. "Oh, no." He fought back the urge to gag.

8

Derelictions

WHY DO SPIRITS ATTACH themselves to certain locations, objects, or people? I have heard it explained with very litigious language: rights, jurisdiction, ownership—even property. When something traumatic, or even downright evil occurs, negative forces claim ownership of the space where it occurred. Exorcists use these concepts to unpack the cause of hauntings—even possessions.

-The Garrison Theories podcast, Episode 3: "Truth and Lies in Gastown"

Sara leaned her head into the driver's side door. She blew out a tired sigh, watching the condensation coalesce on the window for the briefest of seconds before vanishing. *Maybe the cop is right. Maybe I should go.* Doubt crept in and trapped her in the suffocating space of the rental. This entire operation had, so far, been a letdown. Occurrences dashed her high hopes of a breakout story, replaced with a hard-hitting reality that kept knocking down everything she tried to set up. Her mom's face flickered into her mind's eye, grimacing with disappointment. A few scraps of empathy flashed amid her expression, generously peppered with a smattering of I-told-you-sos.

And the RCMP? Accusing her of obstruction for just parking? *More like obstruction of information on their part.* Had she really come all this way to be deterred by a few small-town Mounties? Hands quivering, Sara pressed her face into her palms.

She gathered herself before she snatched up her phone and thumbed her way to a search engine, feverishly tapping in queries related to the kind of consequences she might face if she turned rogue. The data was spotty, but it loaded after awhile: trespassing—no chance of jail time, possibly a hefty fine. *Obstruction of an officer?* Seemed a bit fuzzy. She knew she missed some major details, that seemed a certainty—but it gave her enough. Just enough for that spark of recklessness to catch into a full-blown wildfire. She exited the car, scooping up her messenger bag from the passenger seat.

Taking a deep breath, she stood before the yawning hole in the OSB and the shattered glass, staring into the darkness beyond. *Well, you've come this far, haven't you?*

Her first step towards the lodge stopped, held by a confusion of noise behind that finished with the immense crunch of a snapping log as if something large pushed its way through the trees behind her. Towards her.

Twisting on her boot heels, her attention locked on the towering wall of skeletal trees behind her crudely parked rental, bracketing each side of the lodge. They interrogated her, crowded her against the abandoned resort. It might have been a bear, although she thought that maybe most of them would be hibernating at this point. *Do all bears hibernate?* She didn't know. Or it could have been a branch giving under the weight of some snow, possibly. Or maybe it was a sasquatch, she fantasised. *Been taking too much of my own brand.* Whatever it was, a tingling wave crawled up her spine and pulsed its way down to her extremities.

Nothing came, yet still her breath quickened. Moments passed, frozen, and no evidence appeared to justify the fear she felt. Back pressed to the cobbles of the half-timbered lodge, she closed her eyes.

Her mind groped in the dark, looking for the skills she had learned in therapy, the skills that always seemed to disappear from her tool belt when she needed them most. *Think, Sara*, she pleaded with herself as the stones dug into her spine. *Remember. The forest can't hurt you. There's nothing there. It's just the settling of the trees.*

Her attention shifted weakly to her breathing as she began her body scan. *You don't need to feel this way. You're filling in the blanks with how you're thinking about it, remember?* The voice of her therapist spoke her thoughts for her. *The trees aren't a threat—they simply are. It's up to you to think about them in an adaptive way...* Her eyes squeezed together like they could shut out reality, she continued breathing in, holding, and breathing out. The air whistled out her nose, and she held the emptiness in her lungs for three seconds before filling them again, all the while putting her thoughts on trial. *Is it true that these trees represent a threat to you?* her therapist asked. *What evidence do you have that the trees at the park are worthy of being perceived as a threat?* She thought of her sister, and their family camping trip. *I think I have lots of reasons...* she pushed back. *Yes*, replied her therapist. *Certainly*, that *forest represents something traumatic, something ugly from your past. But why the tree on the veranda? In the dog park, standing alone? What threat could that possibly have in your mind?*

Waves of remembered progress came to her, followed shortly by the echoes of victory. *None*, she replied in her mind. *It is no threat to me whatsoever.* She repeated the words like a mantra, doing her best to rewire her thinking patterns. Sighing, she opened her eyes.

The other pair of eyes were the first thing she noticed. Lidless, cloudy eyes—the same ones she glimpsed briefly on the highway a few days prior. It was *the* elk, the same elk, she had to assume, that was now handful of metres away, staring at her from the greenbelt. It was just as sickly as before, although now she saw it in clearer detail: infected patches patterned its body like extreme mange; its lips had fallen away, exposing its rows of strangely healthy-looking teeth. The antlers seemed overlarge. Its thin, bony body spoke of a deep hunger. The longer she stared, the more uncomfortable she became.

"Can I help you?" she asked. When it didn't budge, she started forward in an effort to scare it off. A branch snapped somewhere to the right of the emaciated animal.

Twenty metres away, she could have sworn she saw a figure slink behind the bole of a thick tree. With a yelp, she twisted round and nearly dove into the lodge, suddenly feeling like whatever awaited her in the darkness was preferable to what was outside.

B lood.
Steve's posture didn't so much relax as collapse. "Oh, Jesus..." he whispered. When he said the name, it was the first time he had said it in a long time that wasn't taken in vain—when he uttered it this time, he was calling on the name of the Lord the only way he knew. If there was a time he needed help from beyond, it was in that moment.

Lauren crept up beside him and searched after the beam of his flashlight. He glanced to the side—her eyes bulged; her mouth hung slack. Cam's face set like stone, although his eyes glistened with moisture.

The already-rotten furniture sagged, soaked in carnage that had now dried to the upholstery in a murky red. Maimed bodies sprawled in a sick, unrecognisable tangle on the floor; they almost seemed to fuse with the recreation room itself—tattered clothes intermixed with pulpy masses of chewed flesh and faux leather. Steve could only identify the head of one victim due to the presence of a single, lidless eye in the centre of a doughy mass near the arm of a couch. He shut his eyes tight. The static continued to burn in the background.

Lauren raised a shaking hand to her face, covering her eyes. "Is it them?"

As if in response to the question, the three Mounties crept around the scene, bending, scrutinising the grisly details. A scrap of cloth here, a torn shirt, a boot.

Cara's glasses.

Steve's voice cracked. "Looks like it." His career seemed shakier than ever. As if the disappearance of the Johnstone boy hadn't drawn enough attention to him—now this. This would be federal news, maybe international. Not that it mattered these days with the way content spread on the web. All news was global now, and his name would be all over it.

Was there a name lower than 'mud'? So much for the peace of the countryside. It had, he supposed, been a good eight or so years.

"This is bad," came Cam's report dumbly.

Breath held fast, Steve encircled the wreckage, taking care not to plant his boots on the scene. The bodies were woven together like wood stacked for a bonfire. How many people died here, he could not guess based on the physical evidence at this point. But he had to guess four: David, Cara, Tanner, and Kimberly. They were a common quartet, and there seemed to be enough flesh and bone to cover them all. All dead.

Steve squatted next to the body he figured to be Cara. Off-white bone glistened through a layer of pink and red, just above the brow line where a dark line of hair clung over where an eye once was. Cam and Lauren stood behind, silent in the static. Lauren's sudden outburst—a muffled, restrained whimper—startled the men.

"Bear?" asked Cam as he edged closer, hesitant as if afraid an arm from the hideous display might grab him. Lauren stood aloof from the scene.

Steve kept his flashlight—and his eyes—on a body part that he couldn't identify. "One nasty bear if it is." He spoke with a hushed tone. "A big maneater."

"How did it get in?" asked Cam. He continued to survey the masses of tattered clothing and flesh, pausing the beam of his flashlight now and again. "I noticed nothing on my run around big enough—"

"Are you both serious?" asked Lauren from further away. She remained at the entrance; her face turned away. "A bear? Bears don't organise their kills into bloody stacks last time I checked."

"Likely less organised than it looks," Steve growled. He wasn't sure if he believed the explanation himself. "I see four young people terrified, clutching together, defending themselves and each other..."

All Lauren did was shake her head.

"Either way," Steve breathed as he stood. "Up for forensics and the coroner to decide. And to your question, Cam, I guess it could have squeezed in the same way we came."

"I don't know, Steve," said Lauren. "Could a bear that fit through that space do all this?" Nausea laced her voice. "And shouldn't it be hibernating?"

"I don't think it's that straight forward," added Cam.

Steve tore his eyes away from the carnage. "Especially not if we're dealing with a maneater." He thought for a minute. His eyes glazed over as he searched the entangled pile of flesh, cloth, and bone on the sodden carpet. He saw a mass of matted black hair fanned out amidst the frozen puddle of blood near the edge of what looked like a sleeping bag. "Hell," he said at last, "better call this in." He yanked his radio from the shoulder of his vest beneath his jacket and clicked it on. The coroner needed to be notified.

Just then, a thump came from beyond the double doors to the lounge, repeating itself as something with weight tumbled down the stairs beyond. Cam burst towards them, throwing both doors wide open and shouting up the stairs, reminding whoever—or whatever—that he was RCMP.

"Go with him, will you?" Steve requested of Lauren. She nodded and scampered after him, leaving Steve alone with the scene.

Uncertainty filled him. But one thought solidified into certainty: that no matter where we went in the future, the Blue Hills Ski Resort would always haunt him.

A single portable generator thrummed outside the doors to the lounge, muffled by the partition and allowing the scattered grunts of Sergeant Robert Harasymchuk to be heard as he squatted, knelt, and hovered his way around the perimeter of the scene. The dark space that hours before had resisted their investigation was now cut through by spotlights, with some help from the early morning light that crept through the gaps in the boarded basement windows crowning the walls.

In the centre of it all was Sergeant Harasymchuk. He was a towering rail, like a scarecrow dressed in the standard RCMP dress. He looked almost spectral as he stood over the edge of the scene. He had left his regimental parka at the door of the lounge; despite the cold, he had worked up quite a sweat. Over the course of many hours, he had bagged dozens of items and snapped countless more photographs. He dusted, sprayed, taped, and measured endlessly. Cameron and Lauren had been put to work, packing clear bags housing crushed cans and empty bottles. But Bob never asked Steve for anything.

It was Steve's turn to stand aloof from the investigation, allowing the forensics unit veteran the space he needed to do his work. Infrequently Bob had asked Steve a few questions, but his answers had fallen woefully short. And based on the sergeant's scrunched, frustrated expression as he approached, Steve figured that the situation hadn't changed much. Bob peeled off his nitrile gloves and huffed.

"So, it was just like this when you got here, eh?" he inquired—again—as he kept his eyes on the grisly display.

"That's right. With the cars outside. The old Ranger is registered to Tanner McCluskey, the Suburban to Rhonda Harvey."

Some forensics elements were undoubtedly challenging and required a heaping dose of technical skill and intuition—Steve could see it at work in Bob as he scoured, sniffed, and glanced his way around like he was a bloodhound working on instinct. But some of it was dead simple: the four phones present painted a crisp picture of high school friends looking for an escape.

"You know them?"

Pursing his lips, Steve gave a shallow nod. "Tanner's a local kid. And that Suburban was likely lent out for the night to a girl named Cara Harvey." Steve kept his eyes on Bob's out of some sense of respect to the deceased. Try as he might to focus, the crimson pile still glistened in his peripheral vision. "Both friends with the other two."

Bob ran a hand over his bald head and winced. "Well, we've got prints here and there. But let's not jump the gun on that one—until I get a positive on these prints, I'm not comfortable confirming it."

"Seems like a lock to me. Car registration, phones..."

The forensics veteran shrugged. "All could be stolen."

"And the parents calling to tell us their kids are missing?"

"Somewhere else, maybe."

Steve frowned. "If only that were true."

Sergeant Harasymchuk acquiesced with a tilt of his head. "Yeah, I hear you. It's likely."

"So how long for the prints?"

"A couple days at the most once I get them back to the lab."

"DNA?"

Bob sucked his teeth. "Months, usually. But the prints should be enough to make a reasonably solid call, one that's good enough for me anyways." He planted his hands on his hips and surveyed the scene. Sergeant Parenteau and Corporal Reid were off in the corner, talking amongst themselves. "Good enough especially when evidence is... sparse. Sparse as to what *precisely* happened, anyways."

Steve cleared his throat. "So—what are your thoughts on the cause?" It was an obvious question, one that hadn't been floated amid the technical examination. It was all bags and dusting and photographs up until now, all begging one glaring question. "Like, what in God's name happened here, Bob? Even as a preliminary exercise, are we talking about a maneater here?"

The thin man let out a long sigh through his nose. "At this point that's where I'm leaning. The bodies have been significantly mutilated," he declared, glancing back at the scene, "not that it takes an expert to see that. The tissue has been torn by the looks of it, shredded in some areas, so nothing clean or precise that would suggest a human. So yeah, I'm thinking bear, but that also raises some other questions." He checked the time on his phone and whistled. "But that's not for me to decide. This isn't necessarily a crime scene."

"I see."

"Just a scene. So, the coroner will investigate. Likely have a conservation officer take a peek, or some other wildlife expert."

Steve listened patiently, then motioned with his hand like he wanted Bob to rewind a tape. "What questions does it raise? About the bear, I mean. It seems pretty cut and dry—"

"Well, there's no evidence of a bear, no fur... no clawing on the furniture—"

"Ah," said Steve with a nod. "But if not a bear, then...?"

Bob shrugged. "If there was someone else here, the fingerprints may tell us. Although I only have four pairs of boots that I can see from the prints on the floor, I imagine I'll be able to match them together back in the office."

"So, four kids came in."

With a lifting of his eyebrows, Bob said, "Four kids stayed." He patted Steve on the arm. "Give it a few days, and I'll have more for you." He strode over to his tools near the entrance to the lounge, squatted and pulled on a new pair of nitrile gloves. "You notified the coroner's service yet?"

"Just before I called you."

"Good stuff." Bob's head bobbed up and down. "I imagine these kids will be moved to Prince George where a forensic pathologist can examine them. Once I'm done, where will you transfer the remains?" He stood and wiped his forehead with the back of his sleeve. "Hell, they might even opt to send them to the National Forensics lab in Edmonton, maybe."

It's getting out of control. The thought came to him as if it wasn't even his own. *Control? How could a staff sergeant be so defensive of an investigation, especially one so close to home? And yet, here I am. Wanting to kibosh this and sweep it under the rug.* His thoughts drifted inexorably to the investigation last year, to his performance that brought him dangerously close to disciplinary action. The last thing on his wish list was another high-stakes case—the kind that invited intense scrutiny.

"I want it done close to home. I've managed to convince them of that, at least. We have a solid surgeon here with training in forensic pathology."

Bob gave an incredulous chuckle. "In Coalbrook? That surprises me that the district coroner went for that."

"I'm sure it does, *sergeant*." Steve enunciated Bob's rank clearly to remind him to keep an eye on his tone. "Edmonton is, what, almost ten hours drive from here? Getting this over there will slow the investigation down. If it *is* a maneater, we need to get on a hunt and get on it fast."

Sergeant Harasymchuk raised a placating hand. "I hear you."

As the day stretched on, Steve found himself fantasizing about the relief he would feel upon the moment it was confirmed that these young lives were, in fact, snuffed out by a wild animal. *And the closer to home we sort this, the better.*

PART TWO

9

Grievances

AND THAT'S REALLY WHAT grief is: an answer to an unsolvable problem. We can't fix death, for example. So, we have to sit with it, feel it, allow the depth of the loss to sink into us. Then, we come to a place of acceptance. If we don't, well, maybe that's what causes some who pass away to remain in this world. And what is acceptance of not a welcoming of truth? Truth, in the words of famous samurai and author Miyamoto Musashi, is not something that we can fabricate—it is what it is. We have to bend to its power, or accept a life defined by lies.

-*The Garrison Theories* podcast, Episode 3: "Truth and Lies in Gastown"

"**F**ather."

The minister whose name Steve had quite forgotten nodded at his greeting as he stepped into the lobby of the small, pearl-painted church. The green-trimmed place of worship stood, old and proud, on the corner of Elm Street and 3rd Avenue in the heart of residential Coalbrook.

Steve kept his hands folded in front of him, walking with equal parts solemnity and discomfort, wrestling with the burgeoning sense of unwelcome that mixed with the grief that hung thick in the house of worship. The lobby stretched wide but not deep, and it ended quickly, with Steve having only taken a few steps from the door. In short order he found himself in the back of the sanctuary. The pews prepared to collapse under the number of bodies in the seats, likely more attendees than the regular Sunday service was used to.

A woman glanced back at him and bounced her eyes away as quickly as possible. *Par for the course.* She corrected, turning to the man next to her and whispering. The man waited, made a show of looking around the room before his eyes finally fell on Steve. But Steve's gaze waited and held on to the man's stare. He broke it off. *So, the blame game begins anew.* Steve sighed below his breath and gratefully found a space in one of the rear pews.

The minister turned from where he stood near the pulpit, nodded, and started speaking in a voice that was easy to hear, clear without being harsh. He spoke of death and the transitory nature of the flesh, his words stoic, stiffened by the solemnity of the occasion. Still the family who had just lost a daughter seemed to take comfort in his presence.

Steve grit his teeth together behind his closed lips, fidgeting as subtly as possible on the pew. He had been to so many funerals in his time, for co-workers and volunteers and donors. The funeral then became an act of respect, but something remote where the words seemed to go in one ear and out the other without dropping down to touch his heart. Vanessa and the kids always came first, and over the course of many years he had unknowingly circled the wagons; nothing else mattered except his wife and kids and the life they built together. The life he tried to build for them.

The words of the minister came simultaneously cold and warm, like he had a deep empathy for the family but also didn't know them very well. It echoed Steve's experience: few people attended church, but when tragedy struck it always seemed like the appropriate place to go. It remained for many a way of dealing with life and its ultimate result. Even for someone like him—a man who had no deep religious convictions—it made sense.

A sermon packed with lofty ideals and an intimation of a distant paradise filled the heavy air. Steve's mind drifted, churning in the knowledge of the horror that this girl died in alongside her friends. *More funerals to attend.* Some here knew, to be sure: but they hadn't seen it firsthand. It felt wrong to be here, knowing what he knew, like he and the blissfully unaware picture of Cara near the front were both sworn into a conspiracy, a dark and dirty secret that they each had to carry to their graves. *Guess it's just up to me and the officers, now.* Cara stared at him, her face split in a candid smile in a beautiful, oversized frame on an easel. No urn, no casket—the coroner's work wasn't done yet.

When the sermon ended, a few family members took to the pulpit and shared their memories. Relatives young and old struggled through their prepared words, fighting to speak through sobs, blubbering more than talking. The last speakers, the mother and father of Cara, wrapped up their eulogy with an introduction to one of their family favourites: a rendition of I'll Fly Away. An older, shapeless woman took to the keys, and two young girls, whose relation to the deceased Steve did not know, began to sing.

Some glad mornin', when this life is over, I'll fly away...

Steve's eyes fixed on Cara's. Like the Mona Lisa, she stared.

To a home on God's celestial shore, I'll fly away...

The innocent image twisted away from him. Instead, images of her chewed face rolled over his memory, her cracked glasses strewn across the floor of the lounge.

I'll fly away, Oh Glory, I'll fly away...

On the stage, Cara's soft skin beamed in the light of the photographer's flash. Her eyes were those of an optimist.

When I die, hallelujah by and by, I'll fly away...

His mind drifted, taking him away from the service. Now he was standing in the basement of the lodge, hand over his mouth, vision watering. Cara's remaining eye stared up at him, lidless and bloody, frozen wide with surprise.

"Excuse me," he whispered to his neighbour as he stood. He sidled past and made his way down the aisle, struggling to make his six-foot frame look smaller. Countless tearful and reddened eyes glared as he went past.

When he pushed through the doors and entered the lobby, he could finally breathe. But he needed more, so he stepped outside into the cold, blustery air. The wind squeezed him and let go like a reassuring hand, the chill cutting down his collar. His skin tingled, almost stung. He took a deep breath. Ice filled his lungs, then tears filled his eyes while the trees around the church yard churned in the wind.

Hands in the pockets of his leather jacket, Steve stood in front of the church for way longer than a non-believing man normally would. Long enough that the service concluded, and many stepped onto the yard out of the too-small lobby. Steve turned and immediately caught the attention of a man ten years his senior. *Roy? Raymond?* The man's name escaped him, but the scowl below his grey hair told Steve that he knew exactly who he was.

"Takes a lot of courage to show your face here, Boyko," he said as he rammed a hand into a leather glove. "I'd have figured that you'd keep your distance this time."

"I'm just here to pay respects, sir. No need to get confron—"

"Sure, sure," mocked the man. "Whatever you can do to relieve some guilt, eh?"

Steve's lips curled. He was no longer an attendee at a funeral—now he shifted into work mode. taking on the recently reluctant role of Staff Sergeant Stephen Boyko. He had to keep it cool. The man's wife, equally sour-faced, came alongside him as he continued.

"Nothing to say, eh? Well," he said as he gestured back to the church, "there's another for your trophy wall, sergeant."

The couple walked off together. Others who stood nearby looked away, unsure of themselves. But Steve knew that a few of them would share the same sentiments, even if they never had the gumption to deliver the message themselves.

Why do I keep trying? He lifted his gaze to the cross that towered above, piercing the grey as it rose from the steeple. Steve kept his eyes there as people filed past him. When he lowered his eyes, the only one standing there was the minister, posturing with folded hands like he had been waiting for Steve, robes billowing in the wind. *Like Saint Peter at the pearly gates; the snow, clouds.* Without thinking, Steve stepped closer.

"Hello again, father," he croaked before clearing his throat. "Beautiful message." Only he couldn't remember a lick of it, and the scant fragments he did swam in the pain of the rejection that just took place.

"Thank you," the man said solemnly, as quiet as he could but still loud enough to be heard over the wind. "Although to my recollection, you don't have anything recent to compare it to."

Steve grimaced. "Yes, it has been a while, hasn't it?"

The nameless minister laughed, an abrupt switch from the dry delivery of his comments. "It is good to see you, Mr. Boyko. How have things been? I haven't seen you since—?"

He offered the priest a sheepish, knowing look. "Easter, I'm afraid. And likely not even the last one."

"Oh no," he mused. "You've become a Chreaster, have you? And not even a consistent one—even worse!"

"Lot on the plate you know. But I'm sure you've heard that before."

"I've heard it all—and I heard that, too," he said as he pointed to the emptying church yard behind Steve. "Come in for a moment, will you?"

Steve shrugged and followed him inside. He loitered in the entrance to the sanctuary, watching the man of the cloth as he busied himself in the quiet space, gathering hymnals and plunking them down into the shallow shelving on the backs of the pews. Steve cleared his throat as the minister rose from the floor, two hymnals stacked in his hands. He beckoned Steve in with a nod. "Come in, come in—have a seat."

In the sanctuary, Steve fell into the olive-green upholstery of the same rear pew he sat in during the service. The minister sat two pews ahead, stretching his arm across the back of the wooden frame. "Difficult thing, memorialising a child."

Steve nodded. He stared at the cross that hung near to the rafters above the stage. "Can't imagine." Weaving his fingers together, Steve continued. "I'm sorry, this is super embarrassing—but I can't remember your name."

"Oh," he responded. "And you also somehow managed to miss it during my introduction? And didn't bother to read it on the provided order of service?" He smiled wide and extended a hand. "It's Reverend Conall. Very pleased to meet you. Again."

"Likewise," Steve said primly with a tight smile. "And I truly did appreciate your sermon today."

Reverend Conall laughed. "I don't think I've ever heard that from someone who didn't have a head of gray hair." The chuckle faded, and his countenance became serious. "I am grateful. Thank you." Looking around the room, he hummed to himself before he spoke again. "Lots of hymnals to gather," he said as he glanced at Steve. "Give an old man a hand, will you?"

"Of course," Steve responded quickly as he rose.

"So, how is the family?" he asked as he continued slotting the books into place.

"They're fine. They're good." Steve stretched across the back of a pew and grabbed a stray hymnal. He stood, twisting around, unsure of where it belonged.

"There," said Reverend Conall, pointing a few paces away.

Steve replaced the book into the slot. "Yep," he continued, "Vanessa and the kids are doing great."

"Two girls, right?"

"Yes, yes. Both teens now. We've got our hands full."

"I'm sure you do," he responded with a chuckle. "Lots of work there." With a big stack of hymnals in hand, Reverend Conall strode to the front of the sanctuary. "And what about yourself?" he asked through an echo as he thumped the books down in a tower on a wooden table. "How are you doing?"

"Well, as you saw," said Steve with a gesture over his shoulder, "things have been better. The last year... well, it's been hell." He cut a glance to the reverend. "Sorry."

"Don't worry—Hell's a good word for it, I imagine."

Slowing, Steve tapped a hymnal on the back of the pew before him. "Yeah. As far as I can tell, this town hates me."

"This town is hurting. It's natural to look for a source to blame in the absence of an answer."

"An answer to what?"

Reverend Conall looked surprised. "The Johnstone boy."

Steve kept quiet.

"Left a big hole," he continued. "And now these four young people. Such pain for these families."

"I can't even imagine," Steve said through a tight mouth as he dropped back into the pew. "From what I've seen, it isn't a hole you can fill."

"It can be filled," said the reverend. "But it isn't easy."

"Hm," acknowledged Steve, clearly unconvinced. If his kids died—especially if they went the way Cara and the rest did—he could never recover. In fact, he might refuse to recover as a way of remembering them. "Well, what about you then, Reverend? What would you fill it with?"

His white collar shifted as he nodded toward the cross that hung above the main stage. "I figured it was obvious," he said with a smirk.

Steve chuckled, shaking his head. "Why did I ask?"

The other man shrugged. "And what about you, Steven?"

With a sigh, Steve leaned back, forcing a whining creak out of his pew. The cross hung before them both, beams outstretched as if waiting to be embraced. "I'm not sure. Family, I guess, is a big one." He glanced at Reverend Conall. "Did I fail that one?"

The reverend shook his head, then nodded. "Yes, family is of paramount importance—one of God's greatest gifts. But something that can be stripped away in a moment," he said, gesturing to where the memorial had just taken place.

"Yeah," said Steve. "Yeah, that's some hole."

The men sat while a strangely comfortable silence grew between them. Steve's eyes focused on the cross, confident that the depths of what it represented was lost on him. A part of him wished that he saw it like the reverend did, but a bigger part of him liked his world just the way it was. Minus the conflict with the town of course. And the guilt—he could do without the guilt.

Or maybe it was shame?

"All of that speaks to a deeper truth, I believe," said Conall at last, pushing himself up with a grunt. "The Scriptures teach us that there is a hole in all people—a deep, deep hunger for something more than what we see around us. And it is incumbent upon each person to satisfy that hunger." He strode away, a single hymnal in hand. He left it on the communion table to the side of the stage. From that part of the sanctuary, his voice carried in the same way it did when he gave a sermon. "Only we have to be wise at what we put into that emptiness."

Brow furrowed, Steve offered the man a cursory nod.

The Reverend continued. "I have what satisfies my hunger and thirst. I have the bread of life—I have living water. You can have it too, Steven. There is rest to be found at the foot of the cross."

Steve scratched his stubble loudly, annoyed at the second use of his full name. "Thanks, Reverend. But I don't know if that's where I am. I'm OK with God and everything, but..." He rose and walked to the end of his pew, raising his hands gently towards the man of the cloth at the front of the sanctuary. "I'll give it some thought, thanks."

Reverend Conall smiled. "Take care, then. Looking forward to seeing you and the family at Christmas. And I hope you find something to fill that hole," he called after him as he strode down the length of the church. "Because if you don't fill it with the right thing, something—or someone—will fill it for you."

The words drifted after him as he opened the door, almost clinging to his back with the intent of riding him all the way home. He rushed out, receiving the wind's bitter greeting as he left Thankful River United Church.

The image clung to her mind.

Four days had passed since she snuck down the bowed stairs of the lodge dining hall. Four days since she peered through the silt-streaked glass and saw the three officers standing around a small hill of blood and bone. Four days since she scrambled to her car and jammed her boots onto the gas pedal.

Still, no one had come calling, and somehow that made it worse. Even though Sara desperately wanted to avoid trouble at this point, to keep her head down... the desire to share the nightmare with someone, to get it out of her head grew with each passing day.

But no such contact came. No peace officer came knocking at her motel room door, no phone call, no email left in her podcast inbox. *They could find me, right? If they really wanted to, they could track me, couldn't they?*

The gentle machinations of a clock whirred from the pallid walls of her motel room. She glanced at her phone on the side table between the armchair in which she huddled and the bed—it was almost eleven. Sleep called to her, but she did her best to resist, did her best to keep her eyes from closing. The images behind her eyelids replayed the scene over and over, and she knew her sleep, restless as it always was, would now be wracked by new nightmares in addition to the old ones.

Sara shivered in her cardigan and the sprawl of thin motel blankets wrapped around her legs, her knees tucked up against her chest. Her fingers hissed over the pages of some foreign thriller, the progress of which took place in some shadowy and wet road in northern Europe. Her eyes crawled from word to word, but she caught herself reading the same page for the third time. Next to her phone on the nightstand, a cup of decaf orange pekoe grew cold.

Focus, Sara. Put it out of your mind. She adjusted her glasses.

Another hiss and a flip. The Nordic hero moved down a darkened hall, pistol ready. A tap-tap-tap came from around the corner, and he burst—

A rushing sound pressed against the side of the motel, shifting the door to the room that was all that stood between her and the second-floor balcony walkway—and the forest beyond across the highway. It crackled as it adjusted in its frame, and her eyes lifted from the page and searched the dim room. She was alone under the lamplight.

"It's alright," she whispered to no one.

A whistling sigh escaped her pursed lips as she slapped her book down next to her neglected tea. Sara took a tepid sip and winced, then replaced the cup onto the coffee table. She took off her glasses and worked her fingers in large circles over her shuttered eyelids, leaving motes of dancing light in her vision.

What now, Sara? Time to pack it in? She finally had her story, something huge and exciting—but terrifying in every sense. The Garrison Theories podcast might grow exponentially if it was to cover something like this; once the news got out, her episode wouldn't be far behind. *I could ride that wave...*

Movement near the front door caught her eye—she jerked her head towards it. The curtains were shifting, almost settling as if from a motion she didn't catch. Jaw tight, Sara stared, hoping it was a simple gust of the baseboard heater beneath them. Reluctantly, she rose and crept across the floral carpet, almost crouching down as she passed the foot of the queen-sized bed. She licked her lips.

She moved closer with tightly held breath. Sara gave the curtains a flick and threw them apart. Her gaze snuck between them, seeing at first her own reflection before her eyes adjusted and peered beyond the glass. Something moved in the moonlit spaces between the shadows of the greenbelt lining the far side of the highway.

A pair of yellow eyes floated in the darkness in the chaotic black and green world outside. Her heart seized a moment before it came crashing down with relief as the eyes attached to the pinched face of a male deer, prominent antlers reaching nearly to low-hanging branches. She held the animal's gaze at length, breath caught slightly as she waited for it to move on. Only it did not move. And she couldn't shake the feeling that this was the same animal that welcomed her to Coalbrook—the same one that met her at the lodge.

"The hell?" she whispered, her breath fogging the glass. "What, are you following me?"

She blinked and pushed herself gently back from the window. The elk remained motionless, obscured slightly by the hanging branches, hidden a few feet beyond the edge of the forest. An electrical sensation grew in the small of her back, climbing up her spine and terminating at the base of her skull, exploding like a slow-motion firework over her shoulders. And then she was still.

The clock clunked again, giving off a gentle chime that shook her from her reverie. She shivered and glanced over to it, releasing the death grip she had on the curtains on both sides. Wincing, she shook the soreness out of her hands.

It was midnight. Either the clock malfunctioned, or she had just stood staring for the better part of an hour. The question hung in her mind as the wind pushed against the motel again. She jerked her head back to the forest. The elk was gone, but there was a figure—

No. Just the trees that continued to rock in the breeze.

The deep cold outside sucked the heat of the room through the glass, so she pulled the thin curtains together. She spun and paced the room, picking up her thoughts. *Remember why you're here, Sara. To jump-start the podcast and to make something of your journalism degree. And of yourself, ethics be damned. If I leave now...*

"I'll be proving everyone right if I pack it in," she breathed as she plunked herself down in the too-small chair in front of the desk. So, what was a little blood, a few trees in the way of her own goals? If she followed this story as it developed, kept herself close to it... yes, that was the ticket.

She cleaned her glasses, cracked her knuckles, and got to work.

10

Cold Storage

WE LOVE TO LABEL AND categorise the world around us, don't we? In the Bible, Adam brought order to the natural world by picking a name for each creature brought before him. We do the same thing today as researchers through the practice of taxonomy. And we do it for more reasons than simple organisation—giving a name to something brings it into the realm of the knowable, the understandable. When we lack a definition for a thing, it remains as smoke, something we can perceive but not grasp. I can't help but wonder if some of the mystery of these phenomena rests in our inability to categorise the experiences.
- The Garrison Theories podcast, Episode 5: "Here Be Dragons"

The atmosphere of Coalbrook Medical Centre was heavy, thick enough to make each step seem like a push through knee-deep snow. Steve did his best to walk tall, shoulders back to express confidence. But it probably wasn't worth it. With all that had gone on—with the horrors that had recently passed through the hospital doors—it felt as if Coalbrook itself was beyond saving.

"Hello, commander," the receptionist nodded, her expression grim. "Follow the red line, it'll take you to the cold room."

He forced out a thanks as he started his journey down the echoing halls, white paint and tile made sickly by the old, yellowing halogens that buzzed each time he walked beneath them. He passed vacant rooms and myriad empty gurneys that lined the halls expectantly, guided by the red strip that looked far too close to a streak of blood for his liking—especially in light of recent events.

The last few days had been hell. And all eyes were on him.

He needed some good news. Something positive, as if it was possible to scrape together something good in all this. *Maybe some revelation that it's not as terrible as it all seems?* He wished—no, he actually prayed—that there would be some relief. The wailing of the families at the various death notices he delivered still haunted him. They had to tell them, though, even though they couldn't completely declare what happened. Not yet. But the prints came through. Sergeant Robert Harasymchuk had confirmed over the phone, and then through documentation, that there were four sets of prints—and *only* four—that matched with the kids. They had to tell them that vehicles registered to them, or their families were found at the site along with some identifying equipment. That they found their bodies—that they wouldn't be coming home. *Likely an animal attack.*

Yes, he needed something good today.

Steve ran his fingers through his hair, scratching his scalp to distract him from the memory of the moment he stepped out of his SUV outside of the Harvey house. He hadn't even given the death notice before Rhonda collapsed in the entrance. It was his expression combined with the removal of his hat that was the dead giveaway—always was.

Shake it off, Steve. You've got work to do.

He rounded the corner, still on the trail of the red line. Further on, a porter pushed an expressionless older gentleman in a wheelchair. The smell of hand sanitizer wafted by, like a trail of exhaust from the seated patient. A murky message rasped over the intercom. Steve strode through it all without a word or a glance askew and found his way towards the pathologist's cold storage. At the end of the red line, he shouldered his way in.

A dark-haired woman sat at a steel desk at the far end of the room. Nothing about her appearance suggested forensic pathology—there was no lab coat or nitrile gloves, only a brown blouse, black pencil skirt, and sneakers of all footwear. Her name was Maryam Haim, and she held all the answers to his questions—at least he hoped. And there were some answers he wanted to hear more than others.

"Steven," she said, half-turning in her chair as she gave him a professional smile. She didn't stand. "Nice to see you."

"No offense," Steve managed, sparing a glance to the steel tables behind glass that were covered in blue sheets, "but I can't say the same."

Dr. Haim raised her eyebrows, smirking slightly as she glanced at him over her thin reading glasses. "Fair enough." Spinning on her chair to face him fully, she took her glasses off and let them dangle on the chain around her neck. "This is a bit unusual. I'm not quite finished my report."

He could never quite place her accent, and he had never asked what country she emigrated from. Their conversation, as infrequent as it was, remained professional and skirted around the reality of death with medical language. Her expertise as a forensic pathologist made her seem cold, a striking contrast to her dusky, warm skin.

"So, what have you got for me so far?"

With a sigh, Maryam turned back to her workstation. Her long fingers flicked over her keyboard, and a few clicks of her mouse brought up what Steve assumed was the makings of her report to the coroner. With an immaculate fingernail she followed a few lines of text, mumbling to herself. "I have to say," she said at last, "I feel a bit over my head with this one. I've had a great deal of difficulty piecing this together."

"It was a scene, all right," breathed Steve. He glanced again to the tables in the cold room on the other side of the glass, his imagination—no, his memory—reminding him of what lay beneath the coverings. "Never seen an animal attack quite like that. What do you think—death by misadventure?"

Maryam looked at him, then turned back to her screen. "It is a bit early to say. At this point, yes, I am inclined to agree based on the tissue damage alone, the broken bones... presumably due to jaw pressure. But—"

"But? What else is there to say?" pressed Steve. Letting loose a deep breath, he squinted like he was staring at the sun. "Each day that goes by, we still have a maneater roaming around outside of town. I've half a mind to get the mayor to close some of the trailheads. We need to come to some conclusion."

"I haven't had the chance to measure the spacing of teeth to get a match to a predator, for one thing. I need some counsel on that piece and I'm waiting to hear back from a particular biologist." Maryam rose and gestured to the cold room. "If you'll permit—"

Reluctantly, Steve nodded and made a similar gesture. "By all means."

Maryam led him over to the steel door and pulled on a thick lab coat. She gave him an amused look with an exaggerated shiver before entering the room and standing at the first of the metal tables. Steve fell in behind her, slowly edging his way closer as the chill of the room sunk into him. He had no desire to go back to that basement in Blue Hills, but here he was. And what did he expect, really? Desperately, Steve wanted to make some sort of official declaration and close the book so he could ease back into things. He wanted to wrap this up before anyone started drawing parallels to last year's debacle. *Let's make it a bear, and be done with it*—after all, wasn't that the most reasonable explanation? But it was like this was becoming a new ritual, a yearly occurrence to welcome winter to Coalbrook.

"You ready?" asked Maryam.

Steve nodded. *A lie.* He removed his hat, placing it solemnly on the edge of the table.

"I hope you are prepared to lose faith in God." Slowly, the reluctant pathologist lifted the sheet, folding it back over itself to reveal the wreckage of contents beneath. Steve took a deep breath and stared. Maryam frowned like she had forgotten just how bad it was. A stretch of silence followed the reveal, a mix of respect and horror, and eventually Steve looked away.

Even though he witnessed this horror already, the sterile setting took away the humanity of it. The discovery of something like this out in the world is a tragedy, a trauma; here, it was another day on the job. The work was now underway that would turn a person into impersonal evidence.

"Mercy," he said, glancing back to the dead face.

"Mh-hmm," hummed Maryam. She stepped closer to the mangled skull, gesturing to a particular section that had collapsed, exposing the backside of an eyeball. "The tearing on the surface certainly looks consistent with the spacing of an animal's bite." She looked to Steve, almost like she looked for confirmation. "But I'm not one for the outdoors."

"The, uh, crushed skull... the result of the pressure of an animal bite, maybe?"

"No assumptions," directed Maryam. "I must do this by the book. I am waiting for an outside perspective."

Steve winced, barely able to keep his eyes on the remains before him. They were like the pieces of a shattered porcelain doll, the fragments disconnected and scattered in a vague testimony to what once was. "Who's this?" he muttered.

"Based on the bone structure and general frame, it's one of the boys." Maryam leaned down towards the red-boned thigh, nearly picked clean of its musculature. Various strands of flesh hung ragged around it, sagging down against the table like a torn parachute caught in a tangle of branches. "I must say that separating these bodies was exceptionally difficult. It was like trying to untangle Christmas lights." She glanced at Steve over her glasses, suddenly looking quite self-conscious. "Sorry. You learn to detach from these things."

"I know the feeling." Steve said. *Another lie.*

"All three subjects each experienced more or less the same severity of tissue and skeletal damage, same level of organ removal, and so on." Maryam roamed around the edge of the table, pointing here and there whenever she made the relevant point. "But the more I—"

"Wait," Steve interjected, shifting his head back and forth, scanning the examination tables. He jerked his gaze back to Maryam. "Did you say there's only three here? Or does one of the tables have two together, or—"

Maryam nodded. "Yes, there are three subjects. I can only examine what I receive."

Steve propped himself against the table. "Why didn't you call me?"

She ran a hand across her cheek, looking fairly flustered. "Well, it was a fairly recent realisation. I suppose I figured you were mistaken, and then I got caught up in creating the report, and contacting—"

"I can't believe it," he said, shaking his head. "How did we—" He froze as he felt a wave of electricity course from his crown down to the back of his neck. He stared at Dr. Haim, his eyes bulging. "Oh god—that means one of them is still out there."

There it is, Steve—you're going to have to go back to one of the families. How could you mess this up? He was so wanting to bury this and move on that he missed a basic detail. *They were so mangled, so intertwined... anyone could have made that mistake.*

"Oh," Maryam responded. "I certainly was not expecting this revelation. Perhaps—"

"Alright, let's wrap this up quick," he continued, switching gears. "I've got to get on this. Do you have any idea of who the survivor might be?"

Maryam pulled the sheet back over the body. "I've confirmed two of them to be male based on bone mass and general musculature, although it was a stretch. That lines up with the names. And for the girl here, based on the positive IDs on her effects—this is Cara."

"That leaves Kimberly Shaw." He edged away, replacing his hat on his head. "Thank you. I'll be interested to hear the results of the report."

Maryam gave him a deep nod.

Without another glance or a word, Steve left the way he came. They had to start the search right away, and this time was going to be different. No assumptions, no exceptions—he was going to tear the whole damn region apart.

It was after she had killed the engine when she noticed the stinging in the pads of her fingers and palms. The joints in her fingers were sore enough from the extended writing session the previous night; now they throbbed. Sara stretched them out, waiting for the blood to rush back into the white creases.

The drive from the motel to the middle of town was barely a blip on the clock, but still she had been strangling the wheel like it owed her money. A quiver passed through her. Relaxing into her chair, she scanned the strip mall that was the commercial heart of old Coalbrook. Across the road was the community hall, a nondescript off-white heritage building. Adjacent to that was the similarly coloured Thankful River United Church, which from what she's gathered of recent events has seen a lot of activity. Then a convenience store, a hobby store, a barber, and beyond that a scattering of old houses with chain-link fences. The coffee shop was further on. Sara took in a deep breath, grateful because from where she was sitting, she could barely make out the sprawl of the surrounding forest. Coalbrook was a concrete oasis in a desert of green nightmares.

The independent grocer pleasantly surprised Sara—she managed to find some of her more urban staples. Even though the tofu was nearing expiry, it opened a lot of options for her. A wave of near contentment rushed through her, as it seemed like things were falling into place—she could hunker down in the motel and start piecing together the text for the recording that would be done when she got back home. *Maybe a tofu stir-fry. I could even get a bottle of wine from the liquor store just across the lot...*

She smiled as she approached the register, surprised by the fact it was genuine. It was especially surprising since there were some recent images that refused to leave her mind.

"Just visiting, dear?"

She snapped her attention to the middle-aged woman running the checkout. "I am," replied Sara, still smiling. "Was it that obvious?"

The heavyset woman laughed. Her name tag said Helen. "Clothes aside," she said as she returned the smile, "I think I know every face in town, and I've not seen you before."

"I guess you would see everyone here."

"That I do. Makes it all the harder when things go bad, you know. Every loss is a loss for all here. Like those poor teenagers."

Sara played dumb. "What teenagers? What happened?"

Helen shook her head, closing her eyes like she was rushing through a Hail Mary. "Nothing official, but word travels fast in Coalbrook—but I heard they got attacked by a bear. Apparently, it killed all three." She whisked a bag of granola over the till with a beep. "Just tragic."

Sara knit her brow together. "Just three?" she asked as nonchalantly as possible. "I had heard there were four of them up there."

"Four? Nope, just three as far as I know." The woman gave her a quizzical look of her own. "Up where?"

"Oh." Sara paused and stared at the woman, scrambling for an explanation that was as far from the truth as she could muster. "I overheard someone mention it at Tim Horton's." *Flawless.*

"Right. Well, I heard three. And now there's a big search out for another one."

Ah, that explains it. "Like a search and rescue type thing?"

"Yup. News spreads through town like wildfire. Police and fire department and search and rescue are all on it apparently—and they're looking for some community volunteers too, just to canvass some areas."

A sense of foreboding rose in her—and excitement. "Who are they looking for?" *Who might have survived that carnage, you mean?*

"Little Kimmy Shaw, although these days she ain't so little, I understand. Gotten herself into trouble again."

Her heart pounded. "I thought—" Then she realized—the information she had up to this point was adequate, possibly even good enough for her purposes. Her plan of leaning back and waiting out the repairs while she worked on the script for the next episode was a solid one. But with this new twist—and if she was to muck in with the rest of the town, she may strike gold, an inside scoop kind of gold. Who knew where this could go?

There was, of course, a bit of an obstacle. Searching for a girl in these parts? That meant being outside. In the forest. Sara's breath lodged in her throat. *Hold on, Sara—can you do this? You barely made the drive here.*

Helen asked her how she would pay. Digging into her bag, Sara asked, "Have they said where the search would be?"

The greying cashier shook her head. "Not sure."

Sara nodded. She wasn't exactly expecting to do any hiking during her time here, but with a few layers, she might be fine—her overcoat was wool and reached past her knees. And then there was the poncho in her emergency kit in the rental. *Thanks, dad.*

But her layering was really the least of her concern showing up there; there was the other obstacle of directly disobeying the man who was likely calling the search. *Are you crazy, Sara? They'll bring you in.* The receipt printer's scratchy mechanism faded into the background as the thoughts rattled in her skull. *No, they would have come already. They've got bigger fish to fry, now.*

"Have a good day, dear."

Sara thanked her and made her way out. The cold air washed over her face and dove down her clothes, tightening her skin. She placed her groceries in her trunk, and then sat in the car for a great deal of time, wondering if it was worth the risk.

Biting her lip, she once again tapped open her phone, hands quivering, and found Coalbrook's social media page.

What a relief it was to not be the point man for once.

Steve stood aloof, off to the side of where Stewart Hannah, the lead coordinator for the Coalbrook Volunteer Search and Rescue Association, was currently giving his go-to speech to the hopeful rabble gathered to assist in a time of need. In his high visibility red-and-yellow jacket, Stewart dictated to the sizable crowd of everyday Coalbrookers the basics of what they would do: canvass as an enormous serpent, one long unbroken chain of boots and eyes. They would segment into pairs of two or three, punctuated by a trained professional to maintain some consistency of searching and to offer on-the-go pointers and radio contact to the different ends.

They would move slowly—poking, prodding, overturning whatever was necessary, looking for all manner of signs of life: a broken branch, a footprint, a sign of shelter. Anything.

And time was of the essence. The entire aura of the scene—with men and women of all ages huddled in their coats and reflective vests, breath steaming like smoke rising from a field of refineries—whispered of desperation.

Headlights beamed through the crowd, cutting through the murk of the grey afternoon as sleet battered the group. Steve tried to hold on to hope, but a big part of his baser self knew that Kim's chance of survival was slim to none, bear or not. It had been five nights of sub-zero temperatures, so unless her survival skills were on point, she was in deep weeds. And if she was in deep weeds, that meant *he* was in deep weeds. Even now, some of the volunteers barely kept their eyes from crawling in his direction, as if to say: *here we are again, Boyko. Let's see what kind of call you make this time.*

"We'll be canvassing from the access road out into the trees, and take some targeted paths that would be easier to traverse and therefore more likely to be one of her chosen routes," Stewart continued, gesticulating with his hands to his captive audience.

"Both sides?" came a question from the audience. Stewart flinched, clearly not used to working with untrained volunteers.

"North and south, yes. It's a start, at least," he said, almost defensively. "We can't assume she would stay near to the road. With the lodge closed, there's virtually no reason for anyone to drive up there and there are no light sources other than whatever's natural." He paused, looking around the audience. "It's possible she never found the road."

"She could be anywhere, then," came a voice from the back of the crowd. Steve winced at the insensitivity of it.

Near the source of the comment, Lauren stood at the ready, somehow all smiles as she bent and ruffled the head of the detachment's German Shepherd—lovingly named Heinz by Corporal Friesen—the lone animal member of the tiny Coalbrook K-9 unit that lived full time at his house. Lauren stood near the dog while Grant held the lead tight. All three were ready to go in addition to an apprehensive Cameron.

Here we are again. None of them relished the idea of another failed search. Behind them, another car rumbled slowly by, the driver rubbernecking to see what the fuss was. It was a blue SUV, and the driver—

Ah. I was wondering when you'd show up.

The car disappeared down the road, obscured by heads and tents and parked trucks way bigger than they needed to be. But a few minutes more explanation passed, with a quick demonstration by another search and rescue professional of what to look for during a search. Flashlights were distributed, and cell phone flashlights were encouraged to be employed when the going got dark. Stewart invited questions. The silence that followed indicated that a funereal readiness enveloped the group.

It was in this silence that Sara Garrison rounded the corner, looking like she was being led to the stand to be cross-examined. She was in a puffy yellow coat this time, swishing beneath a draping clear poncho. It didn't take long for her eyes to meet Steve's through her large-frame glasses, and when they did, he excused himself from the front and worked his way around to the back of the crowd.

"Don't you have any sense of decency?" he began as he walked up on her.

Sara pulled up her shoulders, her yellow coat making a whispering sound. "Um," she croaked, her tongue running over her lips, "I just wanted to help—"

"No, you just want to capitalise on the suffering of others." He didn't look away from the young woman, whose eyes swelled as the conflict developed. Sergeant Parenteau and Corporal Friesen sidled close along with Heinz. Corporal Reid, too, had seen the conflict and decided to join. "You want to help? Stay the hell out of the way and stop interfering with what we're trying to do here."

Sara froze in place. She glanced at the other three officers, who seemed just as uncomfortable. Grant twisted his wrist, tightening Heinz's leash around his forearm.

"Steve," said Lauren, "we're going to need every pair of boots we can get."

He stared at her. "Staff Sergeant."

"We're going to need all the help we can get," she continued, "*Staff Sergeant*. Or would you prefer commander?"

Steve's eyes bulged. "Excuse me?"

"If I may," Sara interjected, sparing Sergeant Parenteau her superior's wrath. Steve glared at her, eyes still bulging. "I... know that I have probably been a bit of an annoyance since I've arrived, but—"

"More than just an annoyance," he said, sticking his head forward. "You've been obstructive. You've trespassed. You've disobeyed a direct command from an RCMP officer."

Sara grimaced. "I took it to be more of a suggestion."

He leaned close. "How you interpret it is irrelevant. The fact is, if I wasn't up to my neck in problems at the moment, arresting you would be my number one priority."

She pressed her lips together into a straight line. "I see."

Steve straightened and read the room. When Christian Johnstone disappeared, there was a distinct sense of camaraderie within the detachment; each constable was behind him every step of the way, championing his decisions and following faithfully. But as soon as things soured—along with the people of Coalbrook—the dynamic changed. They isolated him. And a scene like this was a hearty reminder, as his officers did their best to convince him to another course of action without being directly insubordinate. And it was plain on their faces. They saw him as majoring on the minors—there was a girl out there in need of finding.

It was him against the world—and that was a fight he didn't have the strength for. Not now.

"I suppose my fellow officers are right, though," he said through tight teeth, "as we could use all the help we can get." With a shake of his head, he pointed her towards the vests.

She seemed to think she was on the right side of the law, now—her satisfaction at the invite was plain on her face, palpable in her body language as her shoulders dropped from their stressed heights and the hint of a smile touched her mouth.

She strode away to grab a reflective vest. She stood for a moment next to the plastic containers, staring at the trailhead and the wild expanse beyond. When she turned to look back at him, her smile was gone.

11

Old Hat

INTUITION GETS A BAD rap. It's so often declared as unreliable and fickle, something tossed about like a rowboat in a dark, stormy sea. But I don't think we should dismiss intuition so easily. It's simply a framework built by experience, a schema brought to the fore in an instant to say, "Hey, I know what to do with this new thing here." If you are open and sensitive, intuition can be like a lifeboat. Or a lighthouse. But how does one discern if it's a sign of rescue, or a warning to stay away?

- The Garrison Theories podcast, Episode 1: "Our Weird Frontier"

The grey atmosphere of the forest defied the time of day as the dense boughs refused the sunlight entry, relegating the contents below to an indistinct blend of murky earth-tones. A mist just degrees from freezing still managed to find its way through. At this point in autumn, flashlights would become a necessity within the hour.

Beneath the canopy of the snow-laden evergreens and the skeletal birch, the Coalbrook Search and Rescue task force moved like a sidewinder in slow-motion, a singular vein with hundreds of eyes on the ground. With one mind, they solemnly prodded the frozen earth and underbrush with their tracking sticks, pushing aside bushes and ferns to catch a glimpse of a footprint or some other sign of passage: a mark on a tree, or a broken branch. Each member worked in silence, save for an odd word or two in a brief collaboration with their neighbour.

In the centre of the snaking line of bodies, Sara's eyes absently searched the silvery ground; shadowed snow and the exposed tips of rock and twig alike appeared and disappeared from her field of vision almost entirely unobserved. Hanging over her like a wooded prison, the surrounding trees moaned and bristled, demanding her obedience. Sara shrunk within her jacket and made like she was contributing to the search—but her wide eyes crawled helplessly upwards at the mocking trunks and branches that used the smell of pine and sap to remind her of the power they lorded over her. The absurdly brief training that the officers and the local employed search and rescue personnel had offered her evaporated the moment she stepped into the trees.

Well, if you can't help with the search, Sara, at least pay attention. Take a few notes, even. It was as if her podcast was on life support, begging her for help as it tried to convince her to do whatever she could to save it. Even if it meant being a self-centred jerk.

"First time in the bush?" a husky voice called.

She turned and smiled. It was difficult to recognize him in his gear, but a few links down in the search and rescue chain was her portly interviewee, Clayton Johnstone. Now he was in his element: he was all beard and boots and plaid, the lovechild of Molson and mud. She gave him an unsure smile as he switched places with her closest neighbour.

"First time in some time, anyway," she replied as she stepped over an arched tangle of roots. "Would it be fair to say that this isn't yours?"

He tucked his face into his beard and chuckled, the red of his face deepening. "That would be fair to say." His face grew serious suddenly as he turned to scour the ground, like he had for the

113

moment of talking with her forgotten what they were out there for. Still, he continued. "I grew up in and around Coalbrook. Spent a lot of time in these woods, playin' as a boy and huntin' as a... slightly older boy, I guess." He grunted as he poked at a snag of bush. "And to this day, at that. I got lots of reasons to be out in places like this."

Sara nodded, keeping her eyes low—and not just for the search. Then she remembered why she first exposed herself to this total nightmare. "Thank you again for the interview."

"My pleasure."

"Likewise." She shook out her arms, glancing up and down the line of volunteers. Her neighbour on the other side was just over a knoll, slightly out of view. Over Clayton's head was a row of reflective vests that stretched away in a chain, all capped with hooded or toqued heads with downcast faces. "Clayton, I hope this isn't an inappropriate question—" she began as she lowered her voice. It seemed to grab his attention. "—but in your expert opinion, what do you think are the odds of someone surviving out here this time of year?"

He raised his eyebrows and sighed as he wrestled with the question. "Fair question, considering the circumstances," he said. "Depends on how geared up you are. But most everybody up here respects the cold, since it comes 'round every year with a vengeance and reminds us of who's in charge." He groaned as he took a deep lunge up a small escarpment. "So, all of that's saying—if I understand your meaning—that no, we aren't wasting our time."

"Good," said Sara. "I mean that it's good that she might be OK," she added quickly.

"That it is," he agreed. "Though more can happen out here than you think."

They ambled on in a silence interrupted only by the occasional crack of a stick, or the hollered name of the subject of the search. The background noise of moving branches rustled above them along with the creaking of the tall boles as the wind rode the boughs many metres above their heads. As she walked, Sara made mental notes of every bit of conversation she had and heard. She would have to write it all down later. *Over one hundred volunteers. Search is hopeful. Clayton the hunter's story continues, although he says a lot of cryptic things. Will clarify later.*

Sara took a deep breath, and a notion struck her: during her conversation with Clayton, she had almost forgotten the anxiety that had clung to her so tightly since she left the Lower Mainland. As soon as the realisation came, it settled right back into her. *Maybe I'll get more from this trip than just a few notes.* With another deep breath Sara lifted her chin to the trees, against all instinct. The bristling conifers swayed over her head, coming together as they reached for the grey skies. Her head swirled with vertigo and fear, and she dropped her gaze to the pinecone-covered forest floor. *Baby steps,* she thought as she continued. She steadied herself for a moment, then poked the ground with her stick, scouring the snow-dusted soil for footprints, clues—anything. *Nothing.*

"You alright?" asked Clayton. He stared at her from a few strides ahead, angled off her left side. "You look like you've seen a ghost."

She gave a quivering, quiet laugh. "Um," she started, slowly. "I guess in a manner of speaking, I have."

He shook his head and shrugged, waiting for her to elaborate.

"I have hylophobia," she said. "Fear of forests."

Clayton's eyes bulged, and he almost smiled. "You serious?"

"Unfortunately," Sara admitted.

He took in a deep breath and turned to continue along with the operation. "Didn't even know that was a thing," he called softly over his shoulder. "How'd you come by that one?"

Sara thought of the camping trip her family was on one autumn day. She thought of Andrea. She thought of all the bad things she had visualised when Andrea disappeared from the tent in the middle of the night. She thought of her mother's wails when the search was called off after a week. "Bit of a long story," she said at last.

"We've got time," he replied. "But I think by that tone of voice, your reluctance at sharing ain't got nothing to do with time."

"You might be right."

He nodded. "No worries, then."

"Appreciate it." She kept searching in silence, doing her best to ignore the threats all around.

"I could see how one could grow to fear the woods," he said after a while. "I've spent a lot of time in the woods around Coalbrook, and beyond, even." He stopped walking, one of his legs raised on the incline. He rested an elbow on a thick thigh. "Sometimes I swear these places have a life of their own. Like some consciousness, or something. God, I swear sometimes even I think I'm being watched."

Sara shivered.

"Oh, goddamn—sorry, girl. Got all poetic on you and freaked you out, eh?"

She shook her head. "No, it's OK. Nice to have someone who can relate, I guess."

"So how do you manage it?" he asked as he gestured to the expanse of wood around them. "Takes some balls to force yourself out here."

"I try to remember what my old therapist used to tell me: change happens when the pain of staying the same is greater than the pain of changing." She spoke it like a mantra. And for a time—many years ago—it was. But it was unfamiliar now.

"Sounds like quackery to me."

Sara's eyes widened as she cracked a disbelieving grin. "What? I thought that was a powerful quote."

"Well, it's a fine sentiment," he chuckled. "But look at you. You're terrified." He burst into laughter.

She laughed along, quickly stifling it when her other neighbour gave her a disapproving look. "Yikes," she said as she cringed, "I guess I'm not taking this seriously."

"Ah, to hell with them," reassured Clayton. "As long as you're looking, who cares. We won't miss her for want of talkin.'"

It was the first time Sara experienced some depth of warmth from a Coalbrook resident. The interview he gave was rough, but out here the connection was genuine. Clayton's hard edges had a grandfatherly air about them, like a man who had been through hard seasons of life that have made him stronger instead of broken him down, the loss of his nephew likely being one of his biggest defining—maybe refining—moments.

For the first time since she'd arrived, she had someone in her corner—something that was even a rarity back home.

"It used to be a lot worse. And I mean a lot," she continued. "There was a time, especially when I was in high school, where it was a struggle for me to go outside. At first a tree was enough to give me a panic attack. But then I slowly found myself able to stomach—now don't laugh—to stomach a well-manicured hedge."

He did laugh, but she liked it.

"And I slowly worked through it doing exposure therapy."

"Well," he grunted, "good enough to get you in here. Hell, I would say that's progress."

"I suppose." Her gaze swung up, reluctantly but intentionally as she remembered the principles of her past therapy. The branches spread out above her like a dark web, flicking and swaying in the autumnal breeze. She was drowning, the boughs above like a dark, roiling sea. "Sometimes I feel pretty stuck, though."

"How so?" asked Clayton.

"I'd love to be able to not feel fear. At times like this. It's always running in the background. It's distracting. Uncomfortable."

"Good."

She stopped walking. "Excuse me?"

"Ultimately, I think anyone with any sense should be afraid of the forest. There's nothing irrational about it."

His shift in tone caught her off guard. His jovial edge dulled into a stern bludgeon as he challenged her. Clayton continued speaking as he glared at the snow and soil. "I've spent my whole life in this bush. There's bears, cougars, and even wolves sometimes. They may keep their distance, but they don't always—and if they pick you, you're cooked. And if you don't know what you're doin', you don't know where you're goin', you'd get turned around as quick as you can blink, and wander in circles for days until you collapse dead a stone's throw from a road." He sniffed, rubbing his nose on the back of his sleeve. "Don't get me wrong; believe me, I'm a nature-lovin' man. Love the outdoors. But there are some days—some nights, for sure—where I'm convinced that the forest doesn't want us in it. Sometimes I'm convinced that the forest tries everything it can to kill a man." He glanced at her. "Or a woman."

Sara kept her eyes down as she crept along the forest floor. "I see what you're saying."

"Glad to hear it, city girl," he said, smiling and breaking the seriousness of his monologue. "Don't be too quick to get rid of fear. Sometimes it's worth listening to."

The words had hardly finished sounding between them when a man's voice echoed ahead. Corporal Reid came over a small hill, appearing from behind a thick cedar. "Steve," he shouted across the line of volunteers, "I think we may have a footprint."

Staff Sergeant Boyko worked his way down the slope, hot on the heels of Corporal Reid and Sergeant Parenteau. Corporal Friesen moved behind Heinz on the lead further ahead. His eyes darted up at the cluster of bodies ahead, and down again to ensure he didn't catch his foot on a rock or root hidden beneath the white-grey sea. Cameron moved ahead in his shifting orange vest, eager to rejoin the others who clumped together in a circle, leaning inwards.

"Hey," called Steve as he approached. "Don't crowd it; we don't want to muddy the waters here." A few of the search and rescue personnel stepped back. "This has been hard enough already," Steve grunted again, mostly to himself.

The track was unclear, but it certainly was a track—a fern lay pressed down into the snow, partially buried under the wet powder and frozen into the impression.

"That's a definite boot print," said Cameron, voice heavy with concern. "Good boy, Heinz," he said to the normally stoic German Shepherd who was brimming with energy.

"Alright," said Steve. His head spun, eyes falling to see if the footprint had any siblings. "That's... strange. It looks like this might be a solitary print?"

Cameron pointed up the slope. "No, it keeps going—look!"

The impressions continued up the slope, partially obscured by a recent dusting that managed to sneak through the treetops.

"I see that, but there isn't any prints leading up to it." Cameron shrugged, although his face didn't reflect the same level of nonchalance. Neither did Lauren's. Steve sighed. "Alright, let's see where it goes. Let's take a smaller complement, shall we? Maybe..." he paused to take in the options available, "... let's do us officers, and Stewart. Tell the others to fan out and continue along so we don't miss anything."

"Alright," Stewart began calling through a series of coughs, "let's make two groups on either side of the tracks and work our way up. Business as usual, keep an eye out for any disturbed snow, any indentations, you know the drill. Give us a wide berth here."

The officers and Stewart clambered up the snow-clad slope, followed by the small contingent of volunteers. "There it goes," said Cameron, pointing to a clear boot print. It led into the dense underbrush just beyond them, touched only by a veneer of snowfall. "More over here." He pressed his foot adjacent to a faint impression in the snow. He eyed it carefully.

Steve's gaze narrowed for a moment of silent certainty. He crouched and scanned it like he was reading some text hidden within the print. Then he spoke again. "Looks about a size six, maybe seven," he said as he straightened. "Could be her."

"Where the hell is she going?" asked Cam, mostly to himself.

The others pressed in closer, eager to see what was happening. Steve glanced behind him, mindful of the growing interest. Many of the community volunteers were now phoning it in at the realisation that this narrow strip of travelled land had become the point of interest. Further back, Sara crept forward, nose and eyes red, looking up the slope to see where the tracks might lead. Her new partner, the hunter Clayton Johnstone, was looking exceptionally concerned.

After what seemed like an eternity, the sign of passage continued long enough to make Steve suspect they were hot on her heels, but the slope of the hill was interfering with their view of what lay ahead of them.

"You all work in this area, keep an eye out for any additional physical evidence. Things like discarded items, like a cell phone—anything really," he said to the volunteers, who nodded eagerly in unison. He pointed to his selected group. "To minimise potential disturbance, this group will canvass up a bit further." Without waiting for an acknowledgement, Steve continued up the slope with Cameron who shuffled along through the drifts. Grant and Heinz strode slightly ahead, off to the side, with Grant more focused on controlling the dog than checking for footprints. As he clambered further up the slope, Heinz became agitated.

At the top, Corporal Friesen froze. Heinz began whimpering and railing against his leash, although not in any specific direction. "Steve," called Grant. "You better get up here."

A few dozen metres further on, Steve stood atop a small levee of snow around the trunk of a dead white birch, observing the scene below alongside Grant and Heinz. A shudder passed through his whole body at what he saw. "Damn," he muttered to himself, hardly aware he'd said it.

On the other side of the tree, a dozen or so metres away, a stack of clothes sat on the top of a large, flat rock cleared of snow. Steve kept his eyes on the uncanny display, turned his head slightly to holler back down the slope.

"Cameron," he shouted, "Cameron, get up here. Lauren, you too."

Corporal Reid was panting, with clouds of vapour erupting from his lungs into the air. Still, he was up the slope quickly, gasping and grunting as he did so; he came up next to Steve, and the superior officer simply pointed down the incline. The younger officer's chest heaved as he tried to follow the directing finger.

"Steve, what did y—" he cut himself off, squinting and pushing his head forward. He shielded his eyes from the bright snow as the sun cut through the treetops and blinded him. Then his eyes bulged. "Oh. That can't be good."

"No kidding," Steve said in agreement. He turned and motioned for the neon yellow and reflective volunteers to follow with Stewart at the helm.

Lauren caught up with them, and the three officers carved their way down the slick, snowy slope, leaning into the hill and dragging their hands through the snow. Cameron slipped for a moment, sliding a few feet before catching himself as he hastened towards the evidence. They arrived together, and stood over the sodden, frozen laundry where Heinz waited patiently alongside Grant.

"That looks like a complete outfit, more or less," said Cameron, squatting onto the balls of his feet. "We got... well, the boots obviously. Shirt, pants—sweater on the bottom with the winter jacket."

Using his baton, Steve brushed what looked like days of snowfall from the strange monument. Splashes of damp colour appeared as the flakes fell away in icy clumps. "Mhmm," Steve acknowledged. "Small profile, too." He turned away and ran his gloved hand across his forehead. "Damnit."

"Like it was laundry day," came Cameron's voice, higher than normal. "They're all neatly folded."

Steve sighed. "This isn't right." He walked a loose perimeter around the rocks, scanning the scant snowfall with his eyes. "That's weird."

"That's putting it lightly."

"No, not the clothes—although that is plenty strange." Steve gestured to the ground, furrowing his brow as he looked at his coworker. "No other tracks. Just like when he picked it up, it just... vanishes. Doesn't it? Am I missing something?"

Cameron threw his eyes down, stepping back at an angle that made it look like he was looking under a table, scouring the area in a circular motion with his gaze. "Looks like you're right."

Steve crossed his arms. "Now what the hell does that mean, eh?"

Cameron shrugged, pulling his phone out of his pocket. He took a handful of pictures of the scene, finishing just as the volunteers crested the top of the slope above.

"Everything OK?" came Lauren's voice from above.

Steve said nothing. He glanced at Cam, to the clothes, then back to Cam. The young constable's eyes were downcast, not even looking at the stack of snow-crusted clothing. Words now were unnecessary. If these clothes were Kim Shaw's—and it was likely that they were—then they both knew that she was not going home.

Steve turned around. At the crest of the slope behind, the crowd of search and rescue volunteers, both at the community and organisational level, was burgeoning. Shoulder to shoulder they stood, staring down the gentle incline in disbelief just as Steve had moments prior. Many of the faces were telling as they creased with despair at knowing what the scene meant for the one they searched for.

One face stood out in particular: that of Sara Garrison. She was standing apart from the larger group, coming up the hill just as he saw her. She was already a pale girl, but when she saw the clothes, it looked like the already-scant blood present in her face had drained away completely.

12

Dirty Laundry

WHAT ARE GHOSTS, ANYWAYS? Manifested memories? Personified energy? Maybe both, and more. Well, I have a theory: we tend to see apparitions take root in places of trauma. And trauma is essentially an event turned memory that was too overwhelming for us to process in the moment... so it lingers like a haunting ghost. So whatever ghosts are in essence, it seems to me like they are that which is undone and incomplete—a door unclosed, a story untold, a voice unheard.
- *The Garrison Theories* podcast, Episode 6: "The Jilted Bride"

I t was only Sara and the stack of cotton, polyester, and wool.

The trees disappeared like they were felled, her fellow volunteers and the guiding professionals vanished like vapour into the cold air alongside them. All were there, of course, standing in her peripheral vision. But for her, they vanished. No Clayton. No Steve. Just Sara and the laundry.

Sara quivered as she struggled to regulate herself, eyes locked on what had to be the girl's clothes. Her fur-lined boots stood at attention next to the pile, each one neatly stuffed with gently rolled multicoloured socks. A black puffer jacket comprised the base of the heap, followed by a pair of folded and faded blue jeans; next, a grey hoodie with its arms tucked tidily below. A long-sleeved thermal top served as a resting place for a single pair of black underwear, followed by a nude bra and a Dijon knit beanie.

Suddenly, Sara was twelve years old, cradled in her mom's arms as they crumbled into each other near a fallen tree, staring wet-eyed and bewildered at the clothes Sara had seen her sister in only hours before. It was almost thirteen years ago, but her memory wasn't about to let that image go. It was as clear as the scene playing out before her.

She remembered it was barely into October when it happened. The Garrison family fall camp out was well underway and going wonderfully, as always—only this time the stakes were a bit higher. Andrea was struggling in the throes of teenagerhood, and the struggle was made most obvious in her interactions with mom and dad. Sara was often left to listen and observe from a distance. But the shift away from the day-to-day made a huge difference, as if as a family they went back in time to when things were simpler.

One night, they lazed around the campfire, likely the only man-made light source for many kilometres, listening to dad's terrible ghost stories but loving them all the same. They doused the flames in the latter part of the evening to see the stars as they gathered above the shadowy branches of the cedars. Together they slept among trees and beneath moon and star in their oversized tent, snugly lined up like nesting dolls.

Sara could almost smell the must of the tent lining as she numbly watched Steve and the other officers marvel at the impossible evidence that loomed before them, built up on a flat boulder that looked like a natural altar. While the professionals conversed, Sara could still hear Andrea's youthful voice, whispering to her—because right before they fell asleep almost thirteen years ago, Andrea had rolled over and murmured into her ear while dad snored on the other side of the tent.

"Sara?" Andrea had begun quietly then.

"What?"

"Oh good," she giggled into her sleeping bag. "I hate being the last one asleep."

Inside the tent, silence; outside, a symphony of wind and leaves. The tent bristled under a pleasant breeze.

"Sara."

"What?"

"Do you think we'll be friends forever?"

Sara had hesitated then, unsure of how to respond. Andrea had been so different—but her heart softened. "We're sisters, dummy. Of course we will."

"I know. But not all sisters are friends. I see it all the time at school—you'll see once you hit grade eight. Happens when you get older." Andrea's voice faded to a murmur. "Look at mom and Aunt Bev... and, well, I guess I've been kinda mean lately."

"I guess."

"We have to make sure," Andrea declared with an authoritative whisper. "Promise me that we'll work at being best friends."

"OK," answered Sara with honesty and without thinking. "I promise."

There was a click, and Andrea's face illuminated from below, as if she was about to tell one of dad's awful ghost stories by flashlight. Her extended little finger erupted from her sleeping bag. "Pinky swear it."

Sara wrapped her little finger around her sister's. "Pinky swear."

The light flicked off, and they burrowed into their respective sleeping bags, giggling quietly in the darkness of the tent.

Later that autumn night Sara woke and saw Andrea step out of the tent, presumably to go to the bathroom. She said nothing and fell back asleep.

When Sara woke up the following morning, Andrea was gone.

She left everything behind except an answer as to why. With all the searching, the waiting, the longing, and anguish felt by the

126

three remaining Garrisons, the best answer the authorities were able to give was that she had simply got up in the middle of the night, walked about one kilometre into the forest, stripped naked, and then... nothing. No tracks. No sign of foul play. She was simply, utterly, completely gone.

And here Sara was again. She was older, but she didn't feel stronger—and the same guilt washed over her the same as if it had never left her. The tower of frozen clothes triggered the same bargaining. *She was only going to the bathroom. I was sure of it.* She had felt Andrea rise in the night, watched her pajamaed figure slink to the tent door and peel back the zipper slow enough to be only loose a soft, metallic rasp. *Just a short trip, out past the fire pit to do her business. How was I to know?* Her quivers became shakes, her legs threatening to give out just before a pair of hands gripped her shoulders and held her fast.

"You alright there, Sara?"

She brought her hands up, pushing back her red toque and rubbing her forehead. "Yes," she said with a wince, "I'll be OK. Just need to sit for a moment."

Clayton helped her down after he dusted the snow from a fallen tree. She almost collapsed onto it, holding her twisting body up with one arm.

"Phobia acting up again?" he asked as he stood before her, leaning in slightly to check her pupils.

Sara shook her head. "No. Not a phobia, not really."

"So not the trees, eh?" He looked around, eyes inevitably settling on the commotion a few metres away. Many voices filled the air, with Staff Sergeant Boyko's booming above the rest as he tried to keep some space around the discovery. "Well, that's certainly enough to get someone panicked, I suppose." He sighed, slowly shaking his head as he pursed his lips out from his salt-and-pepper beard. His voice came in softer, quieter, "There ain't no way that girl is OK."

Sara shivered.

"That what eating you up?"

"No," she breathed. "It's just that I've... seen that before."

Clayton stabbed his thumb over his shoulder. "You've seen something like that before? The folded clothes?"

"In the middle of nowhere, yes. A sudden disappearance."

He was within an arm's reach, not too close but close enough to be a comforting presence, as if that was possible. Turning, his gaze didn't waver from the pile of frozen clothing at the bottom of the incline. "Let me guess: long story?"

Sara shivered in her own grip. All she could do was nod, her mind frozen on the moment she watched her sister disappear through the tent flap into the cold autumn night.

Yellow tape shifted in the weak breeze as it hung ragged in a loose circle around the rock. Steve stood back with his hands stuffed into his standard-issue jacket, unable to take his eyes off the unfolding scene.

It looked like a ritual had taken place: the barrier of the space made sacred by an unbroken circle of yellow crime scene tape; the boulder, the altar on which an offering would be made; the clothes, the sacrifice.

Steve frowned. He didn't like where his thoughts were taking him. Only it felt impossible to reign them in—everything he had witnessed over the last few days was... wrong. And wrong in more ways than the obvious. It was wrong in the way his hackles refused to die down. Wrong in a way that brought him back to events over a year ago. Wrong in the way that the discovery at Blue Hills seemed to start something that was very quickly spiralling out of his control.

And he didn't become a cop to feel less in control of his life, and he certainly didn't come to Coalbrook to lose it even more. It was supposed to be a fresh start. And now things were getting weird. His mind quickly went to the face of Christian Johnstone. *Are his clothes out there, too, stacked somewhere?* His heart dropped; synapses fired, and thoughts raced. *Dear God, is the same thing happening again? Is this a pattern—no, for the love of God, Steve, stop killing yourself over this. Don't be irrational. Focus on the facts, not your muddled intuition.*

But maybe his intuition didn't need to be reigned in. Maybe this apprehension, this growing sense of dread was meant to help him. Maybe it wasn't irrational—maybe it was wisdom. Maybe he should have turned and ran out of that forest, ran home, and gathered his family and taken them somewhere far, far away. Only he didn't do that: he simply stood fast and marvelled at the insanity.

Cameron crept closer and stood next to him, silently surveying the scene. A sigh whistled through his puckered lips.

"This wasn't a bear, Steve," he started slowly, "and I don't think it was a cougar or a wolf, either."

Steve gave him a sidelong glance. "Thanks for clearing that up, corporal."

Cameron shrugged. "Sorry, I was just—"

"I am going to wait for Dr. Haim and forensics to tell us about what happened at Blue Hills." He pointed towards the new scene. *A crime scene? Who knows?* "Obviously we have two different concerns here. Some animal did those kids in—" he paused to give Cameron a challenging stare "—one-hundred percent it was an animal. There were no other prints there. That shouldn't be up for debate, it happens all the time up here. But maybe poor Ms. Shaw woke up in the midst of it and panicked and scrambled outside in the dark, got lost, got hypothermic, and here we are."

Cameron was still. He spoke in a quiet voice, "You really think it's that simple?"

"I do," Steve replied. "What else could it possibly be? You ever heard of paradoxical undressing? When hypothermia makes someone undress right before they freeze to death?"

"I have. But not folded so neatly like this, it was more like scattered. I don't know. Just seems like there's more going on here than what meets the eye, you know? Hell, I've been having a hard time sleeping. And Lauren—"

Steve rounded on him. "What about Sergeant Parenteau?"

"Well," mumbled Cameron, "she's been having—"

He almost started growling. "Speak up, corporal. I can't hear you."

Cameron straightened. Steve could see his jaw muscles tightening. "Sergeant Parenteau has been having vivid nightmares. Just like last time."

"Last time?" Steve asked, cocking his head.

"Yeah," sighed Cam. A white cloud obscured his face for a moment. "She's got the same feeling. Me too."

A frown pulled down Steve's face, somehow even further than it already was. Looking at the potential crime scene, he narrowed his eyes at Lauren. She was busying herself about the perimeter, checking tape and exchanging a few words with the local Search and Rescue volunteers who remained behind to do a final scour for signs of movement beyond the site. Somebody made a comment, and a few people chuckled—the standard levity for those in the line of duty. But when she looked around, she made eye contact with Steve. Nothing in her eyes expressed any sense of humour. She busied herself, wide-eyed, somehow more shaken than she was when they had left Blue Hills.

Steve growled and turned back to Cameron.

"Is there anything else you and the other officers are discussing without me knowing?"

"No, Steve—no, sir. It's just... it was only personal, between her and I while on patrol. Didn't seem relevant until—"

"Until?"

Cameron jerked his head towards the altar-looking stone with the strange offering on top. "Until this. Sorry, Steve, but this is freaking me out."

A long, grating sigh rushed out of Steve as Cameron went on.

"I mean, are we dealing with a serial killer here? Someone who runs a butcher and a laundromat that shows up once a year?"

"Cam, we have no idea if these two events are related."

"They seem related."

"They seem related because they happened almost exactly a year apart and they involve a disappearance. But we can't jump to that kind of conclusion."

"I'm not jumping," Cameron protested. "I'm slowly putting two and two together."

Steve held his tongue. It was very clear now that he had lost control of whatever was unfolding around them. Of course, he had made similar connections, but unlike the others, he was fighting tooth and nail to keep these events separate. Everyone else was already seeing the same scenario play out as before, already watching him to see if he would make a bad call. He had to keep these things apart in the minds of others, especially his staff—the more these stories entangled, the messier this would get.

First, he had to keep these events apart in his own mind. *A serial killer? A nameless murderer who appears in Coalbrook once a year to abduct—and now, apparently, to slaughter—teenagers?*

Steve spat on the ground and stormed away from Cam, through the snow and crisp underbrush toward the main scene. He had sent home most of the volunteers while the professionals remained behind, still scratching their heads. The SAR personnel had scoured the surrounding area, and no one could find any sign of passage leading from the clothes. It was like she stripped and flew right out of the forest like an airlifted hiker.

I wish someone would airlift me out of here.

Steve stood, hands in pockets, staring at the strange discovery. The longer he looked, the more uncomfortable he became; the strangeness of the whole scenario spread like an infection in his mind. A pang of nausea crawled up his oesophagus. He tore his gaze away. Blinking, he found himself staring at Lauren, who herself looked like she was fighting off a growing sense of disquiet as she stared right back. Nearby, Grant held fast to Heinz's leash, although the dog was perfectly still and staring off somewhere behind him, deeper in the forest.

Reluctantly, Steve went over to Lauren. *More resistance incoming.* As he came near, she forced a weak smile that didn't touch her eyes.

"How're you holding up, Lauren?" he asked with a stiff voice.

"Well enough, considering," she admitted. "I'd be interested to know how you are holding up."

"Me?" he asked, feigning surprise. "Oh, well, you know me. Just putting my head down and ploughing through."

Her smile weakened. "Hard to keep your head down with this..." she started, "... I just can't help but feel—"

Steve braced himself.

"—you know, like we've been through this before."

"I don't remember this," he said as he half-turned towards the crime scene. *Or whatever the hell they would call whatever this was.*

Lauren sighed like she resigned to whatever she was about to say. "I would be willing to bet a year's salary that there's another stack out there that we haven't found yet."

"Oh, you would, would you?"

"I'm sorry, Steve, it's just that—"

"Nope, nope—no apologies needed. I get it. It's all weird, and it looks like this might be an answer to last year's debacle. I get it, Lauren, really I do. But let's not pretend like whatever this is—" he stabbed his arm towards the scene "—is anything like an explanation."

"Then you tell me what it is, Steve."

"Explanations need to make sense, Lauren. This doesn't make sense."

She looked away, eyes watering as she stared over his shoulder, presumably at the tape-strewn enclosure behind him. "Maybe we need to widen our idea of what an explanation can be," she mumbled.

"Or maybe we should accept that there are some things that don't have an explanation."

Lauren's gaze crawled back to him, her damp eyes full of hurt. "Is that good enough for you, commander?"

He sucked his teeth, doing his best to ignore her emotions. "I don't think 'good' factors into any of this."

Just then, Heinz got up on all fours and pointed his nose further down the incline. Beyond their location, the decline sprawled and levelled out for as far as they could see. Eventually all details were lost to the visual noise and murky blend of brown, green, and white, where one couldn't tell the trees from the ground.

"What is it, Heinz?" asked Grant.

The dog didn't respond. He simply stood, hackles raised, and muscles tensed, staring out into the expanse of woods beyond. His tail was tucked fast between his legs.

He wasn't quite sure, but Steve thought he heard Heinz whimper.

S ara opened her eyes to a grey, sunless sky. Her arms crossed over her chest as if she were interred, and she was powerless to move them, leading her to believe that she may, in fact, be dead.

The tattered remains of an old tent hung around her pharaonic body, the flexible plastic of the poles acting like a cavernous rib cage in an elephant graveyard. She rose groggily. Standing motionless within the decrepit shell, small snowflakes like grains of sand floated and swirled around her, falling and rising as if trapped by the wind, never touching the ground.

Her arms fell slack to her side along with her head, giving her a scant second to stop herself from collapsing completely. On her knees, Sara wretched for oxygen as if she was coming up for water, filling the surrounding frigid air with clouds of her desperate breath. She moved her hands across the cold grass, scattering the pale grains that dusted the dull green surface. Only it wasn't snow—it was ash.

A dead campfire lay before the tent, filled to the brim of the stone circle with black wood and the grey remnants of burnt offerings. Around the site, which was growing uncomfortably familiar for Sara, was an unusual white forest of birch and alder. Not quite how she remembered her family camping trips. But here it was, a loose facsimile of her early childhood experiences.

A disinterested voice called her name, echoing softly as if from a great distance.

She blinked, looking at the trees closely. Sara cocked her head as she cautiously worked her way out of the campsite, keeping her eyes on the trees that seemed to change as she drew nearer—or maybe they were always that way, she couldn't tell—but something was certainly off. She squinted at the blurry flora, looking through the thin sheet of ashfall that danced in front of her face. Brows furrowed, she came upon the nearest tree. Her eyes widened.

She traced her fingers down the linen surface, which shifted as softly as she would have expected from a stack of freshly laundered clothes. Stepping back, she gazed upon the nature of the tree: it was a twisting stack of clothes, piling upwards into a sprawling set of perplexing branches of garments and apparel that terminated as grey-green leaves, swaying like they should in a gentle breeze. All around her, thousands of trees, each an impossible stack of white linen, cotton, and polyester. Hanging from the laundered branches were vines of twisted knots like macramé.

A hissing whisper this time, coming from the trees like rustling leaves.

Sara.

"I can't see you, Andrea."

In the distance a sound pulsed. Sara's eardrums fluttered in response as she tried to triangulate the source; the noise reverberated, growing in intensity, taking form and sounding like a colossal curtain being slowly torn from top to bottom.

Her pulse quickened. A sudden shivering movement in her peripheral snapped her to attention.

The tree in front of Sara began to bleed.

Small patches of crimson grew between the articles of clothing, soaking and spreading across the white, lumpy surface like a spill soaking into a paper towel, filling the cracks between the linens. The crimson stains spread, and Sara watched, mouth agape as the cotton trunks became increasingly sodden with blood. Great flows of scarlet fell from the cracks in the trees of laundry, pooling on the ground and running like sick rivers through the thickening ashfall.

Sara, the voice called again, desperately.

The inchoate ripping grew, filling Sara's mind as it roared from all directions. She threw her hands over her ears, tucking her elbows violently together. The cloth trees began to fall apart like fresh papier mâché, revealing horrid, skeletal cores made of picked-clean human bone. She shut her eyes and screamed, falling to her knees as her own flesh began to bleed and tear.

Sara felt something through the pumping surge of blood; something familiar. She opened her eyes to the ceiling of her motel room, the muffled din of the baseboard heaters filling her head with white noise. She sat up in bed, drawing up her blanketed knees and wrapping her arms around them. *Another night, another nightmare.*

She closed her eyes to fight off the churning nausea that slid upwards along her raw throat. An unwelcome dry cough followed, pushing its way up in the same way. Her fingers found their way to her neck, and she rubbed at it.

Her throat felt raw. Like she had been screaming.

PART THREE

13

Intersections

WE MIGHT LABEL STORIES like this as ill-fated as if the whole thing was doomed from the start. In this case: an ill-fated bride. But was it fate that brought this young woman who now haunts Edmonton's Princess Theatre to her death? Was she destined for this grisly end from the moment this young man proposed to her? Or did she perhaps see the red flags before he broke it off, and persisted because she was afraid to be alone? I would like to believe that she could have chosen other paths along the way—especially when the moment came where she decided to take her own life. I guess I struggle with that dichotomy of fate and free will. And maybe life ends up being a bit of both.
- *The Garrison Theories* podcast, Episode 6: "The Jilted Bride"

Clayton sat in his frayed lawn chair, munching on a crumbling granola bar as he scanned the forest floor a few metres below. It was a muddle of greens and browns, coming into a clearer picture as the climbing, end-of-autumn sun washed it with grey light through the clouds. His rifle rested across his camouflaged lap, in no position to be used for a shot. But that was OK. He didn't construct this tree stand primarily for hunting; it was his home away from home, a place where he could sit like a king on a raised dais as he overlooked the bounty of his kingdom. Sometimes, especially in recent years, he felt like a sentry protecting the borders.

The snacks and beer helped some, too.

Like it had been doing for weeks, a chill wind cut through the spaces between the trees, shaking the lower branches with a gentle, hissing sound. It was all he could hear, except the grinding of the granola in his skull, or the odd creaking of wood or crack of a branch. Largely, the background noise was a constant, rustling whisper—although it seemed to him that it was, as each day went by, getting stronger, like a storm was brewing ever-so-slowly, almost imperceptibly.

But damn, it's good to be out on my own terms.

It had been about a year since he'd been out for a hunt. Killing wasn't his favourite thing, but it was necessary; there was a balance to all things. Sometimes animal populations got out of hand. Sometimes other things got out of hand. Not everyone had the guts to do what needed to be done.

His bait barrel hung empty; its contents strewn about before his arrival. This time he lugged out the best meat and sugar he could and filled the chained barrel from the top before sealing it shut. Then he climbed into his stand and waited. He ate, drank—but mostly waited. And that was alright with Clayton. Hell, if his quarry didn't show, it still might shape up to be a decent day.

Clayton melted into his chair and stared skyward at the web of green and brown above, probably how Michelangelo looked at the Sistine Chapel once he was done. *What a work of art.* Of course, not everyone saw the forest the same way. Not Sara. Certainly not that poor Shaw girl.

Once they discovered the clothes, the search and rescue operation pressed on for three days—and what a sad three days it was. *Frigid temperatures don't pair well with nakedness.* Each passing hour—each passing second, really—felt to Clayton like another nail in the coffin. The girl was probably long gone before they found those clothes, covered with ice-crusted snow as they were. But they had to do their due diligence. And he put in his time, up until the time came when the search was called off. And he would have bailed sooner, had it not been for that Sara girl. She was pale as a ghost and needed all the support she could get.

They only gave the missing girl five days overall, three of which bore the heavy weight of certain death. It was on everyone's mind, and on most people's faces. But no one had the courage—or perhaps the insensitivity—to call it like it almost certainly was. Not even him.

Clayton chuckled. That was Steve's job, after all. *And call it, he did.* He took another bite of his granola bar, and tucked the wrapper, crinkling, into his pocket.

Somewhere beyond his line of sight, a loud crack reverberated through the trees. Clayton snapped to attention and readied his rifle. He waited some more.

He sucked in a bubbling sniff before exhaling a controlled, shaky breath through his mouth, realising that he held his breath for longer than he intended. Now gusts of his breath clouded in the crisp air and curled in tendrils around his raised rifle. He closed his eyes tight, reflecting on the simple truths that were less simple in practice: he relaxed his white-knuckle grip on his rifle and breathed in slowly through his leaking nose. He pursed his lips, allowing a deep breath to exude from his lungs with a low groan. Again, he cycled through his breathing, and slowly he found his centre.

Broad nostrils flared and tingled as his deep, controlled breaths pulled in an unwelcome reek. He recoiled slightly, losing his focus on his breathing as the stench worked its way through the forest and up and around his perch. He swore under his breath, rubbing his nose through its covering and clenching his eyes. The smell came in waves, like tides of hot garbage and rotten meat. He shook his head. Unfortunately, it wasn't an unfamiliar smell.

Where is that coming from?

He opened his eyes with the sound of another crack, this time closer, followed by the rustling of leaves, although he hardly heard it in the rush that surrounded him as an icy breeze cut between the trees. Footsteps, now, a little off to the right of his perch. He adjusted in his seat, licking his lips. The crunching was slow and soft.

He looked up from his rifle and scanned the forest floor below as it held still behind the boughs that undulated around him. His eyes darted between the gaps among the trees, scouring the browns and greens for movement different from the swaying flora. Another crack pealed into the woods, this time followed by a scrape and another breaking branch. He focused his attention on the sound as a small thicket jostled about thirty metres away. He hunched, throwing his eye behind his scope.

His breath caught in his throat.

A pale figure came out of the brush, absently pushing aside the leaves and scraggly branches as it emerged into the tight clearing wedged amidst the thick trunks of the hemlock and other coniferous trees. It was a girl, emaciated and filthy, walking slowly but purposefully down the gentle incline of the forest floor. She was naked, her bare feet ignorant of the fallen cones and branches; each step crunched down with abandon. Clayton pulled his head back and shivered, blinking towards the sickly girl.

Is that—?

He moved his reticle up and down, scanning the scene before him, mouthing a silent expletive to himself as he sat perched, muscles tensed on his tree stand. Her steps slowed to the point where she became still, her dark, oily hair flicked about by the cold autumnal breeze, although she herself gave no sign of feeling the chill. From above, he kept his one open eye trained on her now stoic pose. The knob on the hunter's scope twisted between his fingers, and the image of the girl in his reticle magnified. Her hands and mouth cracked with dark, dried blood; whose it was he could not tell. Grotesque bruises of violet and yellow marbled her bare skin as if someone had taken a meat tenderizer to her body.

Her eyes were lifeless, like she was following something far beyond what he could see, ignorant of the surrounding environment. Her mouth was moving, bloodless lips like worms who came out in a brief summer rain, only to be caught by the sun shortly thereafter. It was barely perceptible, but she was forming words to herself, or to the forest, or to no one, or possibly to the hunter sitting camouflaged above, unbeknownst to the harried girl. The silent words came quicker, her whispering lips quivered like cold flesh as the forest shifted and rustled around her. He sat, unmoving, as his heart pounded in his chest to the point where he feared she would hear it.

It was obviously Kimberly, in the flesh. But she wasn't there—her aimless, confused gaze, her glazed eyes said it all. She jerked her head back and forth, moving her hands and mumbling quietly to herself. Clayton hoped it was to herself. His finger shuddered over the trigger of his rifle.

But there was a nagging, electric tug at his spine, something like an animal instinct, his lizard brain moving into fight-or-flight mode, that told him to choose a third option: freeze, be invisible. *Give her a second, Clayton. Wait and see.* Deep within his thick boots, his toes curled, and he felt that he desperately needed to pee. *She's lasted this long, hasn't she?*

She moved towards the bait barrel. He raised his rifle again, all the while never taking his eyes off what looked like Kimberly, afraid even to blink; his tongue made a soft, slick popping sound as it peeled off his chapped lips. He could barely hear it himself.

Yet, the girl's uncanny whispering ceased. Her head and eyes shifted immediately to his position, despite his camouflage and the obscuring tree cover. He clamped his jaw tight, but her eyes were already locked square onto his through the branches of the tree. As they stared, her distant expression faded along with the black, leaving her very human eyes in their place.

Clayton gasped. *Never seen that before.*

He felt for the first time since she appeared she was in the present moment—and human. Her reddened eyes, wide as saucers, filled with moisture as she lifted her bloodied hands towards him, palms facing to the canopy. As she did, the absent expression on her face crumpled and twisted, her lower lip quivering against her red-stained teeth.

She began to wail.

"Unbelievable," he said, keeping his eyes on the despairing girl. Hair and expression wild, he threw himself awkwardly down the loose nylon ladder; he thudded down into the brush and took a few steps towards the girl, hands outstretched defensively. "Hey," he began weakly, clearing his throat. He looked away from her at the dense woods, searching warily before bringing his attention back to her. "Where the hell did you come from, girl? Are you OK? We've been looking for you."

She continued towards him, hands outstretched, her fingers clawing at the air. Her steps were quick and small, barely holding up her skeletal frame as deep sobs wracked through her. Her intakes of breath were rasping, heaving like she was surfacing out of a frozen lake, her body in shock and struggling for air. Eyes wider than hers, Clayton spread his arms and prepared a space for her to collapse in. She fell into him hard. Through his camouflage jacket, the bones from her shoulders prodded him as he slowly embraced her. She shook in his arms.

"Shh," he whispered instinctively, slowly patting her protruding vertebrae with his fingerless gloves. "Shh. It's alright, it's alright." His nose prickled at the smell of decay that clung to her, and that he was sure would now cling to him, along with the blood. His eyes darted from her to the space between the trees; the forest seemed to draw closer around them, as if the scene were attracting the attention of the wood itself. "Maybe you'll find your way free of this after all, eh?"

Her weeping ended, and she became still. He stayed there, kneeling in the dirt, the waifish girl curled into his shoulder below his neck, deep in the forest, deep in silence. The only sound that hung about them was the rush of the wind, and the rustling evergreen boughs that bent to its power.

Sara took a deep breath and rang the doorbell. She stood, unmoving except perhaps a subtle shiver that covered her flesh, and waited for entirely too long, resisting all the while the temptation to rush back to her car and leave Coalbrook. It wouldn't be a total waste, either; everything that had happened was chock full of paranormal goodness. She could attach all sorts of theories to it, exploring the wildest possibilities to excite the imaginations of those who tune in. It was everything she needed to spin into the creepiest of yarns. And with Kim almost guaranteed to be deceased, it seemed like it was all wrapping up.

So why was she still here?

The podcast can wait, Sara thought. *I need to know. If I can.* While mysteries kept listeners engaged, she herself was looking for answers. She didn't come here looking for them, at least certainly not for herself. But now? The same desperation that led her here had changed course. Now, she wanted answers for herself, the kind of answers that bring closure. Now every step forward brought her deeper into the story. Every step forward brought her closest to her greatest fear, and her greatest pain.

She went to ring the doorbell again, but before she did, the weather stripping around the door crackled as the door creaked back into the house. A woman answered, her face sunken and grief-stricken. She clutched the door like a drowning woman would clutch the floating remnants of a shipwreck.

Sara cleared her throat. "Are you Sharon Shaw?" she asked.

"What do you want?" she snapped with as much grit as she could likely muster.

"Hi—my name is Sara Garrison. I am a freelance journalist working on the story of this town, especially as it relates to events that have taken place over the past year or so—"

Sharon sniffed and spoke with a thin, acerbic voice. "And you want to talk to me about my dead daughter?"

"Well, I was hoping—"

"Get off my property." She disappeared behind the door, leaving Sara standing on the steps.

Sara knocked again almost immediately. A moment passed, and she knocked again. And again. *Come on, Sara, this isn't like you.* But the stakes have changed. The door flew open, and Sharon stood red-faced, eyebrows angled down harshly.

"Can't you see I'm—"

"When my teenage sister disappeared in 2010," Sara cut in, "we found her clothes, too. I was only twelve."

Sharon stared at her. Her eyes were bloodshot, and she was trembling.

Sara continued. "They were stacked. Neatly folded, piled from outerwear up to her underwear and bra." Looking into the woman's eyes, she could see something fall away. Some piece of defensiveness that was already shaky. Sara's own voice broke, only just. "They never found Andrea. I think about her every day."

The grieving woman's lip quivered. She sniffed again, loudly, quickly bringing a tissue to her nose. With a sigh, she stepped back and opened the door. Respectfully, Sara entered. They didn't get far into the house before Sharon turned, addressing her in the landing of the main entrance.

"OK," whispered Sharon, "but I still want to know what you want."

"Like you, Mrs. Shaw, I would like some answers. But I want you to know that I'm coming to you first as a sister, and second as a journalist. I thought we might be able to help each other."

Sharon dabbed below her eyes with a sodden tissue. "And how would we do that?"

Sara raised an eyebrow, adjusting her glasses. "Well, I certainly don't want to intrude," she started, "but maybe we could start with... a cup of tea?"

The beleaguered woman stared at her, lowering her arms limply to her side. She at first seemed incredulous, like she couldn't believe the gall of this young girl showing up at her door. Then Sharon threw up her hands in defeat and chuckled weakly—but chuckled, nonetheless. She turned and strode into the kitchen and filled a pot to boil. Sharon excused herself to the bathroom, and while she was there, Sara took it upon herself to toss in some tea bags and start the steeping process. It was impossible not to notice the collection of empty wine bottles near the sink.

By the time Sharon came back, the tea was ready to go. *Time to put my interviewing skills to use.*

"Sorry," said Sharon. She took the cup gratefully, like she was a guest in her own home. "Thank you."

"No, thank you—and there's nothing to apologise for." Sara sat down at the kitchen table, and Sharon took a seat across from her. "Can you tell me about Kimberly?"

The middle-aged woman began to cry. "To hell with this," she spat out from clenched teeth. "Every time I get myself together, I fall apart again."

Sara wasn't sure what to say. "When you're ready, Mrs. Shaw," she managed, "I'm not in a rush."

She dabbed at her eyes again with fresh tissue. "Call me Sharon, please. Mrs. Shaw reminds me of my age and my divorce."

"Sorry—Sharon."

She scoffed. "Thanks. Why do you want to know about her, anyways?"

"My sister and Kim both disappeared in a similar fashion. Maybe there's something in common, who knows?"

Sharon raised an eyebrow. "How old are you?"

"Twenty-five."

"Did you say your sister disappeared when you were twelve?"

Sara nodded.

"How could they be connected with so much time between?"

"I don't know," Sara said with a shrug. "But the clothes..."

Sharon leaned back in her chair. "Right," she said through a sigh, "the clothes." They sat together while Sharon sniffed herself back together, nodding as she took a deep, quivering breath.

"Kimberly," Sharon continued, her face twisting in all sorts of ways, "was a pain in the ass. But she was my pain in the ass, you know? We fought all the time, especially once her dad left when she was—" she paused to count on her fingers "—eleven. So, a bit more than a few years ago. But oh my god did we fight."

"What kinds of things did you fight about?" *Open ended question. Nice.*

Sharon barked a laugh, bordering on a cackle. "Oh, god—what didn't we fight about?" She splayed her fingers and started working through a list. "Boys, school, chores, booze, what she wore, her language around the house, her attitude... oh, Lord, her attitude was awful."

"The standard fare," Sara joked, if somewhat cautiously.

"That's right, that's right. That's what teenagers and parents do, right? That's what teenagers are supposed to do, they're supposed to push back. But Kimmy, oh my sweet, sweet Kimmy—that's all she knew how to do. She never gave an inch, oh god she was stubborn. And so I would lay into her—" she cut herself off with a wave of sobs that slowly faded. "And for what? It never made a difference except to push her away."

"Yeah," Sara contributed somewhat dumbly, "we tend to push each other's buttons, don't we?" *Empathy. Could have been executed better.* Sharon nodded as Sara scrambled to remember her journalistic skills. "What kinds of things did Kim like to do?"

Sharon thought for a while as she lazily sipped her tea, up until the point where the length of time seemed to dawn on her, bringing with it a new wave of realisation and grief. Then like a lightbulb, it came. "Her drawings. It was one thing I saw as a positive. On my good days, that is. Sometimes I said it was a waste of time, and other times I would ask for one to put on my wall at work, so..."

"I bet that was meaningful for her," said Sara. *Build rapport. Interviewing 101.*

Sharon only shrugged.

"Can I see some of them?"

"I guess," said Sharon. She rose, and Sara followed her down a hall devoid of natural light. "You might need to give me a minute, but you go ahead."

Sara stood just outside the threshold. The atmosphere of Kimberley's room brought Sara to a familiar place and time, almost like she was stepping into her own bedroom. It was familiar because it was all too recent, a stage that she had perhaps only just left. Perhaps one she overstayed her welcome in.

Sharon was quiet now, hovering near the door and looking like she was clutching invisible pearls. Sara excused herself as she sidled past. The bed was the first feature she noticed, and it was a catastrophe. The complex potential of the linen and pillow arrangement was apparent, despite being piled on the floor in a mountain of lace and pastels. Whether it was unmade from Kimberly's last time in it, or from Sharon's own process of grief, she couldn't say. Heaps of young adult fiction books, Funko Pops, and other contemporary paraphernalia punctuated the cavernous shelves that flanked the bed. Most striking of all were the myriad paintings and drawings that dotted the topography of the room like a world traveller might put pins on a map of the globe. Even in her absence, Kimberly was filling the space like the sunlight cutting through the blinds, bouncing off the coral walls and painting the room with a rosy glow.

"She do all these?" inquired Sara as she pointed at a collection of portraits tacked on the cork board.

Sharon nodded. "She did," her restrained voice came. "Every one of them is hers. Hardly a day went by where she didn't draw or paint something." Her eyes were glossy, looking at the pictures but not seeing them. "She does faces the best."

Sara circled the room, which she now realised was actually the master bedroom due to its size and ensuite. At last, she stood before the largest conglomeration of artistry, a smattering of mostly smiling heads in portraiture. The cork wall above her desk looked almost like a detective's investigation board, or the life's work of a cellar-dwelling conspiracy theorist. She gave a vague gesture towards the art. "You know them?"

"They're her friends from school, and some acquaintances maybe. She would often convince them to let her do their portraits, most of them in this room."

"Ah, yes," Sara exclaimed. "There's Christian Johnstone, I think." She gave Sharon an encouraging smile. "She's really good," she declared before she stepped back and took it all in. "She must have been super popular."

Sharon sighed. "She certainly was. And that popularity had no small part in derailing her from school, especially with a certain group. They're probably in that mess somewhere," she concluded as she nodded towards the art wall.

"What group? Was it—?"

149

"Cara, David, Tanner. Her closest friends," she squeaked. Her face tightened as she held back whatever was fighting to come out, but after a moment she sighed again, finally having the courage to step into the room. She pointed to their likenesses, one after another. "That's them. Among others."

Sara continued around the room, taking in the countless knick-knacks one after another like she was browsing at a gift shop, sucking her teeth as she circled the bed. The mother remained aloof just in the threshold of the room, watching Sara as she scrutinised her daughter's most private spaces. Sara ran her fingers across the bed and came to her nightstand, her fingers hovering over it. This girl must have some connection with Andrea. No matter how small, there must be a connection. The disappearance, the piled clothing... it was just too similar.

Teenage girls. Artsy, likely fairly emotional and reflective. Both fought with parent. Or parents. Struggled in school, struggled with substances...

"Did Kim keep a journal?" Sara ventured.

Sharon tightened. "I bought her one a while back. Her request."

Emboldened, Sara changed hats from counsellor to journalist. She yanked open the nightstand drawer, producing a leather-bound book with thin metal bindings.

"That's it," snipped the mother. "Please don't read that."

Sara gave her a sympathetic look. She lifted the journal and spoke with a raised eyebrow. "I take it you've read it already?"

"I made her a promise not to. If you aren't going to put it down, I'm going to have to ask you to leave."

"Given the circumstances," suggested Sara, "I don't think we can afford not to look, with all due respect."

"We? We can't afford to not do anything, thank you very much."

"Don't you want to understand what happened to her?"

Sharon spoke through gritted teeth and glared through wet eyes. "In my own damn time, young lady. Now, if you're done prying into my misery, I think it's time to go."

Sara tightened her shoulders. "I'm really sorry, it's just that there are so many questions left—"

A chime came from the kitchen. Likely Sharon's cell phone.

"Don't touch anything else," she said as she pointed accusatively at Sara before she turned and strode down the hall. "I'll be right back," she called from the kitchen.

Sara moved quickly. She flicked open the journal and began poring over the most recent entries. They were rather venomous, the ire directed towards the mother relating to issues of control. Standard fare. Which household that housed a teenager didn't have conflict? It wasn't too long ago when Sara was arguing with her parents. *Only a handful of days, in fact. Maybe I should start keeping a journal.* A quick glance reassured her that Sharon wasn't on her way back. She cut her eyes left—the portraits stared back, behaving like a jury in silent deliberation. Shaking, she continued to flip back, finding other entries related to... nightmares, of all things. Nightmares detailing a black shape, the forest, staring wildlife, running and going nowhere—and the countless faces of boys and girls, men, and women she didn't recognize, just as lost in the trees as she was.

A blood-curdling wail came rushing down the hall. Sara dropped the journal and burst out of the room, moving towards the kitchen.

She found Sharon collapsed on the floor, shivering and bawling. "Sharon!" shouted Sara as she fell to her side. "What? What is it?"

Deep sobs wracked the woman's frail body. Sara held her for what seemed like entire minutes of silence until Sharon finally croaked out the word *alive.*

14

Visiting Hours

IF YOU'VE BEEN AROUND the paranormal community for a while, you've maybe heard of the concept of "open doors" or "doorways". These are basically invitations for entities to engage with you in some pretty intimate ways. I usually read or hear about this idea when people warn each other about the dangers of Ouija boards—but I think it's broader than that. I think it starts in the heart with what you personally are open to. That, I believe, is where the permission lies. It's like turning the switch that makes the neon sign of your soul say "vacancy".

- *The Garrison Theories* podcast, Episode 10: "A Knock at the Door"

It was all too familiar. The halls of Coalbrook Medical Centre filled with the droning that one would expect from such an environment: muted announcements over crackling speakers, the buzzing and beeping of medical technology, and the trundling of gurneys spoken over with the sardonic remarks of overworked nursing staff.

The receptionist lifted her head as the officers approached.

"Hello officers," she began politely. "How may I help you?"

Steve was too busy glancing around to make eye contact. "Looking for a young girl just brought in by the name of Kimberly Shaw."

"Right," replied the young woman, turning to her computer. Her painted nails fluttered noisily over the black keys, followed by a few clicks of the mouse. "Room 112." She pointed down the hall. "Just follow the green line."

Been doing that a lot lately. Lauren followed him down the narrow hall, seeing the colour moving along the wall like a serpent. They passed several inpatient rooms, many of them with doors ajar, patients sat and laying patiently on their beds, on their phones or watching TV from behind their thin, fabric cubicles. Some were asleep, lulled into unconsciousness by the soft intonations of the medical machines. Another fuzzy announcement came over the intercom: a code blue and an invitation for a particular doctor to make his way to surgery theatre two. Room 112 popped up as they rounded a corner.

How did she survive out there? Steve thought to himself, like he might picture something not quite human on the other side of the slightly ajar door. Naked... for days at a time in sub-zero temperatures. No shelter. No food. He glanced at Lauren, whose expression suggested that she had similar questions. Steve held his breath, not at all sure what to expect. Common sense told him that he was about to see a frozen corpse. But there was nothing sensible about any of this.

Inside, Kimberly lay silently on her reclined bed, head half-cocked on her pillow, intravenous fluids flowing into her arm and oxygen flowing into her nostrils. Her skin was yellowed and sickly, but she was a far cry from a corpse. Her eyes were half-open, but not registering anything. She stared blankly past them all, across the room to the tangle of rollable machines and their sprawl of cords.

Her mother, Sharon sat on one side, her face aglow with the blue light from her phone, which flashed constantly, indicating an impatient swiping of the thumb interminably upwards.

And, of course, on the other side was Sara Garrison. *And why wouldn't she be here?* He thought bitterly. Damn, he was tired of seeing her. But somehow he was becoming accustomed to her presence—and in the grand scheme of everything that was going on, she was no longer his biggest priority. Their eyes met, only briefly before he addressed Kimberly's mom.

"Sharon."

The woman looked up from her device. Her phone dimmed, and she stood, speaking weakly. "Hi, Steve."

And over by the window, staring out into the daylight was Clayton Johnstone, still as a tree like he was standing guard. He gave Steve a brief glance and the requisite nod hello, but nothing more before he turned his attention back to the world beyond the glass.

Finally—and reluctantly—Steve turned his attention to the last person in the room. "Sara," he said with a much lower register. The would-be-journalist gave him the smallest of head tips to acknowledge his words. She looked sheepish. "Why am I seeing you everywhere I go?" he asked.

Sara shrugged as she widened her eyes behind her large, circular glasses. "Fate?" she guessed, although he couldn't tell if she was joking or raising a serious possibility.

"How are you...?" he started, his question trailing off as he swung a pointed finger back and forth between Sara and Sharon. "What's the connection here?"

Sara looked even more uncomfortable and looked to Sharon for support.

"She was with me when the hospital called," explained Sharon.

Steve tightened his eyelids. "Another interview, I presume?"

"None of your business," said Sharon briskly.

Sara uncrossed her legs and smoothed her thighs. "It wasn't quite like that, Officer Boyko. It was more personal—"

Lauren shot her hand forward like she was desperate to change the subject. "I'm Sergeant Parenteau, Mrs. Shaw—we haven't met. Feel free to call me Lauren."

Sharon took it. "Hi, Lauren," she responded, gazing up through dark sockets before cutting a glare to Steve. "I'll bet you're both relieved you won't have to give me another death notice."

Steve nodded, keeping his eyes on Kimberly. Her monitor beeped rhythmically. "A sentiment we all share. How is she?"

Sharon leaned back into her seat with an exasperated sigh. "She was critical, but now she's stable, or so they say." She looked at her daughter and put her hand on hers. "Doesn't exactly look like it, but I'll have to take their word that she'll recover physically."

"Just physically?" inquired Steve.

"Well," continued Sharon, "she's had a few... episodes."

"Do tell." Steve queried, hands on his hips as he looked at the sleeping girl's skeletal face.

Sharon's jaw worked under her skin. She was reluctant to talk, but she kept going. "Been talking in her sleep. And even while she's awake, or maybe she's still asleep—it's hard to tell, but it's like she's hallucinating. I heard the shrink use the word psychosis." Sharon looked at her daughter with watery eyes. She let out a long sigh. "I guess that would explain why she was out there."

Lauren stared at Kimberly's ghostly face. "Or maybe it results from being out there." She rubbed the back of her neck, speaking slowly. "Does she have a history of these things?"

Sharon shook her head.

"Any history of substance use?" asked Steve. He already knew the answer.

Sharon gave him an incredulous stare. "She's a teenager, and we live in the asshole of BC. Take a guess."

He stepped closer to Kimberly, scanning her face. Dark sockets hid her eyes, which seemed to be more sunken than normal—although he had never paid too much attention to the specifics of her face before. She was just another troublesome teenager that made herself a bother along with her friends.

"I'm just glad she's back," said Sharon, her voice cracking as she rubbed her daughter's arm. "Things will be different between us from now on."

"Good," said Steve as he patted the bar across the foot of the bed. "It's good to have good news like this. Glad she's safe." With a nod—and a quick, challenging glare at Sara—he strode over to Clayton, who was still staring out the window. Even as Steve came alongside, he didn't stir. He focused, staring out over the town like he might catch something important.

"Thanks for all you did, Clayton."

He still didn't look at Steve. "Don't mention it."

"So," Steve began, his voice softer as he drew close, "care to give me an idea of what went on out there?"

Clayton cleared his throat and brought Steve up to speed. It was another crisp morning when he went to check on his bait barrel and to hang around long enough get another attempt—possibly a final one—on a bear before the season wrapped. He was up in his tree stand when he heard a rustling and saw a bit of movement from a short way off.

"Only it wasn't a bear," Clayton continued. His eyes never met Steve's; he held them fast on the window, and whatever lay beyond. It made Steve nervous. "It was that poor girl, sick and thin as a rail. Soon as she saw me, she collapsed. I wasn't expectin' it, but she was all there mentally, for a bit—it was a teenage girl, all right. Not the monster I was hopin' to see come up on my bait." He wrapped up the story with an explanation of having to leave his equipment and lug her back to his truck. It was then that she passed out.

"Did she say anything to you?" asked Steve. "Anything about what happened? What she saw, or what went on at the resort with her friends?"

Clayton shook his head. "She just kept mumblin' about the trees. And that she was hungry as all get out, but couldn't find anything to eat."

"Fair enough."

"And when she first came through the bush, she was looking over her shoulder and whispering like someone was following her."

Steve turned and glanced at Kimberly. She was still asleep, or maybe unconscious. Sharon was back on her phone. Sara was watching him of all people. "Guess those are the hallucination they were talking about."

Clayton scoffed. "Guess so."

"Does she know what happened to her friends?"

"Hm," Clayton said before he took a deep breath through his nose. His ample stomach lifted and almost seemed to deflate like a balloon when he exhaled. He glanced at Steve. "I couldn't say. She was distressed, though."

"I'd be pretty distressed if I came out of the woods after a few days naked in the dark."

Clayton nodded and turned his attention back to the window.

"Clayton," Steve began again, "how would a girl like that survive out in sub-zero temperatures without supplies—or clothes, for that matter."

"I suppose," he started slowly, "that someone could find or put together shelter and build a fire and maybe make it work. But that's like winning the lottery."

"Did she stumble across a cabin, maybe?"

Clayton shrugged. "Maybe. But I know those woods," he said as he pointed out the window. Steve wasn't sure if it was even the right direction. "And I don't remember there being any cabins in the general area."

"So..."

"So," Clayton continued, burying his hands in his puffer vest, "she was either saved by God himself..."

Steve leaned his head in. "Or...?"

Clayton looked at him, his face drooping with concern. "Or she had help."

A frown covered Steve's face, telegraphing his comfort level with such a theory. It made sense, of course. In some ways it was the only rational explanation, other than the absolute shot-in-the-dark idea that she somehow managed to scrape together enough resources and shelter to survive in the frigid night air and snow. There's just no way, he thought to himself. Yet he desperately wanted it to be so simple.

"Help, eh?" Steve mumbled.

"Mm-hm."

Steve patted him on the back a single time. "OK. Thanks, Clayton. For helping with the search and rescue, and for the actual rescue."

"You got it," he said, turning back to the window. He leaned in, propped his forearm against the window ledge. And he searched.

"One more thing, if I may?" Clayton didn't respond. Steve wasn't sure if it was permission or rejection. He continued anyway. "You seem pretty glum for a hero. You should be out celebrating—so what's up?"

Clayton licked his lips and glared sidelong back at him. "Just a bit of doubt, is all."

"Doubt about what?"

His lips moved like he was going to talk but froze when he hesitated and seemed to change course. "I suppose I'm just wondering if maybe I should have done more."

Steve scoffed. "More than save her life?"

The large man shifted, turning to stare at the silent Kimberly curled up on the bed. "Sometimes it isn't that simple."

Steve followed his gaze. "I get it. Sure." He gave Clayton a pat on the back.

Back at the bed, Steve planted himself next to Sharon. "Are you OK to keep us informed of what develops?" he inquired. There were some moments where it was difficult to wear the garb of a peace officer—this was one of them. It was a balancing act: human warmth and the cold steel of duty were often antithetical to each other. "I'd like to ask her some questions when she's recovered."

"When she's strong enough," echoed Sharon for emphasis. "Yes, that's fine, of course." She looked up from her phone, her eyes red around the edges of her eyelids. "We all have questions, Stephen."

Before he turned—and after fixing Sara with a warning stare—he gave Kimberly a long, inspecting look. What memories buried themselves in that mind? There was a story there, and in good time he would hear it.

Only now he wasn't sure he wanted to.

Her website lay gutted before her like a cadaver on a mortician's table, its cause of death like a code hidden behind a user-friendly drag-and-drop interface. She fussed over it almost daily, even since her arrival in the unexpectedly not-so-sleepy town of Coalbrook. Even during disappearance and death. But it had been a slog, filled with obstacles both within and without. Coalbrook had sucked the life out of her ever since she sped past the Welcome to Coalbrook sign on the highway, moments before she wrecked her car avoiding what was supposed to be an elk.

But Kim was alive, and the details before her discovery took the work on a personal turn, invigorating her with both good chills and bad. The story of Coalbrook wasn't any longer just the key to her future—it was the key to her past.

Sara tabbed back and forth between the pages of her site. It had her own heavily embellished bio with a photo of her taken from such a perfect angle that someone might not recognize her if they saw her in person. It had numerous links to various podcasts and streaming platforms. It had her crowdfunding patron link. There was some serialised fiction that she had toyed with, but ultimately abandoned. And, of course, the embedded links and archives of all the episodes so far—and the massive gap of time that had developed since the last one.

"OK, Sara. What's it going to be? It's do or die, here." Her mind swam with all the possibilities of constructing her script as she flipped from page to page. This was how it always played out: when faced with a wall that was damming her creative juices, she busied herself about what she called "adjacencies"—mailing list, website, chopping up audio recordings, considering a new portrait, income, website hits and other statistics. It was all important, to be sure, but not what she truly needed right now. She needed to break through that wall.

Only this time the wall was different. At first, the barrier was one of lack, the same lack of content that drove her here. Now she had too much and didn't know how to synthesise it all. What was the theme? What in the name of all that is good and holy was this whole adventure about? And that was the trick: she couldn't put a name to it, because ultimately, she didn't know yet other than the basic details. Whatever was behind these disappearances would give her the answer she needed. It was then, and only then, that she would be able to put this all together.

Well, Sara—looks like you're going to have to see this through.

A light snow was falling outside, the powdery kind that you couldn't make a snowman with. The clock in the corner of her screen told her it was almost three in the morning. Wracked with the jitters that come from exhaustion and excitement, Sara rose from the desk and began pacing her motel room. The window groaned under a breeze; Sara resisted the temptation to look outside to the green expanse beyond that should have swallowed Kim in its frigid labyrinth.

She made her way back across the cheap carpet to the only source of light: the blue glow of her laptop monitor. Sara was about to sit and get back to it when someone pounded on her door, shocking her right out of her skin. The thumping shook the room, sending loud wooden creaks across her wall as the stodgy motel made protestations of its own. The light from the balcony walkway that connected the second-floor suites bled under the door and through the curtains. She sucked in a sharp breath—the light was shadowed in two parts, right where a pair of feet would be. *Maybe it's the overnight receptionist?* Lunging for the lamp, she flicked it on.

The pounding came again, once again in threes. Each hit sent a twitch of fear through her. When the sound stopped, her hackles rose in anticipation of the next triplet, which was almost preferable to the unbearable silence that followed.

"Hello?" she called to her door, mainly to do something, anything to ease the sharply rising tension. Three more strikes railed against the door to her suite. She didn't jump, but instead crept closer. A sense of impatience rose and swirled with her terror. "It's three in the morning, what's wrong with you?" she growled. On tiptoes, she pressed her eye against the peephole. Nothing.

She rested back on her heels and stared bemused at the door. The shadowed feet remained, but only for a moment more—they vanished. There was no scuffing of a rotating shoe, or steps; whoever was out there was gone. After a snap forward to peer out the peephole once more—to find nothing, of course—Sara flung the door open.

Nobody, and nothing. She leaned out, turning her head left and right as she stared down the green-painted walkway, expecting to see other confused and tired faces peering out. All that was there were the time-warped boards and bannisters that were barely lit by the weak bulbs that hung outside the doors. That and the snow, and the occasional hush of a car braving the highway in the small hours of the night. No one else seemed to be bothered by the disturbance. She closed the door and strode across the carpet, then froze as her spine turned to ice.

"Oh, Sara," she mumbled into her palms as she buried her face in her hands. "You stupid, stupid girl." She scrambled to turn on every source of light she could. *How could you forget? You did a whole damn episode on this phenomenon.* Somehow, she had forgotten the number one rule of invisible knocks at the door. "Looks like you've drawn a bit of attention to yourself, Sara." She spoke aloud, hoping that the sound of a voice—even if it was only her own—would somehow be protective. It did make her feel a little better while somehow making her feel weak, like a child would resort to lying to itself to make it feel better while separated from its parents. When the lights in the bathroom flickered, she froze—again; whatever was outside, she had invited it in.

She spent the rest of the night sleeping in her car, head mostly buried under the fleece dragged from her room, having decided to concede the room. Every now and again, as sleep took its sweet time in taking her for the night, she would look out across the highway at the edge of the forest. The first line of trees moved gently in the streetlight, but the rest were lost to darkness.

15

Still Life

WHEREVER YOU THINK Granger may be, this tale speaks to the dangers of isolation. The overwhelming majority of the stories I share with you—especially ones marked by tragedy—happen when the person was cut off from their community in some way. When we are lonely, empty and unsupported, we wither from deceptions both without and within. It's why people struggling with addiction, or some other undesirable behaviour find success in the presence of others. People can bring motivation and accountability, where the problem is dragged kicking and screaming into the light where we can look upon it and see it for what it truly is. But people can bring a lot of pain to our lives, too; trauma usually happens in the context of relationships—but so too does healing.

- *The Garrison Theories* podcast, Episode 11: "The Vanishing of Granger Taylor"

D espite the few splashes of colour staggered around his office, Dr. Senger somehow managed to make the space even more sterile than her corner of the ward. Dull gray dominated, broken here and there by the green of tiny fake plants. One succulent hunched directly in front of her, central on the side table. The adjacent chairs were adjusted to face each other just so, and the little box of tissues was placed suggestively on the coffee table in front of where the client would be sitting. This morning, that client was her.

And what a client she must have been.

Dr. Senger ran a hand down the track of his male-pattern baldness. He had come around from his desk to minimize the space between them. She sat on the other end of the compact space, feeling like a shell of her former self—something she needed reminding of rather than remembering it herself. So much of what came before... vanished. So much of her past was vacant, displaced by a deeper emptiness.

But the man across from her wouldn't have needed access to old pictures of her from before to see how much of a husk she had become; her eyes were sunken, her skin sallow, her arms bony. Dr. Senger had never seen her before, and perhaps even without knowing the backstory he would have guessed that she had sojourned in the wilderness, or perhaps starved in a basement somewhere for a great deal of time.

Her eyes fell to her lap. Skeletal fingers curled and stretched on her spindly thighs, knotted joints poked through a veneer of blue-veined skin that peeked out from beneath the hospital gown that bunched up on her frame like too-big curtains. Her nails were ragged, her knuckles scraped. How it happened, no one was sure. But somewhere deep within her was the answer.

Whatever was lurking inside, she wanted to keep it buried. She wanted to lock it away, wanted to leave this mess behind her and get back to normal. *How could I ever be normal again? All of my friends are dead.* Regardless she had the feeling that Dr. Senger wasn't going to let her find normalcy—at least, not yet. If he was anything like her school counsellor, he was going to bombard her with the kinds of questions that would help her make sense of what she experienced. To process.

Dr. Senger cleared his throat and startled her. Myriad thoughts raced through her mind, barely cutting through the brain fog, leaving her distracted and vague.

"How are you feeling, Kimberly?" he began.

"I'm OK," she stated, slow and dull, blinking way too much. "I'm really tired."

"Yes, you've been through quite a lot. It's remarkable that we're even able to do this." He cocked his head, preparing another question. "Do you remember me?" he asked.

Kim thought for a moment, her eyes looking at him and then through him, like he was a stereogram dipping in and out of focus. Eventually, she shook her head.

"OK," said Dr. Senger. "That's alright. Memory loss can be fairly normal following a traumatic experience. If I may help jog it a little bit—I am Dr. Senger, or Louis if you prefer. I did come see you before for a brief assessment while you were on the mend." Dr. Senger gave her a clinical smile. "And now since you're well on your way, I thought we could have a bit of a longer session."

A tight laugh gusted through her tighter lips. She lifted her hands, allowing the cavernous sleeves of her gown to slink down the pale poles that were her arms. "Well on my way, eh?"

His eyes narrowed slightly. "Of course, these kinds of things take time."

"I thought you might say that," said Kim. The words came out thoughtlessly, like they were just another breath.

"Fair enough," he said as he uncrossed his legs, leaning forward with his notepad. The clipboard was stacked with documentation high enough to make the corners of the paper bulge around the metal clip. He placed a hand over one corner to obscure the sheer volume of notes. "Do you know why you are here, Kim?"

Kim snapped awake, though her eyes were already open. "I guess I must be sick," she said, shaking her arm and the tube trailing from it.

"Well," began the doctor, "maybe that's true. Other than the IV, what else tells you that you might be sick in some way?"

Kim's bony shoulders shifted beneath her hospital gown. "Being in the hospital, I guess." Head low, she ran her fingers over the taped needle in the back of her hand.

"Right. Hospitals tend to be for the sick. Do you know what part of the hospital you are in?"

Kim lifted her head and stared at Dr. Senger. "The psych ward."

"The psychiatric observation unit, that's right."

"Am I insane?"

"I wouldn't put it quite like that," he said. "Kimberly, you've just come through a very traumatic and difficult experience, and other than a few obvious details, nobody can quite grasp the significance of it. Not yet, at least."

Kimberly shook with a violent shiver. A barrage of rapid-fire blinks took over her expression for a moment until she shook her head to free herself from it.

"Of course, the one person who needs to grasp that significance more than anyone else... is you." Louis licked his lips, then continued. "Often when these sorts of adverse events happen in our lives, we find ourselves struggling to grasp the scope of their power to shape how we behave. For example, many people experience flashbacks—it's like their brains, their bodies are still stuck in that time, in that event." Dr. Senger's hands were up by his head, gesturing like he was going to lift his brain out of his skull. He brought them back down, motioning gently towards Kimberly. "This might be an element of what you are experiencing. Does that sound right to you?"

Kimberly gave an unsure nod.

"OK," said Louis. "Kim, how did you come to be in this place?"

"Coalbrook?"

Dr. Senger smiled. "I'm sure that's an interesting story, too—but right now I'm interested in how you came here," he said as he lifted his hands to the walls and ceiling, "to Coalbrook Medical Centre."

"I..."

Dr. Senger leaned in, pen at the ready. Kimberly strained, scrunching her face as she plumbed the depths of her mind. There was nothing there—at least nothing that wasn't obscured by the thick, black clouds of trauma. And it occurred to her that it might have been for the best.

"I'm sorry." She drew in on herself like a guilty child. Louis shifted in his own chair and propped his elbow on its arm.

"Please, Kimberly—no apologies are necessary. I know this can be hard." He pressed on the clip and slid a few sheets out. "Perhaps I'm moving us along too quickly. Let's switch gears for a moment—can I get you a glass of water?"

She shook her head.

"OK. Well, as I understand, you're quite the artist."

Her eyes fluttered, her ears perking up at the mention of her talent. "Who told you I draw?"

"Nobody needed to. Apparently, you've been leaving these—" he held up one of the sheets to her, "—all over the ward. You didn't sign them, of course... but I've been told they belong to you. Is that right?" he asked.

"Yes. I did draw that one. At least... actually, I'm not sure if I did. But it does look like my drawing," she claimed as she pointed weakly to the sketch.

"It's quite the piece," he said, twisting the art towards him so he could get a better look. It was a portrait of a girl, maybe about her age. He didn't recognise her. "Who is this?"

"I don't know," said Kim.

"A friend from school? Or an acquaintance, maybe?"

Kim rattled her head from side to side. "No."

"OK," said Dr. Senger as he placed the picture on the side table. "What about this one?"

"Mm," mumbled Kim. "Don't know."

"Friend?"

Kim shrugged. "Just looks like another face to me."

Dr. Senger smiled. "You're an excellent artist."

Kim smiled too, only more uncomfortably.

"There are a lot of portraits here. Maybe you don't know who they are. Of course, they are drawings... maybe they are fiction?"

"Maybe."

"Which I would find to be a bit striking, because your mom suggested that you almost exclusively draw pictures of people you know."

Kim grunted under her breath. "I guess I never thought of it like that—but yes, I guess you're right."

Louis tucked the images back under the clip. "So, why draw? What does it do for you?"

Kim rubbed her arm. "Feels good, I guess."

"OK. So, it gives you pleasure. What else?"

Kim knit her brow and stared at Dr. Senger for a stretch. "I guess I'm good at it, so it makes me feel... I don't know, important? Maybe? Or capable?"

"Right," he said, engaging his clinical nod of affirmation. "So, using your talent gives you a sense of meaning. And agency, too—it's something in your control."

"I guess."

"I wonder if it helps you make sense of things."

Finally, her eyebrows raised in a way that demonstrated connection. For the first time, Kim gave an earnest and honest nod. "It does, actually. When I draw my friends, I feel like I really get to know them. Look into their eyes and stuff. And we sit for a while, chatting while I work."

"Do you have lots of drawings at home?"

"Hundreds."

"That's a lot of friends."

Kim chuckled. "Lots of duplicates and triplicates."

"Ah," replied Dr. Senger, sharing in her laughter. "OK, good. But these faces," he continued, "the ones you don't know. What do you think you are making sense of by drawing these?"

"I'm sorry, Dr. Senger. I don't know. In fact, I don't remember doing some of those."

"They are very distinct. Some of them you've even done twice, even three times." He tucked his chin into his neck as he stared down at an image on his clipboard, one she couldn't see. "It's like you've met some of these people on separate occasions and have drawn them each time."

Kimberly shrugged. Every word seemed to push her deeper into a hole, scattering her thoughts into a cloud of confusion.

"And these?" He produced some pencilled landscapes, all of them desolate, lined by skeletal trees. "What do these represent?"

She froze. Her eyes locked on the drawing, presumably her own, and cut away—and then back again. The image meant something, that was certain. And whatever it meant, it felt like a threat. His eyes bored into hers for a moment, and almost as in response to something he saw, he lowered the bleak sketch. He raised his eyebrows, his way of inviting a response.

"Kimberly?"

"Yes?"

"Are these images of places you've been?"

Wide-eyed, she shook her head.

"Really? You did spend a great deal of time alone in the forest."

Another shiver wracked her. "No, I didn't," she rebutted.

"Wasn't that where they found you? Out in the woods, a few kilometres from the highway?

"I think so," she said. "And I mean no, as in no, I don't think I was alone."

169

It was his turn to shiver, but only slightly. "When the gentleman found you, you mean?"

Her head shook in a tight back-and-forth, more like a vibration.

"So... who was with you out there?"

She shrugged, then drew herself closer together. "Are we done?" she asked. She stared at the miniature plant on the squat table an arm's length away.

He hesitated and then looked at the clock above her head. He gave her an acquiescent nod, and she rose. As she left in a hurry, she couldn't help but see herself as prey fleeing from danger.

So, what did that make Dr. Senger?

Sara busied herself to the best of her ability, hoping to forget about the previous night's encounter. Her body didn't let her forget it, though—the aches of sleeping in her car continued to remind her of her desperation. But as she ran her errands, she hoped that it would all blow over. The errands included a run to the grocery store, a brief stop at the same coffee shop downtown where she chatted with her mom on the phone briefly, and then a check-in on her car at the auto body shop. It was almost there. The timing couldn't be more perfect. All she had was a few more questions for Kimberly, and then she could finally wrap things up.

And mom said it was all a waste of time.

All positivity drained out of her when she got back to her motel room to make dinner in the tiny kitchenette. The one space that was hers, however temporarily, in this unfamiliar town had been violated. The bed was stripped and piled all over. Her laptop was open—not how she left it. Her toiletries were scattered across the bathroom floor. The closet door was open, too, with the hanging ironing board flung out like a crossing gate next to a train track. Immediately she backed out of the room and closed the door.

Reception confirmed they cleaned her room to the normal standards. The concierge at the front desk took some convincing, and begrudgingly went with her up to her room; when he saw it, his tune changed, telling her he would make sure housekeeping heard her complaint. Sara responded by asking to be checked out, and she quickly packed on the request that he stay with her in the room as she did so. She's researched enough of the paranormal to know that she had invited whatever it was that harassed her the night before into her room without thinking. *Never open the door to a disembodied knock, Sara. That's basic—how could you forget?*

It was time for a new motel. There were options, but it was getting late, and she was burned out and needing something. Her stomach gave her a hint.

Coalbrook had its fair share of standard dining fare, but one doesn't drive this far to eat the same food as back home—not that she would have exposed herself to that slop, anyway. Her phone told her that *The Station* was the place to go in town, a bar and grill that captured the unique "flavours" of Coalbrook. The thought of what flavours they might conjure up in this town made her wrinkle her nose, but her options were scant this far north. Beggars can't be choosers. Only she hoped they might have some vegetarian options.

She was in the rental car and snaking out onto the highway within moments. The drive took her into the heart of Coalbrook, past the medical centre that hunched dimly in the centre of a too-small parking lot. A large red cross crested the old building, letting all who pass know where they should come if the need should arise.

Is that...?

She swung her car by the main lot adjacent to Todd Road on her way through town. *Yep, it is.* It was unmistakable. The old Ford

Ranger, rust red with a white canopy–Clayton's truck. It was still parked at the edge of the medical centre parking lot.

What is he waiting for?

For all his talk of not being afraid, much of his behaviour since Kimberly arrived back in town had been borderline paranoid—not something she expected of him. It was like he was protecting Kim from an unwanted visitor.

But weren't visiting hours over?

She followed the curve that straddled the sidewalk that edged the hospital grounds, the lights hanging over the lot lit the cab from behind. Clayton was there, face illuminated slightly by something–presumably his phone.

It's like he's keeping a vigil.

The street curved away. Sara sighed, struck suddenly by a sense of guilt. She was so quick to make a creep out of him that she forgot his place in the whole ordeal. *Christian. Of course.* Clayton couldn't protect him, so he was doing for Kimberly what he didn't do then. *And I can relate.* She sighed again, deeper, and wished him well as she pulled through the next intersection.

When she saw the restaurant, it dashed her hopes. It was the cattle skull over the entrance and the saloon doors separating the lobby from the restaurant floor that killed and buried them.

The Station was along the edge of Coal Brook Drive, an awkward arm branching off the main core but close enough to draw in weary travellers heading north towards the territories.

Her boots crunched into the ploughed piles of snow that glimmered pink beneath the electric buzz of the neon signage. A handful of cars parked nearby, some of which had their tracks filled in by snowfall, suggesting that some patrons inside might have had a few too many.

Inside, the sound of pool balls clacked over the low drone of country music that came from the speakers in the upper corners of the main bar. Lauren could smell the sourness of beer in the air, along with the faint hint of second-hand smoke that had wafted in from outside. Sara hovered awkwardly in front of the hostess.

"Waiting on someone?" asked a girl much younger, sleeved in a black cocktail dress.

Sara shook her head. "Nope—just me."

"Would you like a table, or were you thinking you'd eat at the bar?"

She thought for a moment, making a show of a thinking expression. "Bar, I think."

The girl stepped to the side and motioned her through the saloon doors. "You can head right over, and I'll send someone to take your order, OK?"

Sara nodded, glancing at the doors. They almost necessitated one make a splashy entrance, and she had to do it alone. Her overcoat didn't help things, either. She wondered if maybe she should have brought a revolver and a bandolier to complete the image.

She bit her lip and bit the bullet; hands in pockets, she shouldered her way in.

For a town this small, the place amazed her with its level of activity. And for a town this small, it shouldn't have surprised her that ahead, sitting together at the bar, were officers Reid and Parenteau—off duty, of course. Their backs were to her as they sat together on wooden stools, giving each other full attention. Their body language screamed friendship, although Sara knew enough guys to know that he would have jumped at the opportunity to make it more.

But the nature of their connection was the least of her concern. Sara was a drowning woman in the middle of a great, dark sea, and these two represented a life raft. She strode over to them, casting the illusion that she had planned it all along. But she didn't care—she was desperate and feeling very vulnerable. Especially with everything that was happening. The stag's head on the bottle of Jägermeister stood out on the glowing surface of the lime-green glass on the wall behind them.

As she approached, Sergeant Parenteau—Lauren was her name—flicked her eyes her way. They widened with recognition, only just. Not making any effort to hide her acknowledgement, she tapped the moustachioed Cameron and pointed at Sara. He rubbed his chin thoughtfully as he held a sleeve of headless beer.

"Hey," Sara blurted.

Cameron smiled, knitting his brow. "Hey," was all he said in response, like a rescuer pushing a drowning woman further away with a paddle.

But Lauren brought her in. "Hello there, Sara Garrison. Looks like you've found the Station at last." She gave her a big-toothed smile. "Took you long enough."

"I've seen it on my drives. I just tend to be a bit thrifty, so I've been cooking in my motel suite."

Cameron swallowed some beer. "So, what's different about tonight?"

Sara froze. "Bit of a story, there, actually."

He nodded, asking no questions as he took another swig.

Lauren was having a glass of red wine, but she hadn't touched it since she walked in. "Are you meeting anyone here?"

"Nope."

Sergeant Parenteau turned to the bartender and asked if it was OK if they switched to a table. He gave them the go-ahead.

"Come on," said Lauren as she slipped from her stool. "Cameron, fall in."

He did so, if not reluctantly. Lauren grabbed her glass and led Sara to an empty booth. As they walked together, Sara felt it was strange to see these two officers in their civilian clothes, as they would have called them. It humanised them. Made them more relatable, although it made Cameron's moustache look even more ridiculous.

Sara slid into the booth after hanging her coat on the end. "This place is nice," she lied.

Cameron plopped down next to her. "No place like it in Coalbrook," he said as he lifted his half-drained glass and took a long drink. "Lots of atmosphere, drinks, good food. It's my number one haunt, anyway."

"It's not possible to have a number two haunt in a town this small," quipped Lauren as she took her seat across the table.

Corporal Reid thought for a moment. "No, I guess not." He shook his head, smiling. "Not of this calibre, anyway."

"So," began Lauren, swallowing a small mouthful of wine. "You said there was a story?"

"Well, I had just gotten back from some errands, and was about to make myself dinner... but when I opened the door to my suite, it had been torn apart."

"Torn apart?" asked Cameron. "Like how?"

"Everything was scattered and messed up, like someone had torn everything up to find something." Sara grabbed a menu. "Or something like that."

"Yikes," said Lauren. "Not too uncommon here unfortunately. Did you make a report? One of the on-duty officers could check it for you. Still can after dinner."

Sara's gaze hopped frantically around the menu. Bison. Beef. She might be in trouble. "Yes, well that's the thing—um, any recommendations?"

"Bison burger," declared Cameron without thinking, giving Sara a powerful, decisive nod paired with a wink. "Best meal in Coalbrook, bar none."

"I was afraid you were going to say that."

Lauren thumped her fingertips on the table. "Look alive, Sara—why didn't you call it in?"

She sighed. "Look, this is going to sound crazy, so bear with me."

Cameron chuckled. "I don't know if you've noticed," he said while gesturing with a finger to himself and Lauren, "but we're in the business of crazy recently."

"Try us," asked Lauren. "You'd be surprised."

Sara took a deep breath. The clack of pool balls sounded somewhere off behind their booth, followed by a burst of victorious laughter. She leaned forward and wove her fingers together, keeping her eyes on the leather of the menu. "Last night I was up working. It was around three, super late, and someone knocked, pounded on the door to my motel suite. And I mean pounded, man it was loud. I called out, no answer." Sara raised her hands as she shrugged. "There was no one."

"Oh, I see where this is going," groaned Cameron, although it didn't seem to Sara it was out of impatience, but rather of discomfort.

Lauren set her wine glass back down and swallowed. "So just random knocking? Pounding, I mean."

"Yep. It went on for a while. Eventually I snapped and threw the door open, and again, no one was there."

"Wind?" asked Cameron.

Sara shook her head. "It was a knock. A very strong knock. No way I could have mistaken it for a breeze." She fiddled with the menu. "But I did make a mistake: I opened the door to it."

"It?" said Lauren.

Sara pressed herself into the corner of the booth. Stifling a cringe, she bounced her gaze between the two off-duty constables, feeling quite out of place. Since her arrival in Coalbrook, she had presented herself as a professional journalist—and maybe that was, in some way, still true. She put in the work after all, and she had a degree behind her name.

But as she sat in a sudden audience with these two peace officers, she became acutely aware of their differences relative to herself. They were good country people, and she was an artsy slacker with a passion for everything that was decidedly not real to most people. Or, perhaps, just not important on a daily basis when concerns for rent and groceries pile up.

She took a deep breath. She couldn't play that part of a professional anymore, and she was about to widen the gap.

"What do you two know about the paranormal?" she asked.

Across the table, Lauren's eyes shifted to look at Cameron before moving back to her.

"Like... are you talking about ghosts, here? Entities, and that kind of stuff?" She leaned towards Sara. "Is that what you think ransacked your motel room?"

"Sure, for starters. I think it was whatever I let in that messed my room up."

Cameron sipped his beer, looking at neither of the women. His expression was grave.

"Look," continued Sara, "this kind of stuff has been my bread and butter for years. I've lived and breathed it."

"The podcast, right?" asked Lauren.

"Right. I've never experienced it personally, though." That was a lie—but one thing at a time. "Or at least I thought that was true. And now this..."

Cameron cleared his throat, dabbing moisture from his lips with a napkin. "Normally I'd investigate something like this. Sounds like a standard B&E on paper," he said. His arms were folded, and elbows planted on the table as he gave a resigned sigh. "But in light of everything we've experienced, hell—I'll believe anything at this point."

"Anything?" asked Lauren, twisting her head slightly.

"For starters," he said, pushing his head towards Sara and lowering his voice, "and I don't care what Steve says, but I'd be willing to bet my truck that what *we're* dealing with is no animal."

Sara spread her hands. "So, what is it?"

"Wait," interjected Lauren, shoving her hand across the table, "are we talking about her motel room, or...?"

"Forget the motel room," he declared. "Let her stay at your place tonight, Lauren. I'm talking about what's going on in this town, with the girl and the dead kids—"

Lauren gave him a look, and a hand motion that said *pump the breaks, man*. He sat back in the booth. Sara bit her lip and raised her eyebrow. Lauren avoided eye contact. After a long moment passed, Sara couldn't keep herself from cracking up.

"You two can't be serious! We have literally seen a girl survive in a frozen wasteland—naked—for days on end after she mysteriously stacks her clothes like she was in some bizarre laundry cult... and now my motel room has been ransacked by an invisible entity." Sara gave them an incredulous look. "And we have to sit here and not talk about it?"

"We aren't supposed to talk about cases," said Lauren. "And that's the end of that."

Cameron let out a sigh that quickly shifted into a groan. "Under normal circumstances, yes. But the girl's right—this isn't normal. And I think I'm going to jump out of my skin if we can't talk to someone about it."

Lauren's eyes bulged. "What am I, chopped liver?"

"I mean someone outside of the detachment. And I know you need to talk to someone, too, with all of your..." he waved his hand towards her, like it might explain everything.

Sara raised an eyebrow. "All of her what?" she asked Cam, first. Then she turned to Lauren. "All of your what?"

178

"Come on, Lauren—tell her about your encounters."

Sara almost shouted, but held herself in something like control, but was just shy—she was almost shaking. "Encounters?"

Lauren glared at Cameron as she rested her folded hands on the table. He gave her a guilty smile, shrugged, and then she seemed to fall into it, too. Her concrete scowl crumbled into a weak, tight-lipped smirk. When she gave an equally weak laugh, that's when Sara knew she was in. No notes this time—just remember.

"When Christian went missing last year, there were a few additional details not included in the press releases. And for good reason, of course: first of all, they were just circumstantial and ultimately had no bearing on the investigation. Second, they were a bit beyond the pale of anything I've ever experienced, so we just ignored them and moved on."

"And move on, we did," declared Cam.

"Don't leave me hanging," hissed Sara.

"It wasn't much, ultimately. And we did move on... until it started happening again."

Sara fell back in her seat. "Let me guess—a short while before all of this started happening?"

Lauren nodded. "That's right. And it was just the presence of animals in strange places, at strange times... and generally just making us all feel... well, strange."

"Let me guess," said Sara, "animals like elks?"

"Particularly the elks. Elks," Cameron paused, leaning his head towards Sara with a knowing glance, "that seemed infected. Sick ones with big networks of horns on their heads," he said as he splayed his fingers above his brow.

"Like my elk?"

"Got to be," he agreed. Cameron smiled at Lauren, pointing at Sara. "See?"

"Alright, alright," she said, raising her hands in defeat. "Yes, it's good to hear that we aren't crazy." She relaxed into her booth seat with a sigh. "Sometimes, I swear that Steve spends more time gaslighting us than he does working."

"Dude just wants to keep things steady. This kind of stuff only gets in the way."

When the server came to take their order, Sara wasn't any closer to deciding. Both Cameron and Lauren ordered a bison burger and then turned to wait for hers. The server stood, tablet in hand, waiting. Only she would be waiting forever, based on the options Sara had in a place like this.

Cameron got her attention and gave her an incredulous look. *When in Rome*, his face suggested, *do as the Romans do.*

Oh, hell. "I'll have the same, thanks."

Cam clapped his hands and hooted. "Garrison, you are a wild card."

Lauren beamed as she raised her nearly-empty wine glass to her lips. "Keeps surprising me, that's for sure." She took a sip, deepening her smile and narrowing her eyes. "She's a bit of a mystery at times, this city girl. You'll have to tell me all about it at our girl's night tonight."

Sheepishly, Sara returned the smiles, horrified at what she was about to eat. But her dietary concerns faded as she mulled over the mystery that surrounded them all, not just her own flippant decisions. There was one more interview she had to do, and it had nothing to do with her podcast.

16

Mentalisation

ONE AREA OF RESEARCH *that we've failed to solidify is the function of dreams. The broad consensus seems to indicate that it is related to learning in some way, but people's subjective experiences point to something very, very different. Lucid dreamers speak of different realities where they are able to discern future events. For some, nightmares take on vivid clarity and move into the realm of spiritual attack. And nightmares are one thing, but sleep paralysis is a nightmare on another level. Most striking of its features is that the experience skews toward the terrifying. And many report that they are able to end the episode with an appeal to a higher power.*

- The Garrison Theories podcast, Episode 7: "Nightmares"

She had gone to sleep in an unfamiliar room, with unfamiliar food—meat, no less—digesting in her stomach. But when her eyes opened, unfamiliar barely scratched the surface as far as a description.

Pristine snow surrounded her.

Sara walked—or was it floated?—between the birch and cedar, their knotted trunks and snow-dusted branches unmoving in the cold mist that clung to her face and arms like a frozen blanket. Disembodied, she pushed through the fog and the trees, hovering noiselessly above the pristine white floor of the forest dimly lit by grey twilight.

The voice came to her like vapour.

Sara.

She could hear footsteps now, crunching and cracking over the snowfall and dead undergrowth.

Sara.

The footsteps were coming closer, right in front, although the snow remained undisturbed. A whimper of panic wove its way between the trees from an unknown source. The gentle sounds of imprinted snow came quicker, and they moved towards Sara rapidly—closer, closer. Silence hung in the air as the footsteps terminated right on top of her.

A chill wracked her body.

Nothing.

Sara.

She turned, and Andrea was there. She stood, bloodless and naked like a statue of marble. Her alabaster backside confronted Sara, her long white legs like the surrounding birch rising out of the clarity of the snow and the mystery of the freezing fog.

Andrea, came her own inquiring voice from afar, a thin echo. Another whisper followed, swallowed by the wood and snow. *Andrea, is that you?*

Silence hung in the air like the mist.

Sara fought the urge to run. She was standing with this figure in the middle of the forest, white mist and snow all around her, wreathed in silence. The curtain of cold moisture that blanketed everything seemed to billow, shift and thicken—suddenly she struggled to see the trees. All that she could see was an ivory woman in a wall of white fog.

She circled her, seeing her black, limp hair and the pallid flesh of the side of her head. Her pearlescent breasts, like her lips and extremities, were devoid of blood and all warmth. She lifted her eyes and saw that the woman's face was a cavernous hole, a convex surface like the curvature of a spoon, polished and opaque like the rest of her white skin.

Andrea, she asked again.

Sara, her name sounded again in response, pleading, louder like it was being projected in an electric fuzz. The buzz became a thunderous rumble, terrifying in its profundity, invading the stillness of the dead place; it twisted and rose into a deafening, lacerating scream that swallowed everything.

Sara threw her hands over her ears. The hollow gaze drew Sara in, pulled her into the space where the face should have been. Shadow eclipsed the alabaster curve, and the darkness overwhelmed her as it sucked her in. A shrill female scream ripped through the air, joining with the terrible chorus that was already moving among the cedars.

The sound ripped her from sleep, jolting her upwards. She was met with the black outline of a spindly figure at the foot of her bed. It reached for her suddenly like it was waiting for her to wake up and notice it. The moment of contact drove her to awaken once more, limbs tangled in her sheets as she cried silently on her bed, alone in the half-light of the waning night.

Kimberly's eyes fluttered open, allowing the sick light of the hospital room to pour in; she winced, squeezing her eyelids tight, lifting her arm to shield her face and give her eyes time to adjust. Blinking, she lowered her arm. The lights were blinding her more and more as the hours passed, like someone was slowly rotating the dimmer dial.

She had been in the psychiatric observation unit for a day. Dr. Senger had recommended she remain under observation, and if her symptoms didn't improve drastically, then they would have to transfer her to a larger city that could offer her the inpatient care that everyone else felt she should have—just another reminder of the limitations of a small town. Another reminder of why her friends resorted to the types of entertainment they did.

She lay alone in the four-bed observation unit where the building's heat apparently didn't reach. She gathered her fleece and cotton over herself, wondering at the value of a place like this, where she'd be left alone for lengthy blocks of time. Her mom had to work, after all, but would be back this evening to spend a few hours with her, even if it just meant scrolling on her phone while she dozed in her bed.

Still, the isolation overwhelmed her. All those old fears and insecurities crept back in the silence of the room. It was her worst enemy, silence—it was worse than anything her mom could throw at her. Silence made the space for worse things to begin to eke their way into her heart and mind, filling every crack. Like a pot forgotten on the stove, Kim began to boil over.

She bit her lip. Her hands knotted together, her legs shook. She ran her fingers over her sternum—her heart was hammering. Immediately, she recognised the signs of a panic attack. Remembering the sessions with her school counsellor, she fell back into her safety net: a grounding exercise.

Five things I can see.

She looked around the room.

Emergency exit sign. Curtains. My feet under the blankets. Nurse moving past the door. The first aid kit on the counter.

There was a slow intake of breath through her nostrils. She held it in her expanded lungs for a moment before letting it out through her open mouth with a whispering sigh. She closed her eyes.

Four things I can feel.

Kimberly shifted her body, moving her fingers and toes. A thin chill coated her.

The roughness of the fabric. My tongue against my teeth. The IV in my arm. The cold.

She shivered under the scant blankets and took another deep breath. In. Hold. Out. Her eyes remained shut.

Three things I can hear.

Her ears tingled as she stilled herself and shifted her focus to the myriad sounds around her, some obvious, some not; she reached out to them in her mind.

My own breathing. The buzzing of the lights. Footsteps down the hall, getting closer.

Another breath, creeping into her lungs through her nose and out of her barely parted lips. Her focus deepened. She felt herself sinking into the thin hospital mattress.

Two things I can smell.

Over pursed lips and under closed eyes, her nostrils flared as she sniffed silently at the air, allowing the ventilated oxygen to flow up her nose.

Antiseptic, and...

She sniffed again. Her face twisted inwards as she wretched, gripping the sides of her mattress, gagging over the edge. Hands over her mouth, her eyes began to water as an unfathomable miasma draped over her balled-up frame. It was the same awful stench that found her in the basement of Blue Hills.

It rolled into her in waves, pressing her into her mattress. She grabbed the steel frame beside her, threatening to pull herself out of the bed, her bony frame poised to flee. But a feeling of futility overwhelmed her, knowing that she would be too weak to get anywhere. She was trapped.

Smell was the sense most strongly associated with memory. And suddenly the memories rushed back to vague images in the forest. Black nights utterly alone, shaking, feeling on the edge of death. And there were those nights, those terrible nights where she wasn't alone—the nights that made her long for the isolation, with nothing but the insatiable hunger and cold to keep her company.

"No, no, no," she groaned. She repeated it like some sort of mantra as she slammed the button on her bed to call the nurse. A moment passed where Kimberly remained frozen, staring at the slightly open door to her room. Her heart filled with tension. She hit the button again. She waited, focused intently on the impending arrival of a nurse. The sudden silence startled her, as if all sound had been sucked out of the world, and she was the only living soul remaining. The halogens flickered in the hall with an industrial buzz.

The emergency lights on the surrounding walls dimmed, the scarlet glow cycling up and down rapidly like circadian waves. Her heart was beating out of her chest. Down the flickering length of the hall, the sound of footsteps continued to echo in a quick rhythm. She stared towards the door, her eyes broad with sick anticipation.

"Hi, Kim," said a green-scrubbed nurse sweetly as she rounded the corner into her doorway. The woman glanced at Kimberly, who was covered in sweat beneath the hospital blanket. "How are you doing?"

Kimberly shrugged. She locked eyes on the nurse.

The professional smiled sympathetically towards the hospital bed as she watched the girl's heart monitor. "It's a normal reaction to what you've been through," she informed her patient. "Try to remember that you're safe here."

"It's not that," muttered Kimberly, still speaking in a low, frightened voice. "I thought I smelled..." The nurse gave her a concerned look. Kimberly swallowed, cutting herself off with a yawn. "I'm just really tired."

"And a little jumpy," the nurse assured her. "Your nerves will settle soon."

Kimberly's distrustful glare shifted towards a sudden change on the nurse's face: a thin red line was emerging above her eyebrows, moving across her forehead like it was being drawn by an invisible pen. A single drop of blood traced a crimson line downwards over the side of her thin nose. Eyes bulging, Kimberly pointed to the woman's face.

"Are you," she began, stumbling over her words. "Your–" The line grew, circling the nurses face. She smiled down at Kimberly with a look of patient confusion.

"Everything OK?" the woman asked with practised levity. Kimberly shrunk back into the reclined portion of her hospital bed, pressing her aching spine against the cold metal guard. Her heart monitor beeped faster. The nurse leaned forward, extending a soothing hand. The red line completed its circuit, leaving a thin, red ovoid surrounding the nurse's features.

"It's alright, Kim." Rivulets of blood streamed down the nurse's face, flowing out of the scarlet circle, pooling around the collar of her scrubs. "Everything is fine. You're with us, now. We've got you."

There was a wet sucking sound coming from her face as she spoke. Kimberly screeched as the traced ovoid and part of her skull fell onto her bed with a light thud, leaving a bloody, concave hole under her tightly pulled-back hair. Kimberly's screech died, twisting into a panicked whimper as she kicked her feet in a desperate attempt to move away. The face rolled on the sheets, staining it a dark red as it kept its eyes on her, making additional attempts to convince her that everything was fine, that she was fine. At the edge of the bed, the body remained upright, busying itself with its nurse's duties, reaching out to stabilise her.

"Kimmy?"

Then the nurse was gone, replaced by her mom and a singular psychiatric aide. The professional hung back, her expression one of concern. Her mom swept in close and embraced her.

"Mom?" Kim whimpered.

"I'm here, Kimmy." She pressed her cheek against hers and rocked her as she sat upright on her bed. "I'm here. Mom's here now."

She breathed a shaky sigh as she melted into her mom. The nurse busied herself around the two women, checking her IV and making sure she was comfortable. Thankfully, her face had found its way back to its proper spot on her head. Through tears, Kimberly sniffed. It was all cold comfort, despite the welcome return to normalcy.

Reality flooded in, confirming in her own mind—however weak it was—that it was all a hallucination.

But her nostrils still tingled with the smell of rot.

17

Windows

WHEN WE SLEEP OR ARE deeply relaxed, the defences in our mind relax... and thus allowing that which is repressed—or maybe even suppressed—to float to the surface like trapped air. Freud called it the "royal road" to the unattended world of the mind. Like dreams, nightmares tend to be more present in those with high-stress lifestyles, or who suffer from anxiety or trauma. It would certainly explain the heightened state of alarm in those states—since to relax is to allow that which is beneath the surface to rise. Sometimes it feels better to let things stay buried.

- *The Garrison Theories* podcast, Episode 7: "Nightmares"

"**C**an you tell me more about that?"

Kim yanked her sagging head up and blinked at Dr. Senger through a tangled curtain of black hair. "Tell you more about what?" she asked in a hushed tone.

The man with gray, thinning hair pushed his thin glasses up on his nose. "The episode," said the doctor as he lifted a printed photocopy of a hastily written report. "Just yesterday, while you were in your room. You mentioned... Kimberly, do you remember what you just told me?"

After a slow intake of breath, Kim shook her head, tossing her hair about her face. She let her head sag once again, burying it in her bony hands. "I can't do this. I'm not supposed to be here."

"Where is it that you think you should be?"

No response.

"OK," continued Dr. Senger. "That's OK. You were just telling me about what you experienced yesterday—what you saw, what you smelled. Do you remember?"

She shut her eyes and searched. It was like groping for something in the middle of an unlit gymnasium, each step an echo, each paw at the air an act of flailing desperation. Kim pressed her temples, running her fingers in tight circles as she scrunched her face up in frustration. She found nothing. There was a void behind, and a void ahead; she was aimless, a ship unmoored in a vast, dark sea.

"The report says you smelled something like rotting—"

Abruptly the smell came back again with such a force that she wasn't sure if she was remembering it or smelling it there, right there in front of Dr. Senger. Wide-eyed, she lifted her chin and stared at him. "Yes," breathed Kim. "Yes, I remember. I smelled it. I was doing a grounding exercise, and it came wafting down the hall. And then—"

Dr. Senger cocked his head, leaning forward ever-so-slightly. "And then?"

"Then... the nurse. That's what it was." With both hands, starting in the centre of her forehead, Kim traced an oval around her features, completing it just above her chin. "Her face."

"That's right," said Dr. Senger with an emphatic nod. "Well done, Kimberly. Your experience of schizophrenia will take a toll on your memory, but always remember that you can think clearly. It just takes more effort."

Kim nodded.

"But please, Kim—be patient with yourself. You've been through an incredible trauma. I know you don't need me to tell you that, but that's the reality of it. Traumatic events demand a great deal from us, and if we don't have the capacity to deal with it at the time, because it was too much too fast, well... we bury it. Compartmentalise. Find ways to cope until such a time comes where we can finally put things in their proper place."

"Place."

"Hm?"

"Place. Put things in their proper place."

"Correct. In due time, of course." Dr. Senger relaxed into his chair. "But these episodes you are experiencing are your body telling you that something is wrong. And it wants you to reckon with it, to understand it." He made a motion with his hand, a swirling one. "And ultimately, yes, to put it all in its proper place."

"Proper place."

Dr. Senger nodded.

"I don't know if there's a proper place to put what happened to me."

Dr. Senger tensed, leaned forward. "And what is it that happened to you, Kimberly?"

"I don't know. Not yet. But you are right..."

"Right about what?" asked Dr. Senger.

Kim turned her head to the side and cut a sidelong glance to Dr. Senger. She clutched her torso and shivered. "Something is very, very wrong."

For a moment, he had appeared a bit too eager for her taste. The previous session had softened her towards him some, but now he seemed to take on a more directive air. His beady eyes searched her face. He was slowly becoming less of a confidant, and more of a scientist. Maybe it would be more appropriate if she dressed as a rat and ran around a maze for him.

As though he could read her thoughts, he relaxed back into his chair and gathered himself, busying about his notes. "Kim, I can see that you are feeling very unsafe."

She didn't take her arms away from her chest.

He put his hand on his own chest. "I do not want to make things harder. But there is an element of our time together that necessitates some level of vulnerability. Largely because of constraints that go beyond the two of us... keep in mind that I need to make a recommendation." Dr. Senger's expression was rueful. "If I have a better understanding of what we're dealing with, I may be able to keep you in Coalbrook."

Kim licked her lips and nodded. *Lab rat it is.*

"I'd like to do an exercise with you, Kim," he began. Dr. Senger detailed the steps of the exercise that would unfold between them, going over a few rules. Together they also went over the basics of some grounding techniques—and then walked through them together. Then they were ready.

"I want to invite you to close your eyes." His voice became like silk as though he were an actor delivering lines. "Now, please bring your awareness to the soles of your feet. Notice the sensation of them resting against the floor. Feel the curve of your feet... each toe as it rests against the floor..." He did a progressive body scan, helping her relax her body piece by piece. Toes, calves, thighs—all the way up. It ended after a few minutes with her relaxing the space between her eyes. "Now, tell me of a place that is safe for you. Someplace you love to be."

Kimberly's face twitched. "My bedroom," she declared with little hesitation.

"OK. Tell me about our bedroom. What makes it safe?"

"It's mine. I can do what I want with it, make it my own."

"OK. Keep your eyes closed please—it sounds like the kind of space you can fill with the things you love."

She nodded.

"Great. OK, Kimberly—I want to invite you to see yourself in your room. To *really* transport yourself there. Take a moment... let me know when you think you might be there."

She shifted in her chair, dragging her bony fingers across an equally bony arm. "I don't know. I may be? I guess I don't really know what I'm supposed to feel—"

"That's OK, that's OK. You're doing great. Why don't you tell me what you see? What are some of the things you might see there, in your room?"

She listed a laundry list of items, almost becoming lost in the exercise. At one point, she even smiled as she recounted her favourite drawings and books she loved.

"Great list, thank you. So, what might you be smelling? Or feeling, or hearing? Go through the senses."

Candles. Her favourite music. The feel of the old shag carpet between her toes, which her mom hated, but she fought to keep. Apparently it was impossible to clean.

"Do you see it now? Among other senses?"

Kim nodded.

"Would you now say that you are in your room? And that you are safe there?"

Kim smiled and nodded again. "Yes, I'm definitely there."

"OK. Is there a window in your room?"

"Yes," she responded. "A big one, just above my bed."

"OK. Now, keep your eyes closed. And remember the safety of your room. In a moment I am going to invite you to look out the window. And when you look out the window, Kimberly, you are going to see the things that happened to you."

Her smile was gone, but she nodded regardless.

"OK, Kimberly," he said, slowly, easing her in. "Please look out the window. What do you see?"

With her eyes closed, she cocked her head. Her eyebrows drew close together, piling up on themselves with equal parts curiosity and concern—like she really might not know what she would see.

"I see trees. Lots of trees, spindly and dark."

"Like the ones you drew?"

"Yes, just like those."

Dr. Senger paused. "OK. What else do you see?"

She was thinking. "I don't..." she sat in the darkness of the memory, in her room as she looked out her window at an unfamiliar vista.

"Move closer to the window, if you are able."

Kim nodded. In her mind's eye, she stepped closer. The window grew, and so did the expanse of dark forest beyond. The trees and their entwined branches obscured much, but she sensed something there. Something that made her want to shut the window and open her eyes.

"Keep it up. You're doing great," said the doctor. His voice was coming as if from a great distance. "Can you see anything?"

Kim shook her head, but then stopped partway through. A shiver ran through her. "There's a figure," she whispered.

"Remember, you can always close the window and come back to me." Dr. Senger paused, allowing his words to sink in. "Now, tell me about this figure."

She scrunched up her face. "It's tall and thin like the trees."

"What else?"

"It's dark. It's hard to see."

"What is it doing?"

"Nothing. It isn't moving. It's just... there."

"What impression does it give you?"

She tilted her head again like she was listening. "Hard to say. I get the impression... that it is very old."

"What do you want to do with it?"

Kim paused, her face relaxing. "Nothing... run away."

"Run? Why? Do you know what it wants?"

The pause stretched, her shut eyes fluttering. "Me."

"And what would such a thing want with you?"

Suddenly she straightened in her chair like a current of electricity ran through her, the plastic frame creaking under her grip. "It's moving towards me."

"Remember, Kim, that this is a memory. You are safe in your room—close the window if you must, and the exercise will be over."

"I can't move," she whimpered. "I can't get to the window." She tried to swing her legs forward, but she froze. The curtains were close yet somehow remained out of the reach of her groping hands. "Dr. Senger, help!"

"Open your eyes. Come back to me, Kimberly. You aren't in your room, you are in the hospital in a private room with me."

"I can't!"

Beyond the window, the trees crawled along the ground by their roots like octopi. They parted before the figure and made a walkway with it at one end and her and her room at the other. With an unearthly gait it came closer; there was no urgency to its movement, which spiked the fear to new heights. It was as if its arrival in her presence was a foregone conclusion, or perhaps something to be savoured. She could not tell which. Perhaps it was both.

The cold grip of a man's hands wrapped around her forearm, bringing her back to the office momentarily. The look on Dr. Senger's face was one of embarrassment.

"Kim," he enunciated clearly and slowly. "You are *not* in your room."

She tore her arm away and huddled her knees to her chest. "Then why do I still see it?" she whispered.

The pair sat in silence for some time. When Kim had finally gathered herself together, she glanced up at Dr. Senger who held the space; the look on his face said it all: she was going to be transferred.

The drive back to Clayton's house was decidedly different this time around. There were no pre-interview jitters, as Sara's intentions with her questions were no longer professional. This was intensely personal. Thoughts of her parents' misgivings had evaporated along with any desire to make it big—the future had lost all meaning. This was largely about the present.

And she didn't realise it until recently, but it had also become about the past.

Other than Lauren and possibly Cameron, her only contact approximating a friend was a retired man with a love of hunting and the town of Coalbrook. Now, sitting at the faded wood of his kitchen table, Sara gave him a sheepish smile. She adjusted her glasses, reflecting on the difference in their current engagement compared to last. It was a funny thing: she had done this with Clayton before, only a week prior. *So why was I so nervous now?* Now she couldn't hide behind a veneer of faux professionalism. Now she was Sara Garrison—and nothing else.

And she wasn't at all sure that was enough.

It was deja vu. The kitchen piled high around them, like a madman's cabin stocked for the end of days. Clayton hovered over a cup of black coffee, his brown eyes trying to figure her out.

"I take it you have some more questions for me, then?" he asked after a bit of small talk.

"Kind of."

"Can't quite get the episode together, eh?" he joked. "And here I was hoping you'd clear our family name."

She huffed. "That's still on my radar. But it really isn't about the podcast anymore for me, it's more—"

"About Kim."

Sara nodded. "About Kim," she said as she straightened, "but I am still going to tell your story. One way or another, it'll get done."

"Good," he said before he took a sip of his coffee. The offering was of the instant variety this time. "And I couldn't help but notice that you're not recording this."

"Doesn't fit the mood," she said with a shake of her head. "I don't think Kim is getting any better. If anything, she's getting worse."

"I know," he said. His shoulders sagged. "It's hard to watch."

Sara leaned back in her chair. "I don't get it. She's got all the care she needs... but it's like all the food and medicine isn't doing anything."

Clayton shrugged and took another sip.

"Is she just too traumatised?" she asked like Clayton might know the answer. "Maybe it's all... psychosomatic."

"Maybe. I don't know."

Sara groaned. "At this rate, she'll be transferred for sure."

Clayton perked up. "Oh? Did anyone say when?"

"Her mom said it could be any day now. Depends on what the assessing psychologist says."

"Hm." His eyes glazed over like his mind had wandered elsewhere.

"But yeah, it seems likely with how things are going."

Clayton downed his coffee. "Well, I guess we better—"

"Can I ask you something?" she said quickly.

He hesitated, then acquiesced. "Shoot."

"You said before, when we were out in the woods... that sometimes you feel like the forest was alive."

Clayton nodded. "That's right." He rose and refilled his mug with a fresh scoop of powdered coffee and a pour of hot water.

She cocked her head. "What did you mean by that?"

He sat and took a sip. When he set his mug down, he didn't take his eyes from the steam. "Well, nothing too specific. Only that sometimes shadows 'n sounds have a way of playing tricks on a man's mind. Especially when one's alone."

"Oh," replied Sara. "I guess that makes sense. And I guess I can relate, too."

"Because of your phobia?"

"That too," she agreed with a shrug. "But recently it's felt more... real."

He narrowed his eyes. "How so?"

"I guess it all started with the elk I hit on the way in, and it's only gotten worse, like something doesn't want me here." She paused, reflecting. "I mean, from the moment I got here it's been one disaster after another. But when I stop and think about it... my attention keeps being drawn back to the trees."

Clayton was looking at her intently. Sara somehow felt the balance of power in the interview shift. "Sounds like your phobia is acting up again. The forest is just that—a forest."

"But you said that we *should* fear the forest sometimes. If that's true, then I'm not crazy. It's not just a phobia rooted in trauma, it's real."

"Well, yes there are times—"

"I just feel like I'm being watched," she said, not even looking at him or bothering to let him finish. "And not just the trees, I mean. By animals, too." She ran her thumb along the edge of the cup. "And I'm having a hard time believing you when you say that it's just a matter of shadow and sound. People don't stack their clothes like that when they're almost dead. And the other night I had some fairly unexplainable things happen to me at the motel, not to mention the weird things I've seen and heard in the trees."

Clayton took another sip of his coffee as he stared into her eyes, almost like a challenge. "Do tell," he asked.

She eyed him, feeling that same feeling she had when she was about to spill the beans with Lauren and Cameron. "What do you think about spirits, Clayton?"

"I don't think about them."

"Do you think they're real? Or at least possibly?"

He shrugged. "Don't know. I heard all sorts of stuff about the spirit world when I was a kid, though."

"Stories, you mean?"

"Yeah. Folklore, that kind of stuff—things my grandmother told me."

"Like, local stuff? Or are we talking some kind of Coalbrook urban legend?" She grinned, the joke being that Coalbrook was far too boring for anything like that. *Well, other than some recent occurrences, of course.* Her smile faded as she adjusted her glasses.

"Nothing too attached to the town itself. But my grandmother was status... boy, did she have stories to keep me from wandering too far into the trees."

"Huh," she huffed, planting her chin on her propped fist. "Looks like some of those stories left an impression on you. Maybe not enough to keep you out of the woods altogether, but..."

He nodded. "Probably more than you'd think. But I'm pretty far removed these days from that heritage, but from what I remember growing up... yeah, there's lots of stories about spirits. Some were tricksters, some were outright malevolent. Sometimes both, I think." He narrowed his eyes. "I guess your question relates to the... fairly unexplainable things you had mentioned?"

Sara leaned in slightly as she continued, "I don't know what's going on, but even though things started weird here, they've been getting a lot weirder since you brought Kim back. I've seen shapes in the woods, heard all sorts of odd sounds, and—"

"Like I said. Shadows and sounds."

"No, no, no," she protested. "Like, I've seen glowing eyes, I've had vivid dreams, I've smelled weird stuff, and I just have the overwhelming feeling of dread. I think there was a presence in my motel room, too."

He only sniffed, twisting his face with something like impatience. "I don't know anything about that. They're just stories, you know? Made up to keep kids from wandering into the trees, like monstrous hags or sasquatches that will eat them, right? That kind of stuff." He went to take a sip but replaced the cup on the table instead. "I just mean that when you're in the forest alone, and the wind's doin' all kinds of crazy things, and all the trees are movin' and things are makin' all kinds of noise... yeah, it feels like it's some big thing and you're just a tiny part of it. Almost like an intruder, where—"

"I get all that. But with everything you've experienced—with the woods, and your nephew, and then everything with Kim..."

"More fodder for the podcast, eh?"

Sara shook her head emphatically. "Not this time," she declared. "I mean, with everything that's been happening... did your grandmother ever tell you anything related to disappearances, or strange animal encounters, shadows in the trees—"

"Lots. Only cautionary tales, though. And lots of spirits took on the forms of animals in the stories. Or maybe they were the animals, I don't remember."

"Give me one."

Clayton frowned, clearly growing tired of the growing interrogation. His massive nostrils flared as he stared her down. As the moment stretched, the emotion she interpreted as frustration seemed to present more as apprehension.

"There was one story... one spirit that left the greatest impression on me. It was the story of the wechuge."

"Way-choo-gay?"

He nodded. "Yep. Supposed to be an ice spirit that represents winter and all that comes with it—isolation, desperation... starvation."

"What was his gig?"

200

He shrugged high, looking away. "I don't know. Same stuff as the rest, y'know—stealing people away, eating their souls. That kind of thing."

"Naturally," she quipped. He spoke with practiced levity, almost as if he was putting on airs. It was beyond silly, but even amid something as simple as recounting an old folktale from his childhood... Sara couldn't shake the feeling that Clayton was holding something back. It was a small thing, to be sure. But at a time like this, who could let even a small thing slide? "Well, great," she said flatly. "All stories aside, I just mean that there is *something* happening here, right? Clayton? You can't be telling me you don't see all this?"

"I see it. Some of it is strange, yeah. But some of this might be the overactive mind of a creative type looking for some new content, eh?" He finished by leaning forward and poking her in the forehead with his fat finger.

Sara rejected his words with a head shake. "Nope, not even close. I've seen way too much freaky stuff these last few days. And it isn't just me, either. Some of the officers have had similar experiences—and not just this time but last year as well."

They sat for a protracted moment, and Clayton's body language told her that he had enough. He shifted uncomfortably in his chair. "So, the RCMP thinks these events are connected?"

"Some of them do. Not all of them."

"Steve?"

Sara raised her eyebrows. "He's wanting to downplay it and sweep it under the rug. Bear attack or something, I don't know."

"Of course he is." He shifted to rise, but she caught him one last time.

"Clayton, if I may—one more question before I leave you in peace?"

He pushed out a lengthy, grating sigh. "Alright, go for it. But then I do really need..."

"Of course." She found herself shifting subtly back to reporter mode and felt the pull of the recording option on her phone. But she resisted and continued. "If you don't think that there's something unusual going on—I mean, other than the deaths and Kim going missing—I was wondering why you've spent so much time at the hospital?"

It was clearly a question he didn't expect. "Eh?" he asked as he went over to the counter to clean his mug.

"I mean, you've been hanging around Kim a lot the last few days since she's arrived. Now not *a lot* a lot, but more than anyone else save for me and her mom. And the police, of course." She watched his hardening eyes. "I know you've been keeping a close eye on her."

It was almost imperceptible, but he froze for a moment at the counter, holding his mug still above the sink as the water poured past it. "You noticed, eh?" He began scrubbing.

"Sorry," she said through a tight smile. "I think it's sweet watching you sit all concerned in your truck." *And a tad overbearing. Or maybe obsessive is the better word?*

He chuckled. "Don't think anyone's ever called me sweet before."

"It must be hard to let her go. Unless you're planning on following her to Prince George?"

He placed the cup in the drying rack, then turned to join her at the table. "Harder than you'd think. And no, my job ends here."

"I guess it's all in the hands of the psychologists and doctors now." She felt her eyes fall to her coffee, knowing her poker face was weak. "Why is it so hard, though? I guess I get that you were the one who found her, but—"

"I feel responsible. Maybe could have found her sooner," he grumbled, voice terse. "Maybe should have done more."

She looked at him. "But that applies to all of us, right? Like, I was out looking too..."

"Hm," he acknowledged. It was his turn to glance away. "Guess it's just different for me."

Careful, Sara. Quietly, Sara took a deep breath. "Is it because of Christian?"

He narrowed his eyes. "You a shrink now, too?"

"Nope," she said, hazarding a smile. "Still just a journalist. And a friend, too."

Clayton sighed as he turned his head towards the kitchen window. A wall of white and green spread from casement to casement. "I guess I was just hoping to do for Kimberly what I couldn't for Christian."

Sara raised an eyebrow. "But... you did. You found her. I don't–"

He waved a hand, batting her words away like they were mosquitoes. "Don't worry about it."

Sara nodded, leaned back in her chair, avoiding Clayton's eyes as much as he was hers. What was happening in this interview was deeply surprising as a sudden wedge of tension had been driven into the table between them. *Am I being overly sensitive? Or is this guy acting far too defensive for a hero?*

"It was a hell of a thing running into her out there."

"It was," Sara echoed dully. "Almost like destiny."

"Like winning the lottery. Like finding a needle—"

"In a haystack."

Clayton smiled. "Right. It's a hell of a thing to be part of."

Sara's eyes fell to her cup of coffee. It had dairy in it, but she couldn't bring herself to care as she took yet another sip. "Did it give you any hope?" she said at last, her gaze still low. She was struggling to maintain a professional composure even as the questions kept coming.

"Hope for what?" he asked.

"That you might find Christian, too?"

An enormous sigh escaped him, shrinking him like a deflating balloon. "No."

She looked at him. "I guess it's been too long, maybe. Sorry, I didn't—"

"It's fine," he said with another wave of his thick hand. "It's just that I feel quite confident that Christian is lost," he then spoke quickly as if correcting himself, "gone, I mean. And my time with Kimberly had nothing to do with me wanting to find answers for him."

Her coffee was almost gone. "So, with everything you've seen—"

"What about you?"

She froze. "What do you mean?"

"Does Kim give you hope?"

Sara only shook her head.

"For your sist—"

"I know what you mean. And no, not hope. Answers, maybe—but not hope."

He pushed himself from the table and rose. "Fair enough. Here's to answers, then," he said like he was proposing a toast. But instead of raising a glass he busied himself about the kitchen, filling a rucksack with some of his shelved preserves. After an awkward moment, he turned. "Where did you say she might end up?"

"Kim? Prince George came up."

"Gotcha," he said with a forced smile. "Alright, question period is over. I've got some things to prepare—so make yourself scarce, and let's do this again real soon."

She rose and prepared to leave without argument. "Another hunting trip?"

"I think it's about time, yeah."

"And what about Kimberly?" she asked, staring at the dark hair cascading down the back of his head.

Clayton planted his fists on the counter. "I guess..." he said, his words punching through a sigh, "...well, I guess it's time for me to let her go."

18

Hunting Grounds

LIKE MYRIAD CULTURES across the globe, the Canadian plains Cree speak of the existence of diminutive humanoid beings that exist in the nooks and crannies of hills, riverbanks, and forests—the home of the mannegishi. Some accounts will identify them as being intensely territorial, marking their lands with strange symbols on rocks and trees. Those seeking passage through their territory would be wise to go around, or at least bring an offering. Otherwise, they may tip your canoe, or steal your food. Missing the markings is an easy mistake to make if you aren't mindful, but the standard of respect remains. For boundaries of this kind, ignorance is no excuse—a standard we can apply to much of what I share on this podcast.

- *The Garrison Theories* podcast, Episode 9: "Fairies on the Prairies"

Moving her feet took a Herculean effort, like bags of sand weighed down her ankles. It had been like that since she arrived in the hospital. Step after shuffling step, each one of her hospital socks hissed over the linoleum as she dragged herself down the halogen halls.

And all of that for a trip to the vending machine for a hot chocolate. She wasn't supposed to have one, but things were quiet this morning and no one was watching her too closely. Corporal

Reid was struggling to keep his eyes open, and the nurses seemed distracted at the front desk of her ward.

Kimberly scanned her options on the dated machine, staring at the faded brown pictures. *Coffee. Cappuccino. Hot chocolate—that's the one.* She tapped her mom's credit card on the card machine that somehow integrated with the old dispenser then promptly punched the oversized button. With disinterest, she watched her steaming beverage trickle into her Styrofoam cup.

Turning, she lifted her drink to her mouth at the same moment she met the gaze of her rescuer, Clayton Johnstone. He was dressed as he always was, much the same as the day he brought her in: he wore his green John Deere trucker hat, flannels, and puffy vest. The smile that crossed his face was the same one he always gave her when he came to check on her.

The only difference this morning is that he was carrying a rifle.

Kimberly blew on her hot chocolate as he strode closer, never taking his eyes from her. She took a sip, wincing at the heat.

"Kimberly," he called to her as he approached. His hands wound tightly around his rifle, squeezing just so as he lifted it. It was aimed directly at her as he came close enough to poke her with it. "I've had one last thing to tell you before you were transf—"

He screamed as scalding hot chocolate splashed full into his face. One hand fluttered over his eyes and cheeks to wick it away while the other hand remained around the rifle stock. Kimberly was already spinning to run when he, blinking, lifted his rifle again.

An enormous pop sounded behind her, echoing in the halls as a metallic *thunk* sounded against the wall directly to the left of her shoulder. Instinctively she twisted away, throwing herself across the hall into the passage beyond—one she hoped desperately would end in either shelter or escape. Each step was laboured, restrictive, like she was trying to rush through knee-deep water on the shore of a muddy lake. It was a nightmare of the kind where you pedal your legs but get nowhere.

She scrambled forward as a nurse poked her head around the edge of a doorway, only to yank it back in with a yelp when another shot rang off further behind. Kimberly scrambled to the end, after nearly colliding with an empty gurney, and the shots arrived successively. She jerked her head around as she reached the stairwell halfway down the hall. He was there, rifle poised. Another shot tore down the hall as she dove into the stairwell and threw herself up the stairs.

She rushed down the white halls like a lab rat in a maze, each turn taking her to what seemed like more of the same, until she came to a dead end that was a supply room with a door left ajar. She ducked in, closing the door as quietly as she could before sidling behind a shelf, obscured by myriad boxes of cleaning supplies. At least that's what she hoped.

Don't let him find me, she repeated over in her head. She did her best to remain still, to steady her breath—it felt like an impossibility with the amount of adrenaline coursing through her veins. Each breath brought a violent shudder through her, vibrating the boxes and the storage rack pressed tight against her as she wedged herself between it and the wall.

Before she could find a comfortable position, the door opened, and she sucked a hissing breath into her lungs. Frozen, she held it in. She squeezed her eyes shut. When the door swung wide, the roar of scattered screams tore into the storage room. The gunfire had stopped, but that was little comfort—all the noise disappeared as whoever entered closed it quietly behind in a manner far too close to how she did. The oppressive hush filled the room, forcing itself into every corner, through the slits of space between the supplies, crowding her. All it left was a ringing in her ears, a thumping in her chest, and the occasional scuffle somewhere else in the room.

Her teeth dug into her lip as she squeezed her eyes tighter.

The lull deepened to the point of absurdity. He must be standing still, scanning the room. *Hang in there, Kimberly. Maybe he—*

The boxes in front of her face shifted apart as the nose of a rifle worked from side to side. Kim whimpered as she locked eyes with her hunter; she was already teary from shock, but now the sobs bubbled up, shaking her frame as she collapsed. At least she would have collapsed if she had space; her body simply went limp and hung wedged between the shelf and the wall with the window that let a sliver of light through onto her shoulder.

"Thought you could run from a seasoned hunter, eh?" he said as he came around the side of the shelf, aiming his rifle down the cinched length of her hiding spot. "I found you once. Now I've found you twice." Like a fish in a barrel, she was caught. "This ain't my first rodeo, you know."

Through withered, twisted lips, she managed to squeak out a fractured, "Why?"

He pulled his gun away slightly as he cocked his head. "Don't play dumb with me, Kim. I know what's got a hold of you." He pressed the gun into her cheek, shrugging as an almost remorseful expression flashed across his red face. "I was a fool, y'know? That thing ain't lettin' you go—"

He ducked his head down as another shot—a tighter, snappier one—burst from the door of the supply room. Clayton turned to the exit just as the shot rang out, and then crumbled to the floor, clutching his side the same way he still clutched his rifle. As he fell, he pressed the shelving into the wall, pinning Kimberly. She yelped and twisted as she jerked her head towards the newcomer, peering through the boxes Clayton parted. Framed by shelving and a mess of containers was a pistol-toting, wide-eyed Corporal Reid stood clear in the open doorway.

"Drop it, Clayton!" the young officer screamed.

From the linoleum, her would-be killer fired off a shot from the hip. Cameron fell back against the door frame as he clenched the side of his throat. Blood squeezed between his fingers, coursing down the back of his hand. Eyes full white, he stared at Kimberly for a moment before he slid down the door frame. His hand fell away from his neck as his blank gaze fell from hers.

Kimberly didn't waste any time. While Clayton was groaning and struggling up off the floor, she thrust her body with all her strength towards him and her only way out. When her hips got caught, she screamed—both at her predicament, and at the wobbly man only a few strides from her. Clayton was unstable, struggling to stand, his hands no longer putting pressure on the red patch that was getting considerably larger. Despite his condition, he still held his rifle like it was a lifeline.

"Don't even think about it, girl," he wheezed, "it's for your own good."

Kim bared her teeth at him as she railed against the shelves. "Come on," she seethed through clenched teeth, tearing her hospital gown as she squeezed her way out. Screaming, she swore at Clayton as she gave a final push and wrenched herself loose, collapsing into him and destabilising him, knocking them both to the floor as she wrestled her way free of the supplies. Half running, half crawling, she burst towards the exit.

Corporal Reid slumped in front of the door, eyes glazed over and mouth open in a soundless cry. She stepped over him and rushed down the hall as Clayton's shouts chased after her.

She ran right into the arms of a security guard, who yanked her back from the supply room and stole her away. The adrenaline buzzed in her system. She felt her mind drift away from reality. Strength failing, she allowed herself to become like a plastic bag drifting in the breeze; where she went didn't matter as long as it was away from him. As the minutes passed, and the gunfire didn't reoccur, Kimberly allowed herself to finally collapse in the hopes that she was out of his reach. Maybe he had cut and run.

It was all too much. The encounter with Clayton in the forest was akin to being shaken out of a nightmare, waking up to a reality so different that it made you realise just how lost you really were. But as the days have gone by, and as things haven't gotten better, she was starting to think that maybe she never really woke up—that maybe this was all a part of the same nightmare that began long before she decided to have a few drinks with her friends in the basement of an abandoned ski lodge.

S teve's head swam with the torrent of information that was coming over his radio.

"Clayton did *what?*" shrieked Lauren from the passenger seat.

"Is she stable?" Steve cried as the dashboard radio took his words in. Corporal Friesen buzzed back with an affirmative. "Thank God," he said. "And what about Corporal Reid?" he asked, his voice cracking. "What about Cameron?"

"Sorry, Steve," mumbled Grant. "We've got lots of professionals at the medical centre to confirm. Cam's dead."

Steve's knuckles paled around the steering wheel. A creaking sound emanated from his jaw as he took the car down the highway, throwing his cruiser onto a back road that cut across town. "Alright," he mumbled. "And Clayton?"

"He took off. We're on his tail—if I had to guess, I'd say he was heading home to set up a stronghold. He knows we'll be coming for sure."

Steve cursed. "I'll bet Rita will be there too. Alright, thanks Grant. You and Mack up for this?" he asked.

Corporal Grant was quiet. "Guess so," he declared finally.

"Good to hear it. Keep on the air, let's coordinate our arrivals. We're heading to the Johnstone place now." Steve killed the radio.

"Oh, God," came Lauren's tearful voice from the passenger seat. "I can't believe it..." Her eyes were red, pooling with water. But her face twisted into a scowl, one that represented the response of a friend and less of an officer of the Royal Canadian Mounted Police.

He could relate: in the heat of all of this, it was easy to forget that he had a job to do. This wasn't about the work—no, this was deeply personal. Kimberly, his victim to protect. Cameron, his friend, killed in action. Coalbrook, his town on the edge of hell.

"Steve, what the hell is happening?" asked Lauren, half-shouting, wholly in disbelief. "This whole thing is spinning out of control." Her hands were balls, shaking in her lap. "Are we cursed, Steve? Is Coalbrook cursed or something?"

"Oh, don't start," growled Steve. His career flashed before his eyes along with all wonderful things it provided him and his family. It was all crumbling down—all of it.

The two officers drove in a tense silence while his head buzzed with rage and fear. Coalbrook whizzed by as they left its limits, heading out into the outskirts that housed numerous wooded acreages. The anguish bloomed in Steve as the sign for Covey Road stood in the distance, standing at a slight angle like it was leaning out to make sure he saw it. The SUV crunched onto the gravel road.

"Look alive, Lauren. Clayton and Rita's place isn't much further." He looked at her. "This isn't going to be clean. We'll wait for Mack and Grant."

Sergeant Parenteau cleared her throat. "OK. OK," she said as she craned forward in her seat. "Let's gear up."

Steve pulled over. The SUV hadn't rolled to a final stop before both officers rushed to the trunk and pulled it open. The back was filled with crates of day-to-day gear. Radar gun. First aid. Pylons. Flares. Ah, there they were—tac vests. They both pulled one on and jumped back in the cruiser, grinding over wet silt as they headed down the unpaved road.

They rounded on the sign and followed the road to Clayton's house. It had been some time since he had driven down this winding path of dirt. It had grown over significantly, like the encroaching woods were in the process of reclaiming the property. Lauren checked her vest, her belt—everything. Adrenaline clearly flooded her and made her unable to settle back into the upholstery, looking like she had a hand on a live wire. As they were pulling up, she undid her belt with shaky arms. "Here we go," she said with a wobbly sigh. She drew her firearm. Steve yanked his standard issue Smith & Wesson free from its holster and piloted the SUV with one hand.

Lauren braced herself against her seat. "Steve, maybe we should—"

The windshield erupted as a heavy round buried itself in the console between them. A waft of ozone filled the cab, rising from the sparking laptop as Steve slammed the brakes and swerved behind a rusted shipping container on the edge of the property. The gunfire ceased, replaced by a gasping silence as if it had never happened.

"Damn," hissed Steve. He yanked his radio in front of his face. "Shots fired, 11 Covey Road. One confirmed shooter, possibly two. Hang back and approach through—"

Another shot roared from the house just as Corporal Friesen swung his cruiser out of the trees onto the Johnstone property. Like Steve, he had to make a split-second call; engine growling, he swung the other direction and crashed through a frozen vegetable garden to the right of the house and disappeared around the side, tearing at the snow and sod. A few seconds passed before more shots rang out from the back of the property. Steve poked his head out and saw Grant and Mackenzie, both hunched down, flying to their position in their bullet-riddled cruiser. It ground to a halt and the two officers burst from the cruiser, taking cover with Steve and Lauren behind the shipping container. Mack was shaking, looking like she regretted the day she considered attending Depot to become a peace officer; that full pension after twenty-five years served wasn't looking so attractive.

Steve struggled to speak through the tightness in his throat. "He's prepped for this," he croaked as he clutched his sidearm, "and there's no way Rita isn't in there with him. We've got to be quick before they flank us here."

Lauren nodded. "I don't think either of them is planning on getting out of this alive."

"OK, so that's two shooters," said Steve to the group. Lauren nodded. "And not handguns, either. Probably the asshole's hunting stock."

They collectively winced as a round embedded itself in the steel shelter hanging over them and their vehicles. Grant shivered. Mack looked like she was fighting back tears. They crouched together at Steve's rear bumper, locking eyes for just a moment as adrenaline forced them to confront reality.

"I don't want to die," Mackenzie whispered. Suddenly, Steve saw a woman in her early twenties instead of an RCMP rookie.

"We've got this," hissed Lauren. "We've trained for this. We've got this." She repeated it to the group, and herself, a few more times.

Steve hung his head. "OK," he began, speaking quickly, "Grant, Mack—you two are going to provide cover, alright?" He cut his eyes to Lauren. "Lauren, I don't expect..."

She nodded without hesitation. "Got it. I'm on you."

"Right." Steve breathed as more shots rang out from within the house. *Could be cover for an approaching shooter. Got to move.* He moved in a crouch towards his SUV and sidled to the trunk. He opened it and snatched his shotgun.

Bullets whistled by and crunched into the surfaces around him, yet his thoughts drifted to Vanessa and the girls. And then they drifted to the absurdity of his desires to find peace up north—and then back to his family. He glanced at Lauren, envying her for not having anyone depending on her in a moment like this.

Other than us three, of course.

A rifle round exploded in the steel near his head.

Lauren leaned in. "We've got to get in that house. Out here, we're just another hunting trip for those two."

He gathered himself. "Right. You and me, OK Lauren?"

Pressing her body against the steel of the box, she checked her clip—again. The thousand-yard stare she had since the first shots rang out vanished, leaving behind an expression of grim determination. When she nodded, Steve's blood quickened.

"On me—" he began as he nodded to the younger officers. Grant and Mackenzie snuck to the ends of the vehicles poking out from behind the container and discharged their weapons towards the house. The nose of a rifle twisted out of sight on the second floor. "—now!"

Shotgun in hand, Steve sprinted for the door and prayed Lauren wasn't far behind. The only shots came from behind them as Steve gratefully shouldered the wooden siding. Lauren squeezed herself against it like it might absorb her. Then Steve tried the door as the exchange of bullets continued above his head. *Locked. No time to waste.* Steve readied his shotgun—after a quick nod to Lauren, he blasted the handle off the door and kicked it wide.

Rita was standing at the end of the hall, rifle raised. She fired off a shot with zero hesitation, and both officers twisted back behind the frame. Steve's face and clothes were now drenched in sweat, and he gasped for breath. A quick glance to Lauren was all that was needed.

"Cover me," he whispered.

Almost without thinking, he twisted and dove into the foyer, rolling into the living room while Lauren rattled off a few shots down the hall. Steve completed his motion in a one-legged kneel, sweeping his shotgun around the living room towards the kitchen and dining room beyond.

A flash of movement came from behind a wall of jar-covered shelves—Steve squeezed the trigger and the huge section of preserves erupted with a bang, sending liquid, glass, and all manner of pickled items across the kitchen. A woman's scream came harried and bubbling from the other side. Lauren—at least he hoped it was her—discharged a single shot from the front door. Out of sight, someone collapsed to the floor with a thud.

Steve crept through to the narrow dining room and searched the kitchen, shotgun raised and ready to go. Lauren was already there, standing over the body of Rita Johnstone. She had been hit in the chest. Her eyes were open but vacant as her body shook on the floor. Beneath the expanding patch of red, her torso inflated and deflated with an ugly cadence. She was a goner. Thus was the legacy of Coalbrook, and his leadership at the detachment.

A bellow came at them from down the hall. Steve had only a second to register the source as Clayton before his rifle roared—Lauren fell back into the wall clutching her shoulder. Steve returned fire with his raised shotgun. The force of the kickback into his torso almost sent him off balance—but he pumped it and fired again. Clayton disappeared through a doorway, his boots clumping up the stairs.

"Put pressure on it," said Steve without even looking at Lauren. Grant and Mackenzie joined them, guns at the ready. "You OK?"

Panting, she confirmed with a hoarse voice.

"Mack—stay with her, would you?" Steve half asked, half ordered. Mackenzie nodded, lowering herself to Lauren's level. "Alright, Grant. Up we go. You two keep your eyes peeled in case he tries to shimmy down the exterior."

"I don't think he's doing any shimmying," wheezed Lauren. "Have you seen the guy?"

Steve smirked. Then he remembered his family and how it was still possible to not see them again. "On me, Corporal Friesen."

The two crept down the hall. Steve left his shotgun in the kitchen, replacing it with his standard issue Smith & Wesson. He needed to be quick. Grant's grip was tight, his own pistol darting back and forth to every likely target. Steve got his eyes and motioned to the stairs. Grant followed, reluctantly. His expression said it all—this was the kind of encounter every officer hoped to never see.

The stairs drew a silent curse from Steve. They went up a few steps to a landing that was in full view of whoever was at the top. It was tight, but the remaining stairs that climbed up to the left gave Clayton a clear shot. It had the feeling of suicide by hunter. That feeling magnified when Steve's boot met the bottom stair—the creak seemed to shake the entire house.

Nothing happened. He took a deep breath and glanced around the corner.

Clayton was in the room at the top of the stairs, sitting on the end of a bed. His rifle was cradled in his lap with the muzzle of the rifle tucked under his chin. He was shaking.

"Drop it, Clayton!" Steve roared as he approached, pistol raised; Clayton didn't budge. Steve shouted again, commanding him to disarm. Nothing. Steve climbed the stairs, peering over his pistol, and noticing for the first time how violently his own hands were shaking.

"Clayton," Steve pleaded. "Please don't do this. I don't want this. You don't want this. Just stop."

Clayton glanced back and forth between the two officers standing at the crest of the stairs, obviously unsure of what to do, looking very much like an animal caught in a trap. The large man released a deep, shuddering breath. A red patch of growing moisture covered his left thigh. Even seated, his shaky posture and fluttering eyelids meant he didn't have much time left.

"Is Rita dead?" he asked. He started leaning to one side, then corrected himself.

"Damnit, Clayton," Steve growled through his teeth. He kept his pistol trained on Clayton as a flicker of mercy came over him. "She is, yes," he said with a sigh.

Clayton gave a rapid succession of nods. "She knew the cost. We both knew it was only a matter of time."

"Matter of time until what? Until you both went nuts and started killing your neighbours?" It wasn't professional, but that train left the station days ago. This conversation was man to man. "Clayton. Talk to me. Why did you do it, man? You killed Cameron while trying to kill Kimberly. Why? What the hell kind of cost are you talking about?"

Clayton scoffed. Tears ran down his cheeks as he winced. "You wouldn't understand. None of you could."

"Try me. I'd love nothing more than to understand this nightmare." Steve's voice was cracking. The sweat on his palms was making his grip slick on his pistol. "You tried to kill the girl you rescued. Why didn't you just do her in the woods if you wanted her dead? Why now?"

"Had to be sure," he said matter-of-factly.

"Of what?"

He closed his eyes and sighed. "When she disappeared, I knew what had happened. People like her... aimless people, fearful people, people with no purpose in life other than to drown out their own misery—they're vulnerable. They're empty." He stopped, considering his next words. "They're prey."

"And you're the predator?"

The hunter gave his head a shake. "No! I'm their salvation. I am the one who comes along, finding them lost in the woods like a rabbit in a trap."

"I don't know, Clay; this is pretty predatory behaviour. So, if not you, then who?"

Clayton closed his eyes and licked his lips. "A being of spirit. Older than you or I could imagine, or so the story goes."

Steve glanced at Grant, his confused look likely a reflection of his own.

"Come again?" Steve asked.

"My grandmother called it *Wechuge*, the spirit of the empty places; a devouring spirit that feeds on vulnerable souls. Its victims know nothing but an eternal, unending hunger that twists them into monsters." He squeezed his eyes shut harder like he was trying to force an image out of his mind. "The only way to save them—*the only way*—is to kill them and burn them." He gave a wet, hacking cough. "But when that girl saw me... it was like she reset. She looked like she became human again, so I thought that maybe she had found another way. I thought that maybe she was strong enough to break free unlike all the others." He shrugged, then shuddered again. "I guess I was wrong."

Steve mouthed a few words, but nothing came. It was clear, now, that all of this stemmed from the mental breakdown of so many in the town. Kimberly, traumatised by the death of her friends, ran away and suffered psychotic hallucinations. Clayton was delusional as well, his mind deconstructed by grief and looking for an answer—however insane—to the question as to why his nephew disappeared. And why he invited Sara here for an interview was beyond him. *Was it to take the heat off him and Rita when they were suspicious? Or is this man simply suffering from psychotic delusions? Maybe—*

Steve cut off his own thoughts. "Wait, Clayton... what others? You've seen this—" Steve cut himself off again with a silent gasp. "Clayton," he said, his eyes boring into the other man's skull, "did you kill Christian?"

Clayton looked at him with bulging eyes wet with tears. His face twisted into a knot. "What choice did I have? I had to set him free." He settled into position, tucking the muzzle precisely under his jaw.

"Where's his body, Clayton?"

He ignored him. "If I didn't set him free, he'd be damned to wander the wilds of this place, feeding incessantly, trying to satisfy a hunger that can never be filled." He sighed deeply and closed his eyes again. "He is resting now. And I pray that you would have the courage to do the same for Kimberly."

Steve stepped closer. He extended a hand towards him. "Clayton. Don't."

Clayton winced.

"*Don't—*"

The large man's muscles tensed, and then instantly relaxed as the rifle snapped a shot under his chin, throwing his head back. He rocked forward onto the floor with a gurgle, then became silent.

PART FOUR

19

Impressions

FOR ME, ONE VISUAL that evokes a feeling of mystery is the footprint. I think of magnifying glasses and Sherlock Holmes as he examines the contents of a muddy boot print and manages to tie it to a particular location. I think of monstrous, demonic tracks left by a spirit moving through flour carefully placed in a haunted home. I think of the too-large footprints of Sasquatch. Each example lets us edge close to the truth but keeps us just far enough away to keep enticing us forward—except in the case of Sherlock Holmes, maybe, as he always sorted things out. Thankfully, I'm not Sherlock, as sometimes I think half the fun of these experiences is in not knowing. Because once we have the answers, then the veil of mystery vanishes, leaving us with nothing but cold, hard reality.

- *The Garrison Theories* podcast, Episode 2: "What's Going on in Sasquatch Provincial Park?"

The tang of antiseptic filled the chilled, circulating air. The fragile Kimberly adjusted herself on the lifeless metal rack as Sara sat hunched nearby, staring at the sterile floor. Head in her hands and short hair caught in greasy tangles between her fingers, she did her best to pass the shift she took relieving Sharon from being a comforting presence to Kimberly; always, someone was with her. These hours following the attempt on her life were long and quiet—the kind of quiet that leaves a mental vacuum where all sorts of cognitive distortions can manifest.

Sara yawned. Kimberley stirred slightly. Even though the physical threat of being gunned down had passed, Sara strangely couldn't shake the feeling that worse things were to come.

What could be worse than being shot dead in a psychiatric ward with no loved ones around? Sara thought, her mind filling in the blanks of the story she heard. Kimberly's mom wasn't there when it happened, and Kimberly was at the mercy of a crazed Clayton—and he'd have to be crazy to attempt something like that. *Didn't he? And it was damn close. Can't get much worse than that.* Like they were a direct challenge to the latter thought, all manner of terrible images coursed through her mind, images that were reflections of dreams she had already lived through. In all of them, Kimberly was alone and naked. In all of them, it was dark and cold.

Sara straightened her back, the metal frame of her chair creaking as she stretched out her joints.

One day had passed since the attempt on Kim's life. And the man who did it—the man who was now dead by his own hand—was the reason she had come to Coalbrook. Someone who she had opened up to, someone who understood her and her struggles and who challenged her in some reasonable, helpful ways, including the offer of the initial interview.

She had come here with a singular question: what happened to Christian Johnstone? That question was entirely displaced by myriad new questions. *Was the interview to throw everyone off his trial? And why throw it all away in such a brazen attack?* She fought off question after question, knowing the answers were just as elusive as the shadows she had seen dipping in and out of her peripheral vision. More than that, she tensed as she fought to squelch the most recent question that had blossomed in her mind: could Clayton have been right in principle, at least? *Maybe there was no salvation for Kim outside of...*

She shuddered away the thought, focusing instead on the girl before her. The real, human girl who was disappearing right in front of her eyes. She took Kim's bony hand in hers and stared at the crudely taped IV in the back of her hand. She had been in the hospital for nearly a week, with a few days in the psychiatric observation unit. Even with the physical and psychological support, however, the stay seemed to do little for her. And the recent attempt on her life seemed to accelerate what seemed like a slow decomposition.

The word felt wrong to use, but given the evidence stretched before her on the bed... what other word would do? The whites of her knuckles were more pronounced, her cheeks and eyes more sunken, her energy levels nearly flatlined. And the smell, no one could explain. Out of care, Sara did her best to pay it no mind—but it was getting to the point where she couldn't ignore it. The nurses had given up on encouraging her to shower; it didn't make a difference.

Sara sat there for a great deal of time studying Kim's skeletal features. *What did she see out there? Where did she go?* What did she know about what was happening... what may have been happening for years—maybe even once a bit more than a decade ago in a similar place with a girl of a similar age. She fought back tears as the questions drew close to her heart. *And what parts of herself did she leave behind out there? What happened to this poor girl?*

"Promise me, Sara," came a whisper as thin as her arms. It was a sudden hiss, startling Sara straight up in her chair. She leaned in. Kimberly grabbed her hands, squeezing them with a child's strength as she drew herself up out of her bed towards her. Her face was close enough to kiss. Her voice softened further, as if the walls themselves couldn't be trusted with the information. "Don't let it keep me."

Sara's face twisted, then relaxed to a reassuring gaze. "I promise, Kim," she said, squeezing and shaking the girl's bony hands. "I'll take care of you. I'll do everything I can." Kimberly fell back down onto the mattress, her burdened face untouched by Sara's words. The younger girl searched Sara's face for a moment before lifting her frail arm. She extended her little finger.

"Pinky swear?"

Sara shivered at the words, but an anaemic smile creased her features as she wrapped her little finger around Kimberly's. "Pinky swear."

The sick girl turned away with a satisfied look and closed her eyes. The monitor beeped as usual. Sara sat there for a few minutes, watching her, not knowing if she was asleep or not. She cleared her throat, but Kimberly didn't stir.

She placed a hand on Kimberly's side, feeling her ribs as she fought back a wave of tears.

The snowflakes were increasing in size and falling in greater numbers. Somehow, despite all the hell that had broken loose in recent days, Steve kept an eye on the precipitation. It dusted the hood and windshield of his cruiser as he sat parked on Coal Street, their white limbs flashing bright for a moment as they passed into the beams of his headlights, and darkening as soon as they exited. It was like the snowfall worsened as the situation fell further into chaos. This time of year it was to be expected, of course. But the frequency, the sheer volume of precipitation... it reminded him of the days he spent out in the trees looking for Christian Johnstone.

If he sat there long enough, he imagined, the snow might have sealed him inside his car. And at that moment, it might have been welcome. *Nobody would ever find me. I'd never have to answer for any of this...*

But answer for it, he would. The district superintendent was now completely aware of what was unfolding in Coalbrook and was sending some higher-ups to oversee the disaster. They were no longer satisfied with Steve's suggestion that this was all a death by misadventure—a simple animal attack. Oh, and what a task they'd have ahead, he thought: first, they'd open a more serious investigation into the tragic deaths of the teens; second, the subsequent disappearance—and reappearance—of Kimberly Shaw and the chaos that followed, leaving one of his officers dead and another injured. And then there was the deaths of Clayton and Rita Johnstone. *And the potential murder of their nephew...*

Steve gripped his steering wheel. *No need to combine it all. The tragedy of the mauling was a spark that set the whole town on fire. But it was still just a spark, and nothing more. The other deaths aren't causally connected...*

Waves of guilt battered him. He had barely thought of Cam since the hospital shooting, and even less for the recovering Lauren. The stress of the impending accountability crushed him. It would be a day or two before the hammer came down.

Another pang of shame tore through him when he had the thought—and not for the first time—of wishing that Kim had stayed disappeared... maybe even that Clayton had just shot her when he first saw her. Thankfully, he was almost entirely numb to shame at this point. It was like white noise to him, a burden he would gladly carry at this point if it would have made his life a lot easier. *Shame, I can deal with... but all this?*

Clayton's words still haunted him. When he asked Clayton why he waited, he said that he had to be sure. He had seen something in Kim that scared him enough to drive him to storm the hospital, as if he couldn't wait any longer, like the thought of leaving her alive was too painful to bear.

A mental breakdown. Nothing more, nothing less. Even his own self talk was starting to wane in its efficacy, like he himself no longer believed his own explanations. And all of it was riding on the coattails of last year's disappearance, which tragically was unfolding in his mind as an occurrence much more sinister than a simple missing person's case. *Wrong again, Boyko.* The thought came to him in what seemed like thousands of different voices, each a representative of the collective disdain of Coalbrook.

Eight years. He sucked in a hissing breath through his bared teeth. *Been a good run, I guess.* He played out the conversation with Vanessa in his head. Once it was all said and done, what would he do? *I could always do drywall with my brother... at least I wouldn't have to deal with the nutcases of this town.* No more psychosis, no more delusions of spirits or monsters in the trees. Drywall was simple. Drywall was real.

His radio buzzed, and he jolted like it shocked him. "Steve, I have Dr. Haim calling for you at the office here," came Corporal Friesen's voice from the dimly-lit dashboard. "Is your cellular OK?"

Steve rubbed his eyes hard. "Sure. I'll expect him." Myriad lights shone and blinked from his cruiser workstation as he sat in the deepening dark. In these parts of Canada, winter meant sunset before dinner. He felt like he would never eat again—felt like his insides were doing just fine eating themselves. His phone buzzed, and he lifted it to his ear after swiping the screen.

"Sergeant Boyko?" the voice crackled.

"Maryam. I take it you've got some updates for me?"

"I will get right to it, Steven. I heard back from my biologist consultant. I showed him some pictures..."

Steve waited. The hesitation on the other end ran like fire over his skin. "... and?"

227

"Well, it took awhile because he wanted a second opinion. He got a colleague on the coast involved, and they collaborated... all of that is to say that they both came to the conclusion that it wasn't a bear."

Alone in his car, Steve raised an eyebrow. A woman with two bags full of groceries passed in front and started loading them into her trunk. "Alright, so what was it then? Mountain lion? Cougar—"

"I'll get there. And keep in mind, the subjects were a mess. It wasn't easy to even identify where the damage started since most of the surface flesh was gone. But based on spacing, and imprints..." she paused again, stretching the time and causing Steve's hair to stand on end. "Steve, the bite marks were consistent with the dental profile of a person."

Steve watched the snow, furrowing his brow further. "Come again?"

Maryam's voice was fuzzy. "Human teeth, Steve. The major tissue damage, and presumably the rest of the damage was done by an individual—a human individual." The tone was flat, like it was a simple matter of fact. She repeated herself, "Human dental imprints line up, although we have no ID."

Somewhere at the base of his neck, an electric prick buzzed and moved like a burning wave over his shoulders and scalp. The frisson vanished and left him with a slow, sinking feeling, like Maryam dropped his heart into freshly poured concrete. "What, are you saying that some person killed those kids?"

"I am not saying anything other than the marks seem to be human. It is not my place to make investigative interpretations—"

"Well where the hell does that leave me? Now you're saying that we've got a killer—"

"I'm not saying anything, Steven."

Steve growled. "This just can't get any worse."

"It's a pain for all of us, Steve. I'm not off the hook, either—I've got to write a report for the chief coroner, and I certainly don't see this looking good on paper." There was a pause, filled with static. "I would not be surprised if there was an inquest."

Steve's heart almost seized for a moment. "God, Maryam, don't say that. I've done everything by the book this time, I'm sure of it." Detectives. Superintendents. An inquest authorised by the chief coroner. *You're gonna catch hell, Boyko.*

"Even if you have," Maryam groaned, "when the chief coroner sees the word *cannibalism* on the report, I think she will just default to an inquest. I would want to know more if I was her."

Silence crackled over the line. Steve thought he heard a sigh from the other end. "Knock on wood," came Maryam's voice at last. "Sorry, Steven. Wish the evidence pointed in another direction. I know this has been hell for you and the rest of the detachment."

"You don't know the half of it," he said, voice weak. "Thanks a bunch. I guess."

"Sure," she replied. "And based on your most recent contact here," her slowed cadence told Steve that she was sitting at a desk, parsing through some emails, "well, it unfortunately looks like we'll be working together again. But possibly a simpler process—gunfire with a clear assailant." There was a long pause. "My condolences for the loss of Corporal Reid."

Steve pressed into his driver's seat, dragging his fingers hard through his hair. He heard his heart thumping through his bulletproof vest, almost reverberating off the upholstery of his driver's seat.

"OK," Steve said, his mouth numb and feeling like the word had no meaning. He simply hung up.

Nothing was OK. He thought of the mess of tangled bodies. He thought of Kimberly, wandering alone, naked and bloodied. He thought of all four teenagers, descending into the lounge of the Blue Hills Ski Resort...

Sergeant Harasymchuk's voice resounded in his memory. *Four kids came in...*

"Four kids stayed," whispered Steve.

His eye bulged. For the first time he had explanation for it all, one that didn't involve an animal. It hit him like a Mack truck that he saw coming from a mile away but refused to acknowledge it until the grill was inches from his face.

It can't be.

Steve flicked on the siren and lights and punched his SUV hard into reverse, his mind racing to figure out the quickest route to the hospital.

20

Silhouettes

BUT THAT'S THE BIG issue with these sightings, isn't it? The footage is always fuzzy, taken from too far off, with just the right amount of camera shake to make it nearly impossible to discern fact from fiction. The Patterson-Gimlin film is a great example of this, or that classic grayscale silhouette of the Loch Ness monster. As far as I am aware, no such iconic shot exists of Ogopogo, except for spurious photographs of unusual parts cresting the surface of Lake Okanagan. But these images are just enough to keep the legend alive. It's important to note, however, that this entity that allegedly exists somewhere in the waters between Vernon and Penticton was not seen as a simple legend to the locals. Historically, Indigenous people would offer animal sacrifices to appease the demon before crossing—not an act typically performed unless one thought it served a very real purpose.

- The Garrison Theories podcast, Episode 4: "The Demon of Lake Okanagan"

Hands deep in the pockets of her overcoat, Sara strode by nurses, doctors, and orderlies without so much as a glance. They were faceless, fuzzy cylinders of blue and white melting past in the halls of Coalbrook Medical Centre, themselves likely heedless of the depth of the situation. Sure, they were all on edge because of the attempted murder of one of their most interesting patients—but it was a shallow fear, a threat to the flesh. The tingling of the back of her neck spoke of a deeper fear, a terror that bored into her core, so much so that her podcast had all but evaporated as a priority. All she could think about was Kimberly. Maybe—*maybe*—one day she would write about it.

It all depended on how it ended.

She was tired of rotting in Lauren's place as she watched the cursor blink in and out of existence in a white haze. The anaemic smattering of paragraphs she had miraculously slapped together during this nightmare had faded to the background. The interviews weren't perfect, but she had something better: she was living the story. And this story would require no embellishment. Still, she struggled to remain cooped up.

So, after finally retrieving her car from the shop, she came again to see Kimberly, the girl she had no connection with—yet every connection with. When she searched Kimberly's broad, dark face, she somehow only saw Andrea's pale freckled expression. *Maybe I need to see her more than she needs my support.* Perhaps Kimberly's story was the key to unlocking her own.

Blinking, Sara shook herself into the present. Further down the hall, a security guard nodded at her as he stood posted at the entrance to the ward, right at the crossroads of the main thoroughfare. She passed him without a word, shouldering through the heavy doors in time to see Sergeant Parenteau coming down the other end of the hall, a ways off, but not too far that Sara couldn't see that she had gone to get a coffee from the basement cafeteria. Lauren moved slowly, taking small steps as she blew over the top of her steaming Styrofoam cup. Her free arm was in a sling. *Not too much help this far north, I guess. Can't even spare a wounded officer.*

"Sara," said Lauren as they converged in front of the entrance to Kimberly's room. "Come to share in my guard duties, I see." She glanced into the room, and Lauren stopped dead, her momentum carrying a splash of coffee over the white edge of her cup. Her eyes widened as she lurched inwards.

Sara leaned and peered in after her. Kimberly wasn't in her bed.

Too-white coffee splashed over the faux-wood grain of a serving table as Lauren abandoned it with a slam, throwing herself into the room to investigate. Sara followed apprehensively with relative inertia. Lauren tossed the blankets about, ducked and scanned around the bed for any sign of Kim.

"Sharon?" she called. "Kim?" There was no answer, and Lauren fixed Sara with a bewildered look. "They were both literally just here. Right here."

On the other side of the observation unit, a splash of crimson grabbed Sara's attention; it was a tiny strip, peeking out from beneath the slightly ajar bathroom door. She pointed at it as she turned and got Lauren's attention—and when she saw, her face fell.

Creeping closer, Lauren tensed. "Kim? Sharon? You both OK?" There was a pause in both speech and movement as Lauren waited on an answer. None came. She strode forward suddenly and yanked the door open. She gasped.

Sara's heart shot up into her throat and then came crashing down into her abdomen as she followed the shimmering trail across the bathroom linoleum. It smeared away into the space in long streaks, ending at the crumpled body of Sharon Shaw, folded over itself on the toilet with her pants around her ankles. There was blood everywhere.

Without missing a beat, Lauren pulled on a single nitrile glove and lifted Sharon's head. She turned her face away as Sara whimpered, almost crumpling herself as she hunched over and covered her mouth. Sharon's eyes stared blindly at the buzzing fluorescents above; she wasn't trying to comfort herself or stop the blood from trickling in rivulets down the length of her neck—the shredded neck that barely remained beneath her chin. It looked like a bear had gotten at her, except for the three pencils that stuck out from the wreckage.

Sara spiralled. It was awful to the point of absurdity. And if it wasn't so horrific, Sara might have even laughed at the fact that Lauren first went to put her fingers to Sharon's neck before hesitating and pulling back. She checked for a pulse on Sharon's wrist instead, confirming what they both knew to be overwhelmingly obvious.

Groping as if in the dark, Sara's hands found the arm of a nearby chair, where she promptly collapsed. Every bit of her shook. She couldn't tell if she was hot or cold; regardless, her skin burned.

Lauren swore. "That girl's lost it," she declared as a curt diagnosis. "Must have been quick. I didn't hear a thing."

Since there were no orderlies or nurses or *anyone* there in response to what would have been a brutal attack, not only must Sharon's death have been quick—it must have been altogether silent. *No time for screams. The pencils probably helped with that.*

Lauren tore her radio from her lapel and rifled off a variety of codes and call signs. It buzzed back—it sounded like Steve to Sara—as Lauren rose shakily to her feet. "Sara, honey—please go back to my place. Wait there, OK?"

"What about you?" asked Sara. Her voice was thin, so thin she had to clear her throat and ask her twice.

Lauren strode to the door. "I'm still on babysitting duties." With a nod, she took off running down the hall, her cradled arm stuck fast to her chest as she swung her still-functioning limb.

Her voice echoed back towards the observation unit where Sara stood alone with the bloodless Sharon Shaw. What Lauren said, she couldn't make out. It certainly caused a stir since moments later a handful of nurses and security guards appeared in the doorway. Even the emergency room hadn't prepared them for what was waiting.

Sara was left alone to the erupting chaos. She crept inwards, eyes fixed on the abandoned station in the corner that was supposed to be keeping Kimberly alive. And safe. The equipment chirped and shrieked like it was grieving her absence. The blue fleece cascaded down the side of her bed, trailing across the linoleum. The departure appeared sudden. It had the countenance of a snap decision, the result of a sudden instinctual impetus to run—after she killed her own mother, of course.

Maybe it wasn't her, Sara. After all, someone made the attempt on her before. Could have been a murder and kidnapping. Somehow, she didn't believe her own theories.

The room was still. Fluorescents buzzed overhead as Lauren's shouts disappeared down the hall along with mixed shouting. Moving towards the window, Sara quivered before she pressed a hand against the cold glass. Overlaid in grim fashion was her own reflection, glaring. Beyond it, Coalbrook, settling into the protracted dark of an early winter sunset. Further still, the wilds of Canada, and whatever they contained. For her part, it seemed to be nothing good.

She felt helpless. She desired so deeply to care for Kimberly, to be there for her and walk her through... whatever she was going through. But something else seemed to desire her more, desire her to the degree that it seemed like nothing could stop it from claiming her. This reality settled into Sara as she gazed numbly out over the parking lot.

Movement below drew her attention.

Heedless of the billowing snow around and ice below, the skeletal Kimberly tore across the ploughed parking lot. She remained in her blue hospital gown and pants, the small of her back exposed by loosened ties as she scrambled barefoot over concrete dividers and between parked vehicles, flashing beneath the streetlamps for a moment before disappearing like a ghost into the dark. Sara only stared, not realising her mouth was hanging open until her mouth dried.

Eventually Lauren appeared below with a security guard, both giving chase. Every few strides Lauren winced and clutched her slung arm. Silently, Sara cheered for the officers. *Go get her, Lauren.* As 45th Ave ran away from the hospital, Sara lifted her eyes to what lay at the end—a wall of cedar and pine which obscured the empty places beyond. Kimberly appeared again in the cone of a streetlight. Sirens wailed in the distance. The chase was on.

But something inside Sara told her that even though she could still lay eyes on her, Kimberly was already gone—and she was gone for good.

Kimberly had just crossed 66th Street when Steve slammed the brakes of his SUV and slid onto the snow-dusted dirt shoulder. Her loose pants billowed around her legs, lit only for a moment as she passed in and out of the headlights. The car had barely ceased its lurch before he was already out the door, joining Lauren on foot to give chase. Hopefully, Corporal Friesen and Heinz wouldn't be too far behind, based on the radio conversation they had moments before.

Flashlights bobbing in the night, Steve and Lauren's voices joined in calling Kim's name as they pumped their legs over tarmac, gravel, grass, and snow. She never once looked back, never once showed any signs of slowing; if anything, she was getting faster.

"What—the—hell—is—she—doing?" panted Lauren.

"She'll slow when she hits the woods," he growled through breaths. "Hang in there." He called Kim's name again. Nothing.

Kimberly was a full ten second sprint ahead, her atrophied and sickly frame flailing wildly as it ambled forward like each step was preventing her from a full-face crash. The ties at the back of her gown came loose and fell away from each other, leaving her bony back exposed to the elements. Steve and Lauren ran full force into a growing snowfall, with Kimberly in a growing lead.

What in God's name—how is she so fast?

Behind them, Grant's cruiser crunched over the loose gravel; seconds later, Heinz let out a bark just before Grant shouted after them.

She can't outrun—

Like a ship sailing into foggy waters, Kimberly disappeared into the trees. The officers crashed into the forest right on her tail, flashlights cutting every which way. Steve's eyes fell to the footprints then climbed back to where she might be. Squinting into the snow, he glanced down again. And up. Down. Back up—nothing, just more white. He passed a tree. Down again. Heinz came up beside him and stopped dead, tongue wagging.

The snow was untouched. Steve jerked his head back, retracing his steps as he could hear Grant and Lauren approaching. He held out a hand, although he was unsure if they could see him. "Stop," he shouted. They slowed as they came into view like ghosts emerging from muslin. Lauren was rubbing her slung arm. "Watch the tracks. Wait—"

Carefully he lifted his boots and replaced them in his own markings, slowly ambling back the way he came until he found Kimberly's path again.

"Right here," said Corporal Friesen. "Oh, that's not good." He pointed to the ground.

Her hospital clothes were there, already gathering snow on their blue pastel fibres. The flakes spun in the beams of their flashlights. Steve bent over and picked up the gown, revealing the footprint of a bare human foot—about a woman's size six. "She was just here," Steve said, moving his head back and forth. "So, she—wait."

"Where did she go?" asked Lauren, her expression contorted. She nodded to the ground, breath steaming. "Her footprints—they just..."

Steve sighed, sending out a cloud of white vapour. "End. Here we go again."

Grant knelt next to Heinz and gave him a concerned look. It seemed to Steve that the dog had almost forgotten its purpose. Grant shook his head, and said, "They can't just—"

A frantic peal of laughter came towards them, weaving back through the trees as the deepening snow devoured the edge of the sound. A prickling cold writhed its way up Steve's spine as he stepped closer to his officers. He gripped a nearby tree before slouching against it, sucking in icy breaths as he attempted to piece himself back together. Grant and Lauren came up behind him. Together, their eyes cutting back and forth between the boughs of the trees now obscured by a curtain of white.

"What is that?" shouted Grant. Lauren covered her ears.

The sound of Kimberly's voice was all around them, pitching and yawing in cadence, a sick cocktail of fear and delight. Her harried cackles climbed into the air before twisting into something closer to a hair-raising shriek—and then back again. With every shift of the voice, Heinz's head lolled in that direction, back and forth at a frantic pace and covering distances impossible to traverse. Even for someone flying, an absurd thought that almost drove Steve to the brink of insanity.

He covered his ears, craning his neck as he looked at the murk of grey above as snowflakes dusted his face. *Is my mind playing tricks on me, or am I out of my depth, here?* He wondered how far away she was from them, how she got there so fast. The assumptions he had made, the theories for this entire nightmare were collapsing. *What the hell is happening?* The question gnawed at his heart, every fresh opening filled with a rush of doubt; the odds were against them, now. Likely always had been.

A smell caught his nostrils, just as Heinz began to whine.

Lauren's face scrunched up. "Steve? What is it?" Even after the wailing ceased, she hadn't unwrapped her arms from her chest.

He sniffed the frigid forest air. It smelled of rot, like piles of maggoty garbage and putrid meat made sharp in the cold. The odour came in hideous waves, so thick he could almost feel it billowing against his skin. A gentle buzz came from below. Steve dropped his gaze to the compass attached to his watch, furrowing his brow as the dial spun in frantic circles. The hair on his neck stood up. Something else had arrived.

"Heads up," he whispered. The wind was so soft that Lauren and Grant heard him and nodded. Heinz shrunk into the snow, whimpering as the officers scanned the tight, foggy area around them. The smell remained, stronger than before, and pushed towards Steve with such cold force that the flashlights flickered like they were flames. Wincing, his eyes moved from tree trunk to tree trunk, skipping quickly over the blackness between them, not wanting to know their secrets. Yet try as he might, he could not prevent some survival instinct from latching on to the thing out of place: behind one tree, a gnarled, black shoulder peeked around the edge. Steve's heart caught—it was at least ten feet up.

It was at that moment that Heinz bolted.

The form stepped out into view with patience. It was there, but not there—it was a shadow, a vaguely human form carved out of the night by a deeper darkness.

His heart sank into a pool of icy fear, and part of his mind broke away like a calving iceberg, dropping headlong into abject terror, freezing him into place. In the focus of three flashlights, it stood; charcoal in colour and texture, a naked and sexless figure that was as thin as it was tall.

Their flashlights went out.

The ghost of its vague form hung in the darkness for a second. Lauren gave a whimpering yelp and scrambled to work her light. Footsteps crunched behind Steve as he himself began to backpedal, slowly—one of the other two was already running. He lunged, groping for Lauren. She screamed when his hand rested on her shoulder.

Steve had enough. He turned and ran.

"Lauren—*go!*"

The forest lit up with moonlight first, and then their recovered flashlights second as they retraced their journey. Steve's instincts were firing out of control, every hair on his body erect and razor-sharp against his skin. Confusion overtook him as every iota of his being told him to never look back.

As the red and blue lights came into view, his thoughts drifted to the girl wandering the darkness alone. Clayton's words of warning drifted into his scattered mind. Collapsing on the hood of his SUV, he stared at Lauren, eyes bulging as he gasped for breath.

"What the hell was that thing?"

She gave him a knowing look, and that was answer enough.

Numbly, she stepped to the mess where Kimberly was supposed to be in respite, a tangle of colourless polyester and fleece capped with far too many pillows. Sara stood at the side of the bed, looking at the impression in the pile like Kimberly was still there. Her eyes welled with tears. She couldn't fight them. She wouldn't—even as activity filled the observation chamber, even when every now and again some nurse would encourage her to leave. Sara was heedless to it all.

It was like this nightmare had turned a key inside her, unlocking a long-buried aspiration to be the best sister she could be. Her hand outstretched and rested on the impression in the blankets. She was the sister to Kimberly she never could be for Andrea—and she squandered it. Like her sister, Kimberly belonged to something beyond her understanding.

Her sisterly devotion expressed itself as she smoothed the blankets and fluffed the pillows as she reorganised the bed. When faced with the overwhelming, unsolvable problem of her circumstances, she reduced herself to menial, adjacent tasks. But that's exactly where she was: there was nothing left to do, other than to fulfil her original purpose. Sara could make it all into a solid episode of a podcast. Hell, it almost would have been wasteful to not use these last few days for something. All that gas, time in a motel, marked up tofu—that stuff needs to be paid for. She stretched out a thin excuse for a pillow and pushed it back together to give it some life. *No dice.*

Like it was a coping mechanism, the thought of channelling her grief and anxiety into her podcast was comforting. This town wasn't her problem to fix, after all. She was just passing through, wasn't she? That made her a true journalist: influencing nothing, turning no tides. Just there to report back to the people what was going on. That was something she could do now. In the end, did any of this *really* matter to her?

Beneath the mountain of pillows was a scattering of creased pieces of white 8.5 by 11 printer paper, dark lines of pencil cut across their angled and folded faces. That would explain how she coped with this long stay. Sara leafed a few together into a short stack and began turning through them.

They were portraits, mainly. Faces she didn't recognise, men and women, mostly young like the ones Kimberly had pinned to the cork board above her desk. Sara assumed these were friends, too, or at least others from her school. The first was a girl with angular eyes and shoulder-length hair. Number two was a boy, full-faced with a crown of tight, pencilled-in curls. The next was a picture of skeletal trees rising out of a thick layer of black lines. Next, another face, this time mostly incomplete. More trees. Perhaps a self-portrait, next.

Sara grabbed more. There were many dozens tucked under the pillows, some even crumpled into tight balls and wedged into the thin line between the mattress and metal frame. She continued to thumb through the pictures, portraits, and landscapes similarly bleak in their design. A theme, a thread of darkness seemed to run between them, weaving each piece into a web of dread. Trees. A dark, faceless figure, cut by shadows and harsh lines. A long, sinewy arm. Black eyes. More trees, more faces, each expression almost one of silent supplication. A stag. A young, freckled girl—

A shrill gasp forced its way out of her throat, cut short by her hand clapping over her mouth. Sara staggered back, awash with nausea, gripping the side of the bed to stay upright. Sara's chest expanded as she forced deep breaths through her system. Like a moth drawn to a lamp with enough awareness that it would kill her, she leaned forward with eyes wide.

That's impossible.

It was Andrea.

21

Penitents

THERE ARE SOME, HOWEVER, who believe that poltergeist activity is not the result of a disgruntled or bored spirit; rather, it is the psychokinetic energy of someone who is among the living. There may be someone in the house experiencing an incredible amount of stress or grief, and the process of wrestling with the emotions releases powerful bursts of psychokinetic energy that sends objects flying, slams doors, or dims lights. If true, seeking to resolve poltergeist activity through traditional spiritual means is the wrong path—looking to the other side when one should look at one's emotional state.

- *The Garrison Theories* podcast, Episode 10: "A Knock at the Door"

Steve had often wrestled with feelings of inadequacy; it had haunted him from a young age, following him through school and to his time in Depot in Regina before he was first deployed in the Lower Mainland. He would make strides here and there, whenever a feeling of competency grew as he grew in his work, becoming more skilled and used to the expectations. But every time there was a slip up, every time there was a miscalculation or an outright mistake, it felt like it dragged him back to square one. Back to when his dad would growl with frustration whenever he didn't do something just right whenever he had the audacity to ask his dad if he could help. *Not that way, this way. Hold it like this.*

But it was all lies, of course—such was the nature of growing up. He had to learn to leave those deceptive messages behind and focus on the positive; at least, that's what Vanessa always told him. *It's not just about focusing on the positive, Steve. It's about focusing on what's true.* The message he repeated to himself over and over again—that he was useless, that he didn't measure up—was a lie ingrained. Over the years, it had become his responsibility to push back. *I'm not useless. I got through Depot. I became an RCMP officer. I got married, I had a family—not everyone gets to do that. I have a house, I'm the staff sergeant in a small town. Would a useless, no-good hack be able to accomplish those things? Maybe. But what's the most likely explanation?*

Steve sighed. Maybe over a year ago, that exercise in self-compassion might have worked. But in a situation like this? He truly was useless. They all were, in the face of whatever it was that they had encountered out there. It was, in some ways, a comfort. A cold, scant comfort—but a comfort nonetheless in knowing that they did all they could. That's all they had as a detachment, and so they had better cling to it. Whatever caused this whole debacle was something from a reality beyond his understanding.

Frowning, Steve did his best to strike that image from his mind. A chill ran through him when he realised that it was preferable to visualise the chewed corpses of the three teenagers than it was to recall the inhuman visage of that... thing. Coalbrook would never be the same for him. Depending on the discipline that followed from the commissioner, he would get out of this place as soon as possible.

"Steve?"

He jerked his head up. In a loose circle, the entire on-duty staff of the Coalbrook Royal Canadian Mounted Police Detachment stood, waiting for their leader to guide them. Following the policing failure of Kimberly's unusual departure and the cleanup of the terrible death of her own mother, he had suggested they all return to the office to regroup. But now that they were here, it was becoming clear to everyone that there was nothing left of them to rally—and no cause to rally for.

All that was left to be done was to apologise. Apologise and grieve. But he couldn't bring himself to do either. First, to admit that he had denied what had become obvious to others, however unbelievable it was, would be an unbearable admission of failure. First Christian, and now Kimberly. And secondly, there were far too many emotions winding up within him, pulled tight and locking him up. He was a tense ball, an object becoming increasingly dense that it threatened to become a black hole.

"Steve, if you've got nothing to say, that's fine. We all saw—"

"We don't know what the hell we saw," he seethed through grinding teeth. "But it sure as hell wasn't a goddamn bear!" he screamed, spinning and launching the nearest steel-framed chair across the floor. He hunched against the wall, agonisingly aware of the silent group behind him. They waited. He was supposed to offer them something, but he was empty.

Steve half-turned and glanced at the constables. A few whispered questions to those present in the woods, yet all stood like fearful recruits at Depot, stiff-backed and ready for direction, afraid to make the wrong move and catch hell. *Was this moment so different?*

The on-duty officers glanced at each other. Sergeant Parenteau glanced at Constable McDonald, who exchanged looks with Constable Campbell and Corporal Friesen. Constable Barchard was there as well, minding the detachment along with Constable Campbell, each oblivious to the depths of what had just taken place.

"What do we do now, commander?" asked Constable McDonald. She was white as a sheet, likely still reeling from the shootout and now having to process the story of what just took place.

Steve straightened and adjusted his belt. It had never felt heavier than that moment, accoutrements or not. "Go home, Mack," he said at last. "All of you. Consider yourselves on call for the rest of your shift, in case of an emergency." He paused and wet his lips. "A solvable emergency, mind."

"What about you?" asked Lauren.

"Don't worry about me. I'm going to hold down the fort."

"Steve—"

"That's an order, sergeant," he said, glaring at Lauren. "You can report my misconduct all you like. But don't get yourself in trouble by being insubordinate, OK?" He looked at them one after another, each one of their faces expressing regret at being scheduled to work this shift and having to witness what they did.

They left as a unit without so much as a word or a glance his way. Grant went to collect his shotgun that he placed on a nearby table, but Steve told him to leave it; he would put it away. He just wanted them gone. Before she was out the door, Steve heard Lauren mumble something about not wanting to be alone tonight. He could relate. There was what felt like an unremovable splinter that he knew he had to deal with tonight. He would be holding himself accountable. He had to take responsibility somehow.

Before she went down the outside steps, Lauren turned. "Steve," she began, her voice thin, "why did she do it?"

Standing in the open door to the detachment, Steve stared at her. He shrugged. "Because it was her."

Lauren only shook her head. "What?"

"Blue Hills," he said. "The kids. It was Kim."

Lauren's face sagged. Eyes vacant, she nodded and slowly descended the steps without another word. She got into her car and was lost to the night.

Steve locked the detachment door and retreated into the shadows. At his desk, he gave Vanessa a call on his personal phone.

"Is everything OK?" she asked immediately.

"Hey honey. Yes, everything's OK." He took a deep breath and let out a deeper sigh. "Just a bit of a lull here, wanted to check in with you. Hear your voice."

She wasted no time in responding. "Talk to me, Stevie. You're freaking me out."

"It's just... I don't really know. Feeling a bit off tonight, I guess."

There was silence on the other end that broke after a brief moment. "Are you overthinking again?" It was an obvious question, one that almost seemed like an admonishment.

"Yeah," he breathed. "Something like that."

It was Vanessa's turn to sigh. "Stevie, you've got to remember, hun—that road isn't going to take you where you want to go."

"I know," he responded. "I guess I just don't know how to turn off of it."

"You'll get there. Give it a little more time."

"How much more time does something like this need? I feel like I'm digging myself further into a hole." The words were flat. His old issues seemed so minor, now. He answered her encouragement in the same way he always did. Her words had lost all meaning, doubly so in light of recent events.

Vanessa went quiet again. After a pall of silence, filled with subtle static, she finally spoke.

"Just give it a little more time, Stevie."

He returned the silence. "OK. I will." *As if I had a choice.*

"OK," she said, her voice sounding like she was smiling. "When can I expect you home?"

"If it's OK with you, I figured I'd put in a few extra hours. Recent events ... have demanded a lot of paperwork. I'm falling behind, and—"

"Say no more, Stevie. I got you. You do what you need to do, OK? Don't worry about us."

"OK. Thanks," he said with a nod, rubbing his free hand over his head. "Alright, well—love you, Vanessa."

"Love you, Stevie."

He killed the call and collapsed deeper into his chair. *Falling behind at work, eh? No, Boyko, you're falling behind in all sorts of ways...* He caught himself going down that same old road, the one his father set him on decades ago with a look. And yet, he couldn't turn the wheel to take himself off it. Further down the road he rolled, hearing the echoes of those careless words, seeing that old shake of the head and the sigh, followed by a soft demotion as dad took the ratchet back. Only now the stakes were much higher. Multiple dead, and one missing. After what he saw an hour ago, he wondered if maybe the dead were the lucky ones.

All he could do now was sit in a pool of horror and defeat and allow it to wash over his mind, to sit and be alone as the night dragged on while others slept, leaving him further behind. And for all he had done recently—and for everything he hadn't—maybe that was his penance.

The drive back to Lauren's was over in a flash. By the time her rental rolled to a stop in the constable's driveway, she realised she had no memory of the drive from the hospital. Sara's mind had been wandering in and out, deadening her to everything outside of her mind. Yet she made all the appropriate stops—even signalled where necessary. She must have, because here she was. She blinked, shaking her head like she was waking up, and suddenly she was outside on the pavement in a car creaking as it settled into a state of rest.

Dinner wasn't an option. The desire to eat had left her, displaced by the growing tangle of nausea in her abdomen. Working on her podcast wasn't an option, either; it felt so far away, so unimportant. Besides, it was hard to tell a story when the ending wasn't quite clear.

But Sara had a pretty good idea of how it might end. Sergeant Parenteau had called the hospital on her way back to the detachment and informed Sara that Kimberly had disappeared—again. Once again, she vanished from existence, leaving behind the coldest trail: one that simply ended with no explanation. Well, Lauren had clarified that there was *something* like an explanation, something that echoed the strangeness that had plagued them all since this nightmare began.

But it left more questions than it answered. Because Lauren had also told her to head back to her place and wait. She had seen something in the woods. And who among them hadn't? Clayton spoke vaguely—*what had he called it?*—of a wild force that resided in the empty places beyond civilization.

And the drawing? The drawing was uncanny, the similarities were too close to ignore. The broad face, the freckles, the ponytail—it was Andrea as she was, over a decade ago. Her sister's face glowered at her as it lay flat on the hospital bed. Her massive eyes dug into her, ripping out the old trauma as if it had just happened. And her hair... she never wore it in a ponytail, yet there it was up on the top of her head. *Just like the day she went missing.* It was like a snapshot, a photograph in smeared graphite, taken by a girl ten years her junior whom she had no connection with before she came to Coalbrook.

She needed to talk to her mom. For the first time in days, she gave her a call. *Now that I need something, here I go.* Without a doubt, her mom would point that out. It rang three times.

The tone cut off, replaced by her mother's voice. "Sara! You don't call, and suddenly at this hour..."

"Hey, mom," Sara said into her phone. "How are you and dad doing?"

Her mother sighed, relenting to the conversation. "We're fine, hun. But you sure don't sound fine. Why are you still awake? Are you getting any sleep up there?"

"Maybe a bit less than back at home. But it's been pretty busy up here, actually..." Sara paused for a moment, biting her lip. "But—uhm—to be honest, it's not going too great."

"Podcast not going so well?"

She shook her head in response, then replied quickly when she remembered her mom couldn't see it. "No," she said in a thin voice, "it's not that. Actually, I've done everything I set out to do. I've got lots of content, I think I can make—sorry, it has nothing to do with all that. I'm all good on that front."

"So what's going on, then?"

Sara pressed her teeth into her bottom lip as the pressure started to build behind her eyes. She fought it back as best she could. "I've started having those nightmares again..." she whispered at last. "And, like, worse than they've ever been."

"Oh, Sara," her mom soothed from thousands of kilometres away. "You must have exposed yourself to too much stress. With your phobia, and everything up there..." she trailed off and paused. "Maybe it really is time to come home."

"I will. Soon." Sara stared at the picture of Andrea she took from the hospital. "Only one more thing I have to do, then I'll be home."

"I thought the podcast was all good?"

"It doesn't have anything to do with that."

"Well, then come home, for Christ's sake—"

"I saw Andrea."

Her mom went quiet.

"Mom, I saw—"

"Don't say those kinds of things to me. You keep your delusions to yourself, Sara. Don't drag me and your dad—"

"Mom," Sara almost shouted, "when have I ever had delusions? And don't give me any bull about me being 'delusional' about my career path or future or whatever," she hissed, "because I know that's not what you're talking about."

"And don't you dare talk to me that way, missy. You can't just call me up and say you saw your dead sister and—"

"And she's your dead daughter, mom. Stop pretending like she doesn't exist."

"Then you better stop pretending like she still does."

Sara's teeth groaned under the pressure of her jaw. "If you'd let me explain..." she mumbled as tears fell from her lashes.

A sigh crackled on the other end. "Sara, sweetheart. I'm sorry. I'm so, so sorry for what I just said. It's just that your dad and I have worked so hard over the years to heal..." she paused to sniff, and presumably to wipe away some tears, "and every time you have an episode, or demonstrate some of that phobia—oh, Sara, it's like you drag me right back there with you. And now this talk of visions..."

"It wasn't a vision, mom. I saw a picture of her, it was just like the day she disappeared. It was her, it was absolutely her. And I can't help but feel like maybe I know what happened—"

"A picture? What are you talking about?" She could almost see her mom backing away from the phone.

"A drawing of her. A portrait."

"Who drew it, Sara? Was it in someone's house up there? Do they know what happened?"

"No, nothing like that. It was—"

Sara pulled her head away from the phone as a burst of static caught her off guard. When she brought the phone back to her ear, her mom was already talking, asking a question in a flat tone.

"Was it Kim?"

"It was, actually. She's had literally the same experience as Andrea, mom, and she survived—" Sara caught herself, feeling her mouth suddenly dry up. "Mom, how did you know about Kim? I never told you—did you hear it on the news, or...?"

A buzzing silence stretched out between them, before her mother's voice finally came through.

"Nobody knows more about Kim than I."

Sara shivered. "What? What are you saying?"

More silence. She pulled her phone away from the side of her head and gave it a glance. The call was still going through—four minutes forty-two seconds and counting.

"Mom, are y—"

"You could have saved her, Sara," came her mother's voice from the other end. "You were right next to her."

Sara's eyes went wide and started watering. "Mom, what are you ta—"

"If you weren't such a damned heavy sleeper," her mom whined, "Andrea would still be here today."

Tears traced wet paths down Sara's cheeks. She could taste the salt in her mouth as they worked their way down to the edges of her lips. "How can you say that to me?" she whispered into her phone, barely able to get the words past the lump in her throat.

"But she isn't here," the voice kept saying as if Sara wasn't responding. The gentle cadence abruptly twisted upwards into a screeching roar, "SHE—IS—DEAD."

Sara let the phone drop to the tile with a crack and threw herself against the wall. Her chest heaved as she stared at the chipped screen on the floor, watching the call continue without her. The timer on the display progressed, and Sara had the distinct impression that whoever was on the other end was waiting for her.

She took a step closer. Eyes wide, Sara snatched the phone from the floor, lifting it to her ear with a shaking hand. A series of high-pitched tones trickled from the speaker, followed by, and mixing with a static rhythm. Then, a distorted voice, speaking slowly.

"Hello—Sara."

She trembled. "Who is this?"

"You—know—who—this—is."

"No, I don't," she retorted shakily, then angrily. "Why do you have my mom's phone?"

The voice came from what seemed like a great distance, pitching and yawing as if a composite of countless voices all trying to make themselves heard. It was masculine one moment, feminine the next. "Do—you—think—I—need—her—phone—to—talk—to—you?"

"What are you talking about? If you've touched her, I swear I'll f—"

"Look—at—me."

Her heart plummeted into her stomach. She flipped around, staring wildly at the doorways and windows of Lauren's house. Nothing.

"*Look—at—me.*"

"I don't know where or who you are, but you n—"

"I'm—looking—at—you."

Her muscles spasmed, giving to aggressive quivers. "Where are you?" she whispered.

"You—know—where—I—am." The dissonant voice paused. The crackle of the receiver was absent, like whoever or whatever talked to her didn't rely on standard cell service. "I—am—where—you—fear—Sara—Garrison."

Like a frigid hand had reached towards her, it drew her attention behind, over her shoulder and to the drawn, pilling curtains. Her skin burned ice as she crept closer. The synapses in her brain fired, spasming like a seismograph, telling her to bury herself under blankets—with a knife—until the sun rose. She buried her instincts instead. She had to know.

She parted the curtains, carefully peeking through the sliver of space between them, straight toward across the street. Lauren's house was in the heart of a residential neighbourhood, slightly treed, but mostly defined by concrete and streetlights. The house on the other side of the lane was, however, on the greenbelt. Towering behind it, blackened by night and lit dimly by porchlight, the trees were as they always were: standing at attention in a row, this time not moving at all on the windless, snowy night. Her eyes darted from tree to tree, to the black slivers between the houses, to shadowed porches and back to the trees from dark space in between to dark space. Every muscle was tense and primed. Hand still holding her phone to her ear, her gaze crawled back and forth...

"Peek—a—boo," whispered the voice.

The slimy words washed over her, eliciting a convulsion. Movement caught her eye, and she froze. She squinted, adjusting her glasses; it wasn't so much movement per se, but there was nothing, and then there was something, like the shadows peeled back to reveal—

Sara screamed and ripped the curtains together. She spun and bolted for the kitchen and grabbed the largest knife she could out of the wooden block on the counter before she made for the spare room, her room. She slammed the door and shoved the dresser in front of it. And then she dialed the detachment, hoping for the first time since she had arrived that she would find herself talking to Staff Sergeant Steve Boyko.

Nobody picked up. She dialed it again. Nothing.

She gripped her hair, almost yanking it as she paced back and forth in her room. "No," she whimpered, teeth clamped shut. "No, no, no." The whimper turned to a growl as her pacing quickened. "No, no—*no!*" She threw her laptop and watched it cross the space into the spare bath where it shattered against the porcelain of the toilet. She didn't give it a second glance before throwing herself on her bed. She wrapped herself in her blankets and wept for Kimberly. Wept for Andrea. Wept for her poor, hopeless self.

You've really messed up again. This isn't just a horror story, Sara—this is real life, and another girl is going to die. Or is dead already. And maybe this time you could have done something...

Face hidden under the covers, Sara pondered the different ways her mother—her *real* mother—would attempt to comfort her while at the same time reminding her of how right she was and how Sara had made a stupid, impulsive decision. How the coffee shop was stable, how she should have tried to find a normal job with her undergrad, how she should have listened to mom and dad. Each way seemed as reasonable as the next, and Sara conceded that she would probably experience them all in due time.

Guilt gripped her. After everything she had seen, this was her greatest concern? There was a girl out there, alone in the woods, just like Andrea was all those years ago. Alone and at the mercy of something that defied explanation. And it had Kimberly. The same Kimberly she promised to never, never let it take her...

Sara stiffened. *No. She had said keep, not take.* All this time, Kimberly had known. The end was already guaranteed, her fate sealed. Whatever was out there had a hold on her. And it wasn't letting go, at least not without a fight.

Backpack strapped tight and knife in hand, Sara eyed the dresser. There had been no sound or indicator of entry since she spotted that... thing in Lauren's neighbours' backyard. And she doubted, too, whether the thing had the ability to physically harm her. Or would a dresser even stop something like that?

All I have to do is make it to my car.

With all that her adrenaline-infused strength could muster, Sara shoved the dresser aside and threw open her bedroom door.

Nothing. Sara lurched after the front door, bulging backpack tight to her back with the steak knife still in hand.

She was inches from the knob when the front door swung wide—Sara screamed. Her reaction brought a similar yelp from a wide-eyed Lauren who shouldered her way into her own house, a large black duffel bag hung heavy on her remaining useful arm.

"Give a cripple a hand, will you?" she grunted.

Sara dropped her own bag and relieved Lauren of hers. "Sorry—let me!"

Lauren adjusted her sling and melted onto the loveseat next to the entryway.

"What are you doing here?"

Eyes closed, Lauren shook her reclined head. "What, are you looking to take Steve's job? Set my schedule?" She frowned, then sighed. "Steve sent us all home."

Sara jutted her head towards her. "What?" she asked incredulously. "Kim is out there by herself with barely a stitch, and he sends you *home?*"

Lauren gave her a challenging stare. "She's gone, Sara."

"Gone like before, like right before Clayton found her? That kind of gone?"

"At the very least, yes. And maybe a bit more..."

Sara crossed her arms. "What do you mean?"

Still reclined on the loveseat, Lauren stared straight ahead at nothing, her eyes full of memory. "Like I said on the phone," she mumbled, "we saw something tonight." Lauren glanced at Sara, who wore an expectant expression. "Right. Well, after Kim's footsteps disappeared—and I mean, her trail just ended—after that, we floundered about for a moment before this ungodly stench hit us. And that's when we saw it."

Her skin crawled in anticipation. "Saw what?"

"A black figure. Some shadowy thing... who knows? I only glanced at it for a split second before I ripped it out of there."

"Did it... say anything?"

Lauren kept her eyes forward. "Nope. Didn't need to, anyways. I think I understood it loud and clear." Her voice was flat, her eyes unblinking.

"So, what was the... message?"

The weary officer shrugged. "It was a big *get-the-hell-out* as far as I could tell. So we did." She finally glanced at the knife in Sara's hand. "What's with the knife? You OK?"

"Better now that you're here." She left the knife on the dining room table. "Well, OK—but that doesn't mean that Kim's a done deal, does it? I mean, she got away from this thing before, right? So she can—"

"Oh, come *on*, Sara. I absolutely love how far you'd go for this girl, but seriously? After all this, we're talking about redemption and recovery?" Lauren shook her head at Sara. "You saw what I saw at the hospital earlier, right? Her own mother?"

"Well, maybe—"

"And the forensic pathologist..." Lauren hesitated, licking her lips as she bounced her leg nervously. "Ah, I could catch hell for sharing this—*she* says it wasn't an animal that killed those kids. Steve just got confirmation, so even he's finally let go of his theory."

"So—?"

"Human dental imprints," Lauren enunciated. "Confirms what we saw with Sharon. Confirms everything. It was Kim all along."

Sara quivered. Myriad stories and urban legends suddenly rushed into her mind to fill the gap that had been there since the oddities began. The elk. The weather. The smells. The black shapes. Kim's emaciated form... and now this. *Cannibalism. She killed and ate her friends?*

She almost laughed. Even though truth often seemed to be stranger than fiction, when faced with the strangest truth she failed to see it—like she herself didn't believe the stories she told. Every step of the way she had reasoned with herself, trying to figure out an explanation. And after all this time, in the absence of a rational explanation... the most irrational, the most unbelievable becomes the most likely.

And the most irrational-seeming explanation? Her listeners would undoubtedly know this as a story of the wendigo. *Or, according to Clayton, known locally as wechuge.* And she knew it as such... and how could she not? She had done a whole podcast on the wendigo and other similar wild spirits. *How did I not see it?* Suddenly, her podcast felt so small.

"Sara?"

Lauren's words shook Sara into the present. "Sorry."

"Are you OK? Did you hear what I said?"

Sara nodded.

"I had a similar reaction, to be honest. To think that such a tiny girl could do that... and this thing in the woods. It's all so... impossible."

Sara frowned as she pulled on her bright red toque. "That's the thing with this kind of stuff," she said as she lifted her bag. "But believe it or not, I believe every word."

"Hey," said Lauren as she leaned forward, "where do you think you're going this time of night? Especially with all that's going on—"

"It's *because* of all this that I've got to go. Lauren, we can't just leave her out there."

"Yes, we can."

Sara gawped at her. "You don't mean that. You're a police officer, Lauren, you've got to—"

"She's gone, Sara."

"We've got to do something."

Lauren stood. She gripped Sara's shoulder with her unslung hand. "Sara... you didn't see what I saw. You didn't see what I *felt* out there. That... thing took her. She was *flying* Sara. It took her right up into the sky, and—"

"Stop."

"—and Kim was *laughing*, somewhere above the trees..." Lauren paused, wiping a tear away from her cheek with a shaky hand, "...and we just ran as fast as we could with her laughing the whole time, and Heinz ran away and—"

"OK, Lauren. Stop. Please, just stop."

The officer took a deep breath. "Sorry. I'm just really shaken."

Sara responded with a deep breath of her own. "Maybe you're right. I haven't experienced that, but you know I've seen some things since I've been here. The elk, my room, the figure."

"It's all the same nightmare, isn't it?"

Sara nodded. "Maybe I've seen and done enough. Maybe it is time to go home."

"Really? Now? And just like that?" asked Lauren.

"I think so. I can't stay here another minute, and if I start now, I could be home for dinner tomorrow." She hiked up her backpack. "Thanks for taking care of me, Lauren."

Lauren gave her a weak, one-armed hug. Sara rested her chin on her shoulder.

"You got it, Garrison." She pushed Sara back, holding her at arm's length. "Is it fair to say that you won't be finding yourself in Coalbrook anytime soon?"

Sara shook her head. "I am never coming back here again."

"OK." Lauren pressed her lips together. She looked at Sara with longing. "Drive safe. Straight home, OK?"

She hoisted her bag. "Straight home. No elks this time."

Lauren looked after her as she walked down the drive and got into her car. She was going straight home. Only she had a few stops to make along the way.

22

The Fifth Stage of Grief

THE WORLD OF THE PARANORMAL will sometimes overlap with psychology. When it does, it gives credence to the strange and discredits the scientific. There is no finer example of this than the culture-bound condition known as wendigo psychosis—a state of being where one is driven to insatiable cannibalism. As they sought to proselytise the Indigenous population of pre-Confederation Canada, the early Jesuits witnessed a litany of examples of executions of alleged wendigos. Despite being spiritual men, they largely perceived it as being the result of a mental disturbance. Still, the legend of the bloodthirsty spirit persists. Some see it as the spirit of desperation, either itself being the devouring culprit, or it being the one to instigate and empower the weak-minded to indulge a hunger that can never be satisfied. And for what? I imagine the answer, if it was even knowable, would be largely unpalatable to you and I.

- *The Garrison Theories* podcast, Episode 8: "Perspectives on the Wendigo"

By the time the orange aura of the sun had disappeared from the horizon, Steve had already had too much to drink. As it turned out, it was even too much for him to simply sit and experience the weight of his guilt and the shame of his poor choices. So he drank, slowly, leaning back in his creaking chair as he waited for the liquid to work its magic, to smooth out those rough emotional edges.

Numb to it all, he sat deflated in the yellow half-light of his office desk lamp. What he would do if he got a call, he didn't know. And at that moment, he didn't care. His heart and mind swam in whiskey, drifting like the tiny snowflakes that battered the large window in front of him.

Coalbrook was quiet, taken by a deep sleep as the winter deepened around it. Across the street, in front of the family development office, a single streetlamp lit what was otherwise a pitch-black road. A car hummed further down the way. The headlights pierced through the thickening snow, casting enough light to make him squint. He thought it might go past; he frowned as it pulled in front of the detachment. Tensing, he stood and hid his glass in the drawer of his desk—he couldn't see the driver behind the headlights. Instinctively, his hand went to his sidearm.

The driver door opened, then shut, and then Sara Garrison walked up to his window, now buried in a bright yellow coat but still wearing the same red toque. She was already significantly shorter than he, but the difference in height from the front walkway outside to the level of his office made her look like a child. He stared down at her like a king from an ivory tower, feeling like it would be more appropriate if it were reversed.

She pointed to the door. Like it was a question, she cocked her head towards it. His frown deepened, but he nodded and went to meet her there. Sara was already standing at the front door by the time he arrived and unlocked it.

"Ms. Garrison," he said flatly as she squeezed past him. "Usually when there's an emergency, we encourage people to call 911. It's more efficient."

"Don't even—I just tried calling you. I don't exactly know if what I'm dealing with is an emergency," she said with a shiver, dusting herself off, "and even if it was, I don't think there's anyone around who could deal with it."

He turned and walked back towards his office, beckoning her to follow him past the secure doors that led from the phone booth-sized lobby. "Sounds like you've lost confidence in your local law enforcement."

"Well," she began, stomping the snow off her boots, "I wouldn't say it was a matter of confidence. Or competence. I think my issue—our issue—goes beyond the RCMP handbook, wouldn't you say?"

He shook his head, feeling the liquor slosh back and forth in his brain. "I don't know what to say anymore." Back in his office he collapsed into his chair, spinning it to meet her as she settled into the one facing his desk. It wasn't exactly a textbook interaction with a member of the public. Lazily he folded his hands together, blowing a raspberry as he sighed, doing his best to figure out the young woman before him.

"What brings you here, Sara? One last interview?"

She shook her head. "No more interviews."

"All done, then? Got everything you need?"

A weak smile curved her lips. "Not quite. Not yet."

"Alright," he said, leaning forward and supporting himself on the large, flat desk calendar. "So, what do you want from me?"

"Nothing, Staff Sergeant Boyko. I actually came here to give you something."

"Oh?" he said, cracking into a smile. He wasn't sure if it was the alcohol or the absurdity of the past dozen or so days, but he felt like he was on the verge of bursting into laughter. Or tears.

"Yep," she said. "I just wanted to tell you that I think she knew."

With his eyes threatening to close on him, Steve lifted his eyebrows. "Knew what?"

"She told me not to let it keep her," said Sara, "as if it already had her. Maybe this was set from the start. Maybe there wasn't anything we could do."

His eyes glazed over as he stared ahead, looking through Sara more than at her. She searched his face, most likely knowing exactly what he was thinking—and that he had been drinking. He had the distinct sense that although he had implicitly forbidden any discussion on the matter, the two of them were on the same page of this horror story. It was written all over her face—the burden of terrible knowledge.

He had to force himself to talk. "And what do you mean by 'it'?" A part of him desperately clung to material things, to reality—that this was all just some horrible accident, where some stupid kids got mixed up with sex and alcohol and wound up dead from some act of nature, some wild thing. But that was gone. All that remained was the unexplainable, and the feeling of being terribly, terribly small.

"You know what I'm talking about Steve. I know that you saw it, too."

His face buckled in on itself. "I don't know what the hell I saw."

"Neither do I. I know I only got a glimpse of it, but I know it is real, and I know it made a claim on Kimberly, and I know it isn't a problem you, or I, or anyone could solve." Sara's watery eyes drilled into his. "At least not in the way we've been trying to." He felt profoundly insignificant, and he imagined she did as well. But at least she was trying to do something about it.

He had nothing to say. He looked away from her, resisting the temptation to turn his chair around and stare out the window. Suddenly, he felt exposed. There were many things in his life he could fix, could reason his way through; and many more problems that he couldn't. But this was a problem of an entirely different calibre, something far beyond him or any tool he had.

So why do I still feel like I failed?

"I should have started the search sooner," he said. "I shouldn't have called it off. I should have found her—I should have found Christian, before…"

He glanced back at her eyes, still locked and boring a hole deep into him. Her lips curled inwards and covered the tops of her teeth as a tear fell onto her jacket. "Maybe," she stated resolutely as if she wasn't crying. "But maybe when she came to the hospital it was already too late." Her voice cracked as she finished her sentence. "I guess we'll have to find some comfort in that."

"Some comfort."

In the weak light of the detachment, the two sat in silence and stared at each other.

Finally, Sara spoke after clearing her throat and rubbing the tears from her cheeks. "You asked me why I came here," she said. "I think that it's too late to solve whatever is going on in this town—to deal with that... thing. But I think we owe it to—"

"Other than my wife and kids, I don't owe anybody a damned thing," growled Steve, pushing the grotesque image out of his mind, the thing that called to him whenever he closed his eyes. "Like you said, I've done my job. Mistakes were made, yes—oh, hell, mistakes were made. And we'll answer for them, all of us here will. Myself especially. But as far as... that—" he hissed, pointing out of the window to the blackness beyond, "—well, I think it goes without saying it's a bit beyond my purview."

He forced himself to stare at her. He wanted to look away, but he resisted. *Penance.*

"*I'm* not done, Steve." Her voice cracked, tears welling in her eyes. She gestured toward his desk. "The case is closed for you, I get it. As closed as it can be right now—what will the official word be? Some form of psychotic break from trauma?"

Steve nodded. "Probably."

"Well, it's still an open book for me." Sara leaned in, hand on her chest for a moment before pointing out towards the same spot he had gestured to seconds before. "She's still out there, Steve."

A wordless pall hung over the office.

"And like you said," he whispered at last, "she's in the hands of something far beyond us." He stood up, shakily, coming around his desk. "So we're done. The RCMP is done—and the freelance journalist is free to go. You got your story, go on and publish it. Make your podcast." He scoffed, shaking his head, once again moving to the edge of laughter. "Slot it in alongside Sasquatch—nobody is going to take this seriously."

"What about Coalbrook?" She was starting to raise her small voice. "Are you going to tell me that you're just going to leave Kim out there to die—or God knows what else?"

Steve stared at her with hard eyes. His face ached with the pressure that mounted behind it, the tension in his features tugging at his temples and the hollows under his cheekbones. Her pleading expression did not waver—but his did. Tears pushed out from behind his eyes, despite every effort he made to hold them back; his face broke and fell, and his rigid stance crumbled. He turned away, putting his hands on his desk, hanging his head. Cruelly, she said nothing.

Almost collapsing on his desk, he said, "I'm sorry, Sara. I can't go back out there." Tears dropped silently onto his workstation. "I have to move on. We have to move on." Again, the silence covered the room. Then she spoke; her voice was small, coming from behind.

"You're right," she whispered. "It is time to move on." Then her tone became level and controlled, as if she had the words rehearsed. "I'm on my way back to Vancouver, then."

Steve turned, his expression soft as if he expected the revelation. Either way, he was grateful for the change in the subject. "So, what's next for you?"

She shrugged.

He fixed her with a long look. "Well, although you've been a real pain-in-the-ass... I wish you all the best." He gave her a sad smile. "Sara."

"I hope you find everything you are looking for here, Steve," she said quickly. "I wish you and your family health and happiness."

She was gone as quickly as she came. He remained in his office for a while, turning his glass over in his hands, running his fingers over the texture of the crystal, feeling the weight of it in his palms. He sighed, tapping the belt against his thigh, looking around at the black-and-orange room, his dim office lit only by the ageing lamp and the single streetlight whose sickly light snuck into the room through the cracked blinds. He heard the ignition of Sara's repaired hatchback firing before the engine hummed to life. There was a slick grind of tires on the gravel in front of the detachment, and then the fading hiss of Sara driving away.

When he had metabolised enough whiskey and emotion, Steve lumbered through the detachment and prepared to drive himself home, confident in his ability to make it home safe, knowing he'd be out of a job—perhaps more—if he bungled it. He chuckled to himself. It was a strange feeling, not caring about himself or anyone else. And really, what's the worst that could happen? He couldn't quite think of any answer to that question other than to know that at least he wouldn't be alone in the woods at the mercy of some ancient spirit.

As he made his way through, he glanced to the table where he told Grant to leave the shotgun. It was gone.

Gently, she pressed her boot into the brake, bringing Silver to a slow, grinding halt. The transition back to her old car was a rough one—everything was a little slower, a little weaker, and definitely louder. A piercing squeal shot into the night as the brake finished the job.

It served as a reminder of her lack of funds and forward progress over the years: same job, same car, same bedroom at her parent's house. All the things that drove her to get creative and get her breakout success. Imagine—hundreds of patrons paying her to do what she loved. That desire lit a fire in her, propelling her to do some admittedly absurd things.

Things like what she was about to do.

Undoing her seatbelt, she twisted to the side and checked her supplies one last time. Even though she hadn't quite decided around two hours prior, she wanted to be ready, just in case. Who knew what might be ahead? As if by divine intervention, the fragments of memory of the family camping trips rushed back. Another key turned, unlocking a vault of uncomfortable memories that flooded into her, the rush of pain carrying with it long-forgotten skills. Her mind raced through scenarios, responding with solutions and necessary supplies. Thankfully, there was one singular piece of advice that her parents—particularly her dad—had given her before she left: pack the trunk with emergency supplies, just in case.

Matches. Foil blanket, to go along with her sub-zero temperature sleeping bag. Flares. First aid. Food and water, and a headlamp with more lumens than she had ever seen. Single person tent. She had rifled through them all and confirmed their presence in her trunk prior to seeing Steve at the detachment, while rehearsing what she was going to tell him.

So much of that conversation didn't go the way she expected it to: she tried to accept this new side of Steve, one of abject weakness and withdrawal, but she was having trouble reconciling it with the man she knew, however distantly. His inaction, his resignation was so much more unsettling than his practised aggression and pushback, and it brought her to a place she didn't want to go. The urge to shake him, or yell at him had bubbled up within her like a pot boiling over, hissing with screams of blame for this mess, accusations of weakness and cowardice. And most of all, she wanted to yell at him for not being strong for her.

Now, she was entirely alone.

But she had at least made her point. And she had followed through on her decision to walk away. What was next for her, Sara didn't know. One thing was certain: Coalbrook had changed her. What she experienced had gnawed at her, eaten her alive from moment to moment—there was the darkness within, and there was the darkness without. She came to the forest to deal with both, as much as she could.

Among her supplies was the newest addition: the shotgun. She rested her hand on the stolen weapon, an electric feeling rushing up her arm as her fingers touched the cold steel. There was no memory there—only what she had seen in the movies. But it was the last tool she needed, and she had to trust that if the time came, she would figure it out.

Sara knew that Staff Sergeant Boyko wouldn't follow, that he would simply cover up the disappearance of the weapon. His fear of failure would drive him to bury it if he could, a thought she found both encouraging and incredibly crushing. Despite her initial dislike of the man, she had nothing but empathy for him. She whispered something like a prayer, that somehow he would find whatever he was looking for—that he would stop running like she had been running.

She cleaned her glasses on the loose base of her sweater. Holding her breath, she got out of the car, going around to the passenger side to grab her bag and the shotgun that felt heavier than it weighed. Shrugging on her bag as she turned, she exhaled a rush of white, moonlit smoke that twisted upward into a mess of tendrils before disappearing into the night.

At the edge of the forest, Sara stood. It was where they had gathered to begin the search less than a week ago, here at the mouth of the Crucible trailhead. Only this time she was alone. No reflective vest. No professional SAR personnel. No peace officers, and no K-9 units. It was only her—her and the empty places beyond, and whatever they might contain.

You could leave, Sara. Right now, you could leave. You've got your car; you've got your story. And for the time being, you've still got your neck...

The wall of trees loomed only steps away past the shoulder of tussocky grass. The pines huddled close, rocking gently in the chill air, glowering at her like they were daring her to enter. Their evergreen branches hissed as they jostled like hecklers to her performance. And after all, wasn't this a performance? It wasn't like her to do anything like this, and yet here she was, playing the part of the reckless, rebellious journalist.

Got to fake it 'till you make it.

Although she took that journalist hat off a little while ago; that job was done. So what hat was she wearing now? Daughter? Individual? Good Samaritan?

Sister?

Despite the ravenous chill, her palms were growing slick in her gloves as they gripped the shotgun. Sara knew the longer she waited, the harder it would be to make the choice; her thoughts would wander, start distorting the truth, and before long all manner of catastrophic scenarios would drag her mind away into the woods and do with it what they willed. She shook herself and walked toward the forest, pulling her steps only slightly.

Sara stepped over the threshold of the woods, enveloped at once in darkness and the towering trees that leaned overhead, coniferous boughs weighed down by powder, swaying imperceptibly above, threatening to dump their burdens. Her tall boots crunched in the snow that managed to reach the forest floor as she followed the blinding beam of light that flashed before her from her forehead, cutting it back and forth as she got her bearings, keeping her hands gripped around her shotgun and her mind gripped around the equipment that she had in her backpack, not wanting to be unprepared for whatever was coming.

The sounds of her movements were the only discernible noises in the area as she forced herself to plunge deeper into the wintry wilds, up the powdery slopes that reached up towards the northeast range of the Rocky Mountains, far from the reach of everything that was known and safe. As far as she knew she had left the main body of the Crucible trail behind long ago.

She was of a singular mind, unconcerned that Steve would know exactly what she was doing; unconcerned that the law might hold her accountable for absconding with and being in unlawful possession of an RCMP-issue shotgun. And that was just the beginning of it. Her mind was on fire, but the burning in her legs pulled her back into the present moment where nothing mattered but what was unfolding.

The tree supported her weight with ease as Sara pushed her body against it, breathing heavily, exhausting gigantic clouds of cooling vapour into the frigid air. She glanced up at the illuminated bottoms of the branches that jutted out of the hemlock above her, contrasted against the blackness of the forest. Eyes straining to see the stars in the spaces between the trees, she clicked off her headlamp and allowed her eyes to adjust. The darkness was complete, devouring everything beneath the trees, but not ravenous enough to push back the pale moonlight that dusted the whitened tops of the wood.

The Milky Way was visible in the clear sky, draped like a blanket of diamonds over the cosmos. A rapturous smile filled Sara that did not show on her face. The stars made her feel small, smaller than the immense forest ever could—but the vista offered a sense of freedom, of beauty, of incomprehensibility that brought her heart close to something like a prayer. It helped draw her out of the darkness. For a moment, she believed she was brought here to bear witness to this scene.

Nearby, there was a soft crunch that sent Sara's heart pounding, displacing the peace she had felt as if it was never there. She struggled her headlamp on, and scoured the snow and trees for the source, shotgun high and pointing forward. She licked her lips as her eyes darted to what she could, and sometimes couldn't see. Sara stepped away from the tree. She forced herself deeper in.

"Hello?"

Nothing. The surrounding snow seemed to swallow her voice the moment it took to the air. Everything felt so close, as if the trees themselves were being dragged by the roots to surround her. The only perceptible noise was the rasping of her breath, coming fast, steaming out of her nostrils, and the shuffling of her hands on her gun, her boots in the snow. The silence was overpowering, leaving nothing more than a buzzing in her ears. Her steps came quickly, as her heart began to fill with the sick impatience and perverse desire to see something, anything, no matter how terrifying it may be—anything to end the torture of the noiseless anticipation.

"Show yourself, damn it!" she screeched into the night, her frantic voice carrying far beyond the reach of her headlamp. "I know you're out here, you twisted... whatever you are!" Her words died between the trees, pulled down by the snow. She thrust her shotgun forward, threatening the darkness. "Give her back, damn you!"

Again, there was nothing.

What felt like hours passed in much the same way: Sara wandered the forest, shouting at the darkness, her heart filled with anger and fear, eyes filled with tears that stung in the freezing air.

Eventually she collapsed against a small outcropping, allowing herself to slide slowly down into a squat, lips chapped, and emotions spent. She stared ahead, following the light of her headlamp as it pierced forward into the shadows, revealing nothing but the same scene, the same staggered pines and birch, among others. Her face twisted, hopeless. She gasped for breath.

Finally, a sound came in response, followed immediately by the appearance of a large, antlered elk—an emaciated one with infected patches covering its face. It walked silently into the path of her headlamp, as if it was alone in the forest, uncaring of Sara's disrupting presence in these untouched spaces. It stopped in the centre of the cone of light and turned its head to stare at her. Its lidless eyes glared, glowing in the lamplight. Still against the tree, she gathered her shotgun into her lap, moving her gloved finger close to the trigger.

She met its gaze with her own stare of intense distrust, her eyes wide and holding on its state of decay. Like the other encounters, its lips were absent, leaving its teeth bared in a sick grin. Her breath quickened and shot into the light of the headlamp like smoke billowing out of a steam engine. "What are the odds," she whispered, voice clenched. "Fancy meeting you here."

It walked out of the light, disappearing without a sound into the darkness. She remained for a fleeting second dumbfounded, breath held and unable to move until she turned her head, casting the light to where it should have been—but it wasn't there. Instead came a thick snowfall, slowly at first, with thick flakes that floated in and quickly out of the beam of her headlamp.

Just as I arrived. It was like another invitation. She took it as a warning.

"Perfect," she mumbled. She cast her light upwards with a crane of her neck to catch the growing rush of snow that managed to sneak through the forest. She frowned as she watched it churn overhead. It came at her not through the tops of the trees, but rather it almost seemed to rush towards her from some place deeper in the forest, pushed by a growing wind.

Whether it was a push of her own intuition, or the beckoning of something else, she couldn't say—but something told her to find the source.

23

The Empty Places

BUT LIKE THE EXPLORERS of history who often encountered disaster instead of what they built up in their discussions and dreams, our encounters with the paranormal can leave us broken and horrified instead of inspired and invigorated. It's the ultimate thrill on paper, but in practicality it can be more like peeking through a hazy window of some condemned building and seeing something you weren't meant to see—something that left an imprint on your mind, something that changed the way you looked at your own existence. For better or for worse.

- The Garrison Theories podcast, Episode 5: "Here Be Dragons"

The door to the master bedroom stood ajar, and Steve only had to give it a nudge to open it without a sound, allowing the light from the hall to spill inwards in a luminous wedge filled with his shadow. Dimly he saw Vanessa curled on the far side of the bed, wrapped in the duvet, knees pulled up to her chest. The hum of the sound machine on her nightstand—tuned to brown noise as usual—covered whatever small sounds he emitted as he ventured closer to his side of the bed. With an awkward gait he crossed the room as the whisky did its work. He undressed and joined Vanessa under the blankets.

He should have gone after her. Now there was a girl out there with an RCMP issued shotgun. Yet nothing could drag him out of this bed. *Not now. Perhaps never again.*

On his side, he gently stroked his wife's hair, neck, and back, something he often did to help her fall asleep; but she was already gone now, and his touch didn't cause her to stir in the slightest. He gave a shaky sigh, and his eyes watered from a confusing mix of gratitude and shame: grateful for his family, his home, his ability to support both; ashamed for his tendency to cower, to run, to take the easy road. To leave that young girl alone in the freezing forest, and to allow Sara to do what needed to be done by herself.

He took a deep breath in a last-ditch effort to quell the urge to cry, an expression of his guilt and his shame of his shortcomings in the face of disaster. Then he gave up, pressing his lips together and rolling onto his side. He covered his face with his hands and wept silently, gently shaking the mattress next to his wife of twenty years.

And sleep escaped him once again.

The wall of snow that pressed at her made it feel like she was wading through waist-high water, washing over her like waves in the shallows. She came close to abandoning the shotgun in order to cover her face, but she clung to it, allowing the short strands of her hair to freeze against her temples and forehead. She grit her teeth. She leaned into the wind.

It had gone on unabated for long enough, coming with such a horizontality that she was now confident that this was another expression of all the weirdness she had experienced so far in Coalbrook. Through gasps of breath as she turned her head to the side, she silently hoped it was the final bit of strange.

And then as quickly as it came, it stopped with a suddenness that left the flakes reeling downwards. With the longest portion of night behind her, she slowed. In the silence, the buried exhaustion rose to the top. A part of her hoped to be in and out, but she left that behind hours ago; she was in deep—it was time to make camp.

With her boots she cleared a plot in the snow for a fire and her tent. With her matches and kindling she was able to get a small fire going under a pile of damp wood. While the inadequate fuel hissed, there she pitched her tent and unrolled her sleeping bag, every moment feeling the tug of the devouring darkness around her. By the time she turned back to the fire she was relieved to see it had blossomed.

Dad would be proud. If that was something he even cared about now—they hadn't been camping since Andrea disappeared.

Feeling unreasonably safe in the confines of her tent and insulated sleeping bag, Sara drifted off, her last thoughts of her parents.

She burst awake. The side of her tent still flickered orange—it couldn't have been too long since she had gone to bed. A wave of electricity ran over her, tightening her pores and causing every hair on her body to stand up underneath her winter clothes. It was overwhelming. A prickle in her neck told her that if she looked outside, she might see something—no, it wasn't even a question of if. There was a terrifying certainty to it.

She held her breath while she dragged the tent zipper down as slowly as possible. That familiar awful stench poured in, smelling like a failed deep freeze filled with expired, thawed meat. The fire was weak, but still going. The nearest trees were only barely visible in the utter black, the firelight scarcely touching the boles. Somewhere in the distance there was a hollow sound, like a strong wind rushing and echoing through a tunnel of ice. Yet everything was still.

Her intuition tugged at her from somewhere to the left of the fire; she followed the invisible line with her eyes. There was nothing there but the bare trunks of the towering coniferous trees whose boughs fought each other for moonlight high above the forest floor. The bark flickered with the radiating orange of the fire in stark contrast to the infinite darkness that stretched beyond them, punctuated with dim trees that sunk further away from the light, deeper into shadow.

In a sudden wrinkle of darkness, it was there.

It stood in the devouring gloom between the trees. Sara stared at it, seeing it there where it wasn't a moment before, like the shadows peeled back to reveal a deeper darkness. Blood drained from her slack face. She had seen it before, but obscured. Now it was laid bare. Sara tried to make sense of its form—she desperately searched for some frame of reference, some schema to cling to that would place this thing somewhere safely within the realm of known existence. In the absence of an answer something deep within her shattered.

Get away, Sara. The single thought came forward like a rebuttal to the instinct that held her fast. But the latent familiarity of the thing also told her that it took Kimberly—possibly took Andrea. *Get away before it takes you.*

It was very tall and vaguely human, with legs, arms, long-fingered hands, and feet attached to a body and a head—but that was where her connection to it ceased. The frame of it was absurdly thin, almost skeletal, although no bones made themselves known under the surface of its smooth, dough-like skin. It was a matte black, with the orange glimmer of the campfire dancing on the surface of it in an unusual way, as if the light itself didn't know how to interact with it. Where a face should be, there was a cavity like an ice cream scoop; the belly was a similar hollow space.

Her body was on the verge of a shudder, but terror froze her—she simply stared and waited, unthinking in her tent, still cocooned from the waist down, leaning back slightly on her arms, staring at the empty space where a face should be

It began moving towards her.

A switch flipped, and she scrambled free from her sleeping bag and tent, dragging herself to her feet with her stolen shotgun clutched to her chest. Awkwardly, she brought it into the position that seemed like proper form. She kept the muzzle trained on it, her entire body trembling—unlike the thing that advanced out of the trees with an unearthly yet strangely calculated movement. It was sturdy and focused, never turning away. She watched, wide-eyed as the dark surface of its opaque skin shimmered like the outer layer of the thing was shifting in some way.

Her mind emptied as it drew close. Her heart hammered like it was going to crack a rib, creating such tension in her torso that she couldn't make a sound. Breaths came in shallow, short gusts as her vision blurred in and out of focus—unable to concentrate on the thing one second, and unable to not concentrate on the thing the next. It stopped at the edge of the campsite, bathed in the orange glow of the flames, a tower of obsidian over the dying fire. It bored a hole of fear into her heart with its eyeless stare.

Sara licked her dry lips, her tongue struggling to move across the cracked and trembling surface. "Where is she?" she croaked in a half-whisper, surprised by her own audacity at addressing the thing. "What did you do with Kimberly?"

Nothing. It simply stood, as motionless as the surrounding trees.

Sara began to cry. Face twisted, she lifted the shotgun and fired. The roar filled the tiny clearing, sent the butt of the weapon hard into her shoulder and caused her to stumble back. Her boot caught the edge of her tent, and she crashed down into a tangle of polyester and rods. Disarmed and sputtering, she worked her way back to her feet.

Again, there was nothing. It hung over the flame which seemed to be fading quickly. Sara retrieved the shotgun and tried again, this time anticipating the recoil. She made a clean shot and pumped the 12-guage forward, back. Then she stopped. The entity gave no acknowledgement of the noise, let alone whatever firepower may have found its way to its body. She fired again, screaming.

"What do you want from them, huh? You took Christian?" she screeched as she sent yet another shell spinning from the chamber. "Kimberley? Did you take Andrea? Did you take my sister?"

No response. All her assaults, whether they came from the shotgun or her mouth, failed to register. The entity almost seemed to be waiting, an act more terrifying in her mind than anything she could imagine. Desperately she hoped it would give her something, anything that would indicate it was listening. Anything that would suggest a connection. Anything that might suggest it could be reasoned with. A moment of panting, sniffing, and crying followed.

And then it moved again.

Without taking its vacant glare from her, it worked its way around the fire with its uncanny gait. Her thoughts scattered, but the instinct of flight was undeniable. How far could she get? What was this thing capable of? The plans and possibilities came crashing in; her ideas fell into pieces on the floor of her mind, like small glass splinters that pricked the base of her skull. In a time of fight, flight, or freeze, her lizard brain chose freeze. A deep shiver wracked her body, and she followed it with a deeper, shaky breath.

It stood a few steps away and regarded her. Sara's blinking ceased, her gaze never tearing from the thing's tarry surface for a terrifying stretch of time. Then, it leaned towards her in a subtle way, gradually, carefully, giving Sara ample opportunity to back away or run. Every inch of her, every pore on her skin, every molecule in her body screamed a plea of escape, begging her to take them away from whatever this was. She didn't. Her body would not obey her

280

command to flee as if on some deep level her instincts knew something she did not, a piece of occult knowledge imprinted in her DNA from the evolution of aeons past that knew exactly what was about to happen.

The arms crept forward, the thin, tar-like surface stretching out and curving like the tongue of a chameleon extending towards a fly in slow motion. Her mouth opened and closed as she tried to work it to form some words. A small whimper escaped from her throat, pumping icy vapour into the small hours of the precocious winter night.

"No," she pleaded faintly through tears and saliva. "No, please. All I want is Kim. I want—"

Her eyes bulged as an obsidian hand cupped her skull without taking its focus off her face. Both black hands wrapped around her head, pressing her glasses into her skin, covering her ears and her hair with its icy grip. Her face collapsed in dismay, and Sara began to sob wretchedly, filling the space between her face and where its face should be with spittle and vapour, screams and whimpers. She stared wide eyed at the thing, and although its hollow glowered directly at her, there was no engagement with her being, no recognition of her humanity; it pulled her effortlessly towards itself, dragging her by her head towards its own, forcing her to hang onto its arms to prevent her neck from stretching. Sara howled in pain through sobs as it wrenched her upwards. She clung to black hands, trying to support herself as it lifted her.

She stared deep into the hollow of its face as it yawned above. The back of the head was a vitreous black that reflected and distorted everything that was within. She saw her frenzied face there, concavely reflected, flashing faintly in the firelight as it screamed hysterically, drawing closer to her own until a soundless dark swallowed it.

24

The Promise

SO, WHAT DO WE MAKE of all of these stories? Wendigo, sasquatch, dogman, chupacabra, mothman—so many of these encounters have a few things in common: they are wild, yes... but they often leave those who walk away from such encounters with a newfound respect of the uninhabited places far beyond the safety of our own homes. There is an energy there that reminds us of our place in the order of things. And we would do well to respect that hierarchy.

- The Garrison Theories podcast, Episode 1: "Our Weird Frontier"

Sara woke herself with a scream that seemed to have begun before she opened her eyes. She was as she was when she laid down to sleep a few hours prior: her red toque was on her head as she wrapped herself like a chrysalis in her sleeping bag within the protection of her single-person tent. Shivering, she sat there for a great deal of time, doing her best to wrap her mind around what had taken place. *If it even did take place.*

Eventually—after hovering her quivering hand over the zipper for a moment—she yanked her tent open and peered out into her campsite. Her fire was still smoking, but out. Sara twisted her head back and forth, and even amid the darkness of the small hours she could see that the snow was significantly deeper, piled up around the boles and her tent like a snowstorm had passed. The sun was just climbing over the horizon, hidden still in part by the mountains and trees, casting a green-grey pall over the whitened forest.

Sara's eyes welled with tears of gratitude towards the growing daylight. *Takes the edge off the nightmare.* She wasted no time in packing her camp. She shook off the drifts and layers of ice, hastily rolling everything into crude shapes and cramming it all as tightly as possible, all the while glancing here and there and over her shoulder to catch a glimpse of any—

In the snow a few strides away, she saw a red cylinder—and then another. She reached to grab it, examining it with broad eyes. *Shotgun casings.* A wave of ice rolled over her hunched back. She let the casing drop to the snow and rose to her feet. *It wasn't a dream. So why didn't it take me?*

The question overwhelmed her as she pulled on her pack. A few strides away, a trail of deep shadowed imprints continued up the incline, stretching far beyond where she could see. In addition to her hellish encounter, someone had been through her camp. They didn't stop, either—just strolled on through. Clayton's words came back to her. *A needle in a haystack. Like this was all meant to happen.*

She followed.

The blackness of the wood gave way to the grey light of early dawn as Sara continued her journey along the stretches and slopes of the woods, in deep places entirely untouched. The quivering sensation that covered her skin was like another jacket that she couldn't take off, although it had slowed some. *Exposure therapy works, after all.* It was usually baby steps; this was an absolute swan dive into fear. Long draughts of white vapour poured from one side of her reddened nostrils between the stinging intakes of frigid morning air laced with the fragrance of pine. The light of the headlamp grew less useful, and when the time came for the pale morning light to begin to glow yellow on the exposed snow, Sara switched off the light and put it in her bag. Deeper still she trekked, shotgun at the ready, eyes searching.

She came to a gentle slope, and the shadows laid down by the dawn stretched out across the smooth, glinting snow that wrapped around the trees and rocks. Sniffing, she pressed on beside the trail, following it up the incline for a time, until she could see a collection of large boulders in the distance, gathered at the base of a tree-covered ridge.

There was movement near the rocks, thin and pale.

Sara quickened her pace, tapping into what scant resources she had remaining, lifting her legs high to step over the calf-deep snow that gathered in billowing drifts. She stumbled often in her haste, losing her grip on her shotgun, placing it down into the snow as she pushed herself up to try again. Above, the figure had turned its head to observe her approach, but it did not move to compensate or prepare as Sara ploughed upwards, swinging her shotgun back and forth in front of her as her boots drove into the snow.

She slowed her advance.

It was Kimberly. She was leaning on one skeletal hand against the largest of the rocks, the rest of her naked and frail form was hanging down into the snow that gathered around her bony knees and thighs. Her black hair hung around her gaunt face like a tar-drenched wig, obscuring most of her features, dripping over her sick, white body. Her extremities were gangrenous, displaying a deep frostbite that ran almost to the elbows and knees. Her white chest, splotched with sickly colours, would move in and out in long, ragged breaths—but no vapour came out of her mouth. Every bit of this girl was dead.

"How are you still alive?" Sara whispered, her mouth slack and eyes wide, filled with tears that threatened to freeze on her lashes.

The girl's limp head turned towards her. She had only been out of her sight for a single night, yet she looked like she vanished out of time to rot for months, only to be reimposed upon the living. Her nose was absent, leaving behind a great black and crimson cavity in the centre of her face. Her eyes were a deep red, bordering on black, as if someone had filled them with paint. A dead tongue worked behind her tattered lips and red teeth, and she tried to speak; a guttural sound emerged like cracking ice, like she was clearing her throat of some hideous blockage.

After a struggle, she swallowed, and looked Sara in the face. A noise emerged from her throat, something like a voice with words beyond comprehension.

"I'm sorry, Kimmy," moaned Sara as she shook her head, her tone anaemic. "I don't know what you're saying." Tears dropped from the ends of her eyelashes, and she worked her gloved fingers beneath her glasses to keep them out of her vision.

The green bottoms of the snow-dusted branches swayed above their heads like an awestruck audience, filling the air with a gasping silence as if the trees themselves were waiting for whatever came next. A breeze came from further up. It hissed, clambering over the rocks before Sara, pushing the tips of her tangled hair back as they poked out from beneath her toque.

Like a marionette, Kimberly heaved a lifeless arm, holding out her black hand towards Sara. She slowly curled in all her dead fingers, save one: she left her little finger, bloodless and shrivelled, outstretched.

Sara's face fell apart as streams of tears poured down her cheeks amidst gasping sobs. She wiped the snot gathering below her nose on the yellow cuff of her jacket. Sniffing, she raised the stolen shotgun to what was left of Kimberly's face.

"Pinky swear," Sara whispered.

She squeezed the trigger.

THE END

About the Author

SINCE HE WAS YOUNG, Landon has loved all things spooky. He devoured the Goosebumps series as a kid, and once gave a speech to his seventh-grade class on the 1961 abduction of Barney and Betty Hill. Today he keeps those traditions alive through his continued consumption of horror in all its mediums and creating his own stories. Other than the work of R. L. Stine, Landon has found inspiration in the works of Algernon Blackwood and Shirley Jackson among many others too numerous to list.

Despite the nature of the subject matter he deals with, Landon's existence is a far cry from horrific. He lives in Alberta, Canada with his wife and children. When he isn't neck-deep in all this horror stuff or working, Landon loves playing with his kids or playing board games with his wife while drinking tea and eating popcorn.

Visit him at landoncrook.com and sign up for his mailing list to see what comes next!